# TH
# GOD

## Thomas Norford

Copyright © 2023 Thomas Norford

All rights reserved

The characters and events portrayed in this book are fictitious. Any similarity to real persons, living or dead, is coincidental and not intended by the author.

No part of this book may be reproduced, or stored in a retrieval system, or transmitted in any form or by any means, electronic, mechanical, photocopying, recording, or otherwise, without express written permission of the publisher.

ISBN: 9798386885045

*For Wendy, Lilybo and Jack*

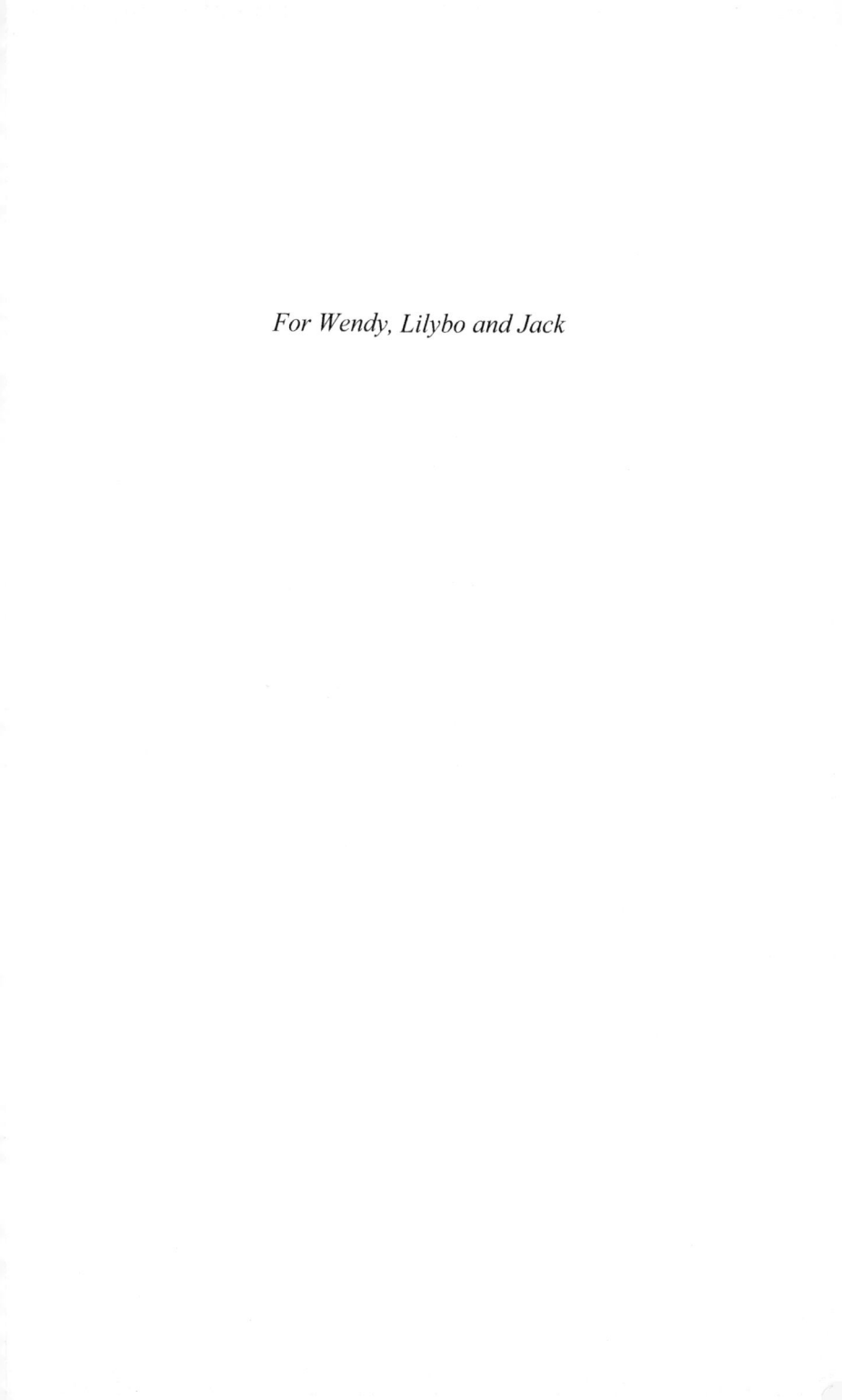

# 1. UNDER GOD'S BRIDGE

*7th day of Morshugr, 893 After Zarat.*

Lamplight glinted off the brass, puck-shaped object which Canna Dawn turned over in his hands. One side of the object was highly polished and featureless, aside from a brief inscription in a language he did not understand. The other was engraved with swirling designs, suggestive of order and movement. On the edge of the object was a pupil-sized hole, and a quarter of the way around, a delicate clasp.

He manipulated the clasp with dextrous fingers and the engraved cover swung open on a hinge. A satisfying movement, smooth, but with a reassuring resistance. Canna's face was cast in ochre by the lamp's dim glow, and a bowl of lumpy stew lay cooling and forgotten on his battered table. The hearth burned low, smoke curling through a hole in the ceiling of his wattle and daub home.

Canna found the object glinting in mud at the small Riverbend dock as he helped unload the barges, as was expected of all able-bodied villagers. Metal tools, trinkets and weapons from Arada; smoked and salted fish from Gallr; wine from the loamy soil of Lepe; spices and silks from Sardan in the east. Weary bargemen mopped their brows and took draughts of cool wheat beer from fussing Riverbend girls while the emptied barges were loaded with furs and Kyr leather, to be transmuted by the tailors of Silves and Teoton. Patient kyrs stood harnessed to wooden carts, their tails swishing at flies. Bent like a crone, catching his breath with hands planted on thighs, Canna had flinched as the half-buried thing caught the sun just so, blinding him.

A thin arm extended from the centre of the brass puck's face. Twenty symbols were arranged around the edge, numbers he supposed. Peering at the small hole on the edge of the puck, he saw a tiny cylinder inside. From a mess of objects on the table (tools, nuggets of coloured glass, leather strips) he took a pair of long-nosed tweezers. Squinting with his tongue poking from the corner of his mouth, he reached into the hole with the tweezers and turned the tiny cylinder, keeping a firm grip with strong fingers. The object began to tick. He turned a little more until he met resistance, stopped with a wince, and placed the tweezers aside. The ticking continued and he made a mental note of the arm's position.

A boy materialised in Canna's doorway. His face was scrubbed, his clothes neat and clean and his hair slicked into obedience, yet he radiated childish grubbiness. He grinned, peered at the objects on Canna's table, and fiddled with the clasp of the oil lamp.

"Hier Poesha sent me. He said to remind you to come to the Moon Pool before you gets too gross in your work and forget."

Canna rubbed the bridge of his nose. Closing the face with a snap, he slipped the puck into his pocket. "Stop fiddling with that. I assume you mean engrossed in my work, Taffa. And it's traditional to knock."

They left, following the rock-lined south bank of the Odel River, uphill through the quiet village. Taffa kicked at a flapping hokr and cleaned his fingernails with a tiny blade.

"Got a girlfriend yet, Canna?"

"What? No, have you?"

"Two."

Canna rolled his eyes. "You should focus on smithing."

What passed for Riverbend's government, culture and industry were clustered north of the Odel: the gauldrhouse and temple of Svangur; the blacksmith's workshop; the marketplace; grain houses; Javic's wardenhouse with its huge, fenced garden. Worshippers leaving the temple of a Zarday morning immediately saw the statue of Zarat, imploring on its knees, framed by Yfir in the southern sky. South of the river was smellier, noisier and muddier. Rashes of wattle and daub huts bustled among tiny crops of grain and vegetables, strutting hokr and bleating heidrn. Faye's farm and orchard sprawled over the south-east of the village, with the Horn Tavern nestled behind it. The north was traversed by semi-maintained cart tracks, the south by a hectic array of muddied desire lines.

Nodding to the bored-looking drengr atop the western watchtower, Taffa and Canna passed through the village gate and followed a cart track for half a mile, past the dock and through meadowland, to a clearing a short way into Haugr Wood. Reflected torchlight wavered in the water of the Moon Pool.

A few hundred people were gathered in their modest finery; women in patterned strap dresses ornamented with plaited leather belts, bead necklaces and brooches of coloured glass; men in neat, plain tunics and loose trousers with decorative woollen wraps about the ankles. Some were shining-eyed and mellow, splayed on rocks or logs, pulling on pipes. Others stood in clusters, shielding jugs of beer from stray elbows, leaning into each other to be heard over the revelry. A few young couples whirled and cavorted to the strains of inexpert but energetic lyre music, giggling apologies as they collided with stern-faced elders.

A heidrn roasted over a spit, and a stout, cheerful man carved off dripping hunks for the revellers, with warm bread from a table under a striped awning. Massive sarsen stones, topped by a lintel, bridged a stream which wound through the trees to feed the pool from the river. Barrels and crates were stacked against the stones, and children clambered up and leapt into the pool with shouts and giggles. The younger ones were bare-chested, and shook dripping backfur as they clambered from the water.

In the southern sky, the shadow of the Earth kissed the upper edge of Yfir, the Great Bridge. This was Ostarnight, celebration of the vernal equinox.

Canna slouched on a wide slab of rock in the shadow of a low cliff, a couple of man-lengths high, and watched Taffa yell to a friend and disappear into the crowd. Javic Tor, Bridgewarden of Riverbend, moved among his people with brief nods and tight-lipped salutations, fingering his ceremonial chain.

Poesha Cairn sat, and elbowed Canna in the ribs. He spoke around a mouthful of flat-cake and swept crumbs from his chest. "Thought you'd never get here. You missed the wood chopping. Keren won it, that streak of piss. I couldn't believe it."

"God's ribs, I thought he was a weakling."

"All in the hips, he reckons."

Canna began filling a pipe, his fingers working automatically. The lyre player struck a discordant note and a few people laughed.

"You actually taking part tonight, lad? Or just observing?" Poesha said.

"A little rich coming from you, Poesha."

Poesha wiggled his eyebrows. "I'm just keeping an eye on silly bollocks over there," he said, pointing to the bridgewarden. "Full-time job, it is." Javic was cornered by a group of men, who spoke at him with earnest gesticulations.

Canna tipped his head in the bridgewarden's direction. "How is he, then? Looks like he'd rather be somewhere else."

Poesha took a swig of something and belched. "You know how he is. Not great with people. *The* people. He's not a bad sort."

Javic Silver, the bridgewarden's son, strolled among the crowd. Young women worried at their hair, adjusted brooches and laughed as he spoke. Their mouths opened a little when he smiled. Men maintained eye contact when they shook his hand, fretting over their grip strength. Canna noted the tiny gestures and glances, a turn of the shoulder, a touch of a forearm, with which Silver created an exclusive, dedicated space for each interlocutor.

Poesha slapped his thighs, moved off, then returned with a thin, flaming stick. He helped Canna light his pipe and sat with an ankle propped on a knee. "I can't help feeling sorry for him, to be honest. Javic. You'd think the oldies would have let Red Harpal go by now, but he still gets it in the neck." The downturn of Poesha's mouth made him look older.

Canna opened his mouth to riposte, bracing himself for a re-tread of a familiar argument, as well-worn as their usual chairs in the tavern. He stopped himself, and rummaged in his pocket. "Ever seen anything like this?" Canna said, holding the brass puck up to the light and flicking it open.

"It's an Austeri timepiece. Where'd you get it?"

"Found it by the dock. Nice, isn't it?"

Poesha grunted. "Easy to make such stuff when slaves do all the shit work, wiping your arse, keeping your wife happy in the sack."

With a start, Canna looked up to find Gauldr Moshim Vitchum staring at him, expressionless. The gauldr's vit was being fussed by a group of children. Its whiskers twitched, scaly tail whipping about, as it nuzzled their thighs and begged for treats.

Poesha followed Canna's line of sight. "Moshim's giving a sermon later."

"Joy."

"Friend of mine's got something lined up as well. Skuld Heel. Sea captain from Silves." Poesha pointed to a tall, powerfully built man who stood aloof, commanding the space around him, observing proceedings with dour appraisal. Two men slinked to him, their demeanour obsequious yet menacing. He said something to them, clapped them on the back in turn, and his face broke into a grin. They scurried away. With an effort, Canna averted his gaze.

A young woman approached the rock where Canna and Poesha sat, and smirked down at them with her arms folded. "You'll never find yourself a woman, Canna, sitting there listening to my brother's conspiracies. He'll turn you cynical."

Poesha slapped Canna's knee. "Don't blame me, Jalana. The bits of animal stinking out his hut might be a bigger a turn-off, I feel."

"You are an oaf, Poesha," Canna said, with a sniff. "I probe the intricacies of God's creation that I may illuminate his design. The noblest of callings. And my samples are stored with requisite care."

"That's the only probing you'll be doing."

Poesha and Jalana drifted away, laughing, and Canna twirled the timepiece in his fingers, spinning and catching it like a coin. What does this object say of its designer and his world? he wondered. Surely, only a people of luxury who delight in creation for its own sake, could manufacture things of such intricate beauty, a people who have outgrown suffering and petty rivalries. He looked at the crude stone arch in the clearing, an astronomical clock left by the first inhabitants of Ibr, some reckoned. The diminished heidrn turned on its spit.

Are the Austeri and Widdith not the same species of being? One, capable of this timepiece, epic poetry and colossal engineering, the other flailing around in kyr shit. If the artefacts of their cultures are indicative, they must have faced wildly different tribulations, same flesh or no.

A bug with spotted wing cases landed on him, and he followed its struggles over the hairs of his arm. Reasonable to assume that this, its daunting complexity, was also designed. An inimitable, perfect creation by a designer of formidable capability. To illustrate such workmanship is an act of creation in itself, he thought, worship and communion. Behind Canna, the jagged rock of the cliff face was criss-crossed by twisted striations, attesting to immensities of heat, time and pressure. Running through it was a distinct line, black and very narrow.

#

In the shadowed brink of the clearing, Canna bit through warm bread and meat, and wiped his mouth with his sleeve. A small crowd guffawed around the lyre player, who was now juggling apples, taking bites of them while singing a nonsense-song. Fruit sprayed from his mouth. Poesha pushed through the crowd with the big man, Skuld Heel. Although they moved at the same speed, Poesha rushed while Skuld sauntered.

"There you are, lurking as usual," Poesha said. "Skuld, this is Canna."

Skuld's voice sucked the air from the surrounding noise. "Poesha tells me you're an amateur naturalist."

Canna nodded, still chewing. He pointed to his mouth and made a circling gesture with his hand. Skuld raised his eyebrows and smiled.

"Canna got his vital name trekking to Vitgut Lake," Poesha said, "to watch insects having sex. Stayed there all night, hence Canna Dawn. If you want to know anything about juggler beetle cocks, he's your man."

Canna swallowed with a pained expression. "Clown beetles. But yes. Their penises break off inside the female to stop them mating with other males." He wiped greasy fingers on his trousers and shook hands. "Watha, Hier Skuld."

"And you make jewellery."

Canna nodded, unable to place the man's accent.

"Very fulfilling, I'm sure." Skuld just looked at Canna, who raised his meat roll to take a bite and then let it fall again. "Would you like to discover animals that no one's ever seen? To name them?" He let the question hang for a moment. "I'm leading an expedition. South, down the coast of Eyra. An exploratory venture, commissioned by His Vitality the Overdrengr himself. I need a naturalist to record observations."

Canna blinked over and over, like there was something wrong with him. "I've no training, Hier Skuld. Surely there's someone at Silves more qualified. A seidhr."

"I need fresh eyes. The seidhr are blinkered by zealotry and devotion to the Overdrengr. They begin with answers and assemble facts around them. I care for quality, not qualifications." His voice slowed and the scene around him seemed to lose focus. "Poesha recommended you to me, for your integrity and clarity of mind. He says it would be good for you, that you're stagnating here. And I admit, I'd welcome an able conversationalist aboard, and I hear you're good company. It will be a long journey."

"What's the, um, purpose of the mission, exactly?"

Skuld shrugged, dug in a pocket and pulled out a small tin. From it, he pulled a wedge of sticky brown leaves, placed them in his mouth and started chewing. "Whatever I deem it. Identify opportunities and exploit them. Natural resources, animals, trade. I have total discretion. Eyra is unexplored south of the great desert. We've no idea what's there, so we'll go and see, yes? Your gauldr is coming, to spread Widdernity to the uncultured hordes, if any are to be found."

"I've never sailed, Hier Skuld. Never been further than Qeren."

Skuld spat a foul, brown liquid and grinned. "You've never been with a woman either, but I bet you'd give that a go." Canna glowered at Poesha who shook his head and raised his palms in a gesture of innocence.

Skuld waved a dismissive hand. "Just a guess, Canna, forgive my crude sailor's humour. You'll be in good hands, lad, don't worry. Ulter Wan is the finest navigator in the world and my shipbuilder, Knuld Calldr, is an engineering genius to whom wood bends its knee. But I wish to tame the world, Canna Dawn, and for that I need you.

Would you like to see Yfir, edgewise?" He jabbed a thumb at the gauldr, who was looking their way. "I have to go. Think on it. Godo'lade, Canna." Skuld headed for Moshim. Canna stared at his roll for a moment, then tossed it away.

Poesha wagged a finger and backed away. "Don't pass this up."

Canna muttered and rubbed his forehead. A thin, tired-looking woman waved to him and approached, nodding a greeting to Poesha as he passed her. The boy, Taffa, balanced on the stone arch, then backflipped into the Moon Pool, to laughter and curses.

"Watha, Canna," the woman said, joining him under his tree.

"Kerat Alina, good to see you."

Alina nodded and pointed to the brooch pinning her shawl, a design of three interlaced crescents. "Thank you for this. I know you undercharged me for it."

"It suits you. Lamir's getting big." A gawky youth carried a giggling little girl on his shoulders through the crowd.

"Aye. Shedding backfur all over, he is."

"How are you managing, Alina?"

Her smile faltered. "It's hard, Canna. The boys help, but with Reed gone...it's just hard." She folded her arms and looked away, as if conversing with the darkness of the woods. "It's not right. I despair at what life my sister must be enduring, now. Cursed, she was, the day she met Bradden Scar. If she'd died, I could mourn at least. And if she'd stayed, the world would think her an undutiful wife, would it not?"

She turned to him and he held her gaze, surprised he could do so. "I know he's damaged from torpor," he said, "but I never learned what happened to him."

Alina huffed. "The northern woman who came to my door, I could barely understand her, but she said he raved about monsters or some nonsense."

#

A dusty track curved through the trees, up a short, steep incline to a grassy space upon the miniature cliff, under which Canna had sat. It was a natural stage, overlooking the clearing and the Moon Pool. Gauldr Moshim Vitchum and Bridgewarden Javic Tor walked side by side, negotiating their way by lantern light, pushing branches from their faces and passing a flask of beer back and forth. The former wore the featureless, brown robe of his calling, Javic, the heavy, ornate chain of his station. Each man's facial features seemed more attuned to the other's dress. Moshim, the elder of them, was full featured and handsome, eyes soulful and expressive. Javic was thin-lipped and sharp-nosed, with a forehead of lines that lingered when he relaxed.

"Silver's grown into a fine man," Moshim said. Javic swatted at a moth that darted at his face, and nodded in the dim light.

"I'm proud of the boy. Fast learner, like his mother. He'll do well. Spends more time roaming the hills than learning the ways of rule though. Folks will have to tolerate me a few years yet, mind. Aester keeps my vices in check." They grunted as they leant into the steep incline up to the stage.

"And how is the wardenwife?" Moshim asked.

"Formidable. Nags at me to give up the kyr cheese. And milk. And bread. Red meat, baccy, booze, slouching, loud noises. She should wear this at home." He jingled his chain and groaned. "Ah, shut up knees. You know, Moshim, instead of a flowery speech, I'd get a warmer reception if I stood up there and told them I had the wasting disease." Taking the arm Moshim offered, he said, "This thing you're doing, with the wagon. Sure it's a good idea?"

"It will illustrate my point."

"Alright. I'll be brief, then the floor's yours, gauldr."

Emerging from the trees, they looked down to the crowd milling around the clearing. Younger children had been sent home, leaving the adults to dedicate themselves to drink, revelry and courting. A man snored at the base of the rock arch, sick decorating his torn undershirt. Javic grimaced, caught the eye of the lyre player and the music ceased. A few heads turned his way but the crowd continued to entertain itself.

"A moment, please," Javic called. The last syllable jumped an octave and a few people tittered. Javic cleared his throat and tried again, louder. "Please."

"Don't fall," someone yelled, to another smattering of laughter.

Javic winced and smiled. Nearly half the people were listening now. It would have to do. "Yes, thank you. It's wonderful to see you on this Ostarnight. God hone your blades, all of you. Now, registration will soon be upon us, and we'll bid farewell to four of our best as they make a new life in Silves. They'll become learned seidhr, formidable drengrs, musicians or trade envoys. With glad hearts we'll wish them well." A grumbling from those in the crowd who were paying attention.

"Thank you Hier Faye Gheren for the generous donation of food, and I am pleased to see you all enjoyed the barrels of ale. They did not come cheap, I assure you." Javic swallowed, muttered to himself and continued. "Now. I'm delighted to announce young Calick Spiller, son of Hier Calick Gren and Frei Calick Valia, has completed his overcoming this night and gained his vital name." At this, a cheer from the crowd, and an embarrassed teenager endured a swarm of hands slapping him about the back and head. "Young Calick delivered a worthy effort in the wood chopping contest earlier, putting some of you older fellows to shame."

Javic paused, sucked in his stomach and spoke in the most commanding tone he could muster, while the throng quietened. "Young man, you leave your childish name behind this day, and with it, childish distraction. So, I welcome you, Hier Calick Splinter, on your journey to the Bridge." Another cheer, and the boy was hoisted aloft on shoulders, swayed and then crashed to the ground to general hilarity. A flask was thrust in his face and he gagged as some foulness was poured into his throat.

Javic raised a hand, with little effect on the crowd's unruliness. "I remind you, it would be greatly appreciated if, before tonight's gone, I mean, before the night is done, you could leave your rubbish in the empty barrels here, and…" He trailed off. Turning to Moshim, he said, "All yours," and stalked away through the trees.

Moshim chuckled. On another stage, he had completed his own overcoming. Fresh from novitiate college in Silves, with rivulets of sweat weaving about his pimples, he quivered on Janna Square and stuttered through the preamble of his first public sermon. Words came out of his mouth, but his mind was disconnected from their meaning, despite having composed them. Parchment fluttered in shaking hands while a stray vit, scarred and mangy, sniffed around him, and pissed on his novitiate robe. The crowd fell about as blood thundered in his ears and the acrid stench of piss watered his eyes. For a moment, he could only watch the clouds trailing about Yfir's eastern base, willing Dregva to take him. He breathed in, then out, in, then out, forced a smile. I am not the writer, but the page, he thought, allowing the concept to mature from a string of words into a pure feeling. His fear left him.

He ignored the parchment and reconnected with the sermon's essence. Words submitted to his will, flowing through him as he reshaped the sermon on the fly; he was but a conduit for Svangur's Intention. A deft segue steered the sermon into a droll acclamation of God's meekest creations, and the crowd's amusement moved from mockery to a wry acknowledgement of their own fallibility. He took the vital name Vitchum, a lifelong reminder of the humility the moment taught him.

Moshim stood there above the Riverbend populace, doing and saying nothing. In short order, the crowd stilled, almost as one, and every face turned to him.

He boomed, "Svangur was compelled by His master, Dregva, to fashion a beautiful meadow, with trees bearing plump fruit, pools of clear, sparkling water, and flowers of every hue. Dregva wallowed in sloth, and where he trod, grass turned yellow and brittle, flowers died, and where he drank, the waters became poison. To indulge his pleasure, he sent a swarm of bees to torment Svangur, whom he had chained to a rock. Bees stung God, and died, stung Him, and died. Svangur whispered to a bee the secret of making honey, and the bee flew far away, and upon its return, placed a single drop of honey on the starving God's tongue. Svangur taught the bee to dance, and said, 'Dance, little one, for your queen, for your brothers, and teach them the secret of honey.' Soon, the bees brought a wealth of honey to Svangur, and God's ribs no longer protruded from His chest and He gained the strength for His unbinding.

"As the starved God suffered, our people have suffered. But hardship is the anvil upon which our souls are forged. The great famine brought death and penury, and many descended into torpor, proving their souls unworthy. Like Svangur, and His prophet Zarat, we persisted. Our crops flourish and the fruits of our labour are valued across all Ibr. But remember, friends, that vitality, perseverance and humility are all that keep Dregva's ruin at bay. Vitality and perseverance are two ends of the same bridge, or as you might say, Elder Calick, two cheeks of the same arse!"

Moshim smiled and took a swig of beer while the crowd settled. "But humility unites them. On this Ostarnight, we are reminded that though Dregva may take your body and cleave your flesh from your bones, your soul will cross the Bridge, to fight by Svangur's side to defeat Dregva, for ever."

During a strategic caesura, Moshim wondered if the crowd's silence was a mark of their understanding, or of his stage presence. "After Svangur's unbinding, He wished to fashion a world, to give vent to his creativity. His first effort failed, and the cold, dead Moon reminds us of His imperfection and our own."

Moshim nodded to Skuld, who gestured towards the trees. Two men pulled a tall, covered wagon into the clearing. Drunken people scurried out of the way. Noises came from the wagon and a murmuring arose.

"After He created the waters and the land, God's first attempts to create animals and plants were failures, twisted things that could not live. He buried them in rock, curiosities for inquisitive minds to pore over, like our friend Hier Canna." Canna's eyes widened as heads turned to him.

"After filling the Earth with things of living wonder, God resolved to fashion a being of His own ilk, a steward to assume dominion over the Earth, who like himself, could feel the joy of creation. Again, His first attempt failed. The creatures were beautiful and proud, but Svangur had not mastered breathing soul into flesh, so the creatures were beautiful and soulless. In His mercy, He cast them down to dwell beneath the Earth, where the passage of ages and Dregva's ruin transformed them into distorted things. Slipskins."

Skuld yanked the cloth to reveal one half of the wagon. It was a cage, and therein cowered three humanoid creatures, clearly an adult of each sex and a child. They were white, wrinkled and pasty, with broad, flared ears and vestigial eyes set deep in faces of complex, folded flesh. They squeaked and gibbered and the female's hands whispered over the infant's body as it pressed against her.

Skuld whipped the cloth from the other half of the wagon, to reveal a massive flightless bird, taller than a man, separated from the slipskins by a thick curtain. At the apex of a long muscular neck, a curved, red beak dominated a bright blue face. Iridescent green and yellow feathers shimmered in the torchlight. Each powerful leg terminated in three wicked claws the length of a child's arm.

"I present to you," Skuld bellowed, "the inside-out bird. Bane of the frigid forests of northern Ibr, they are so named because if you suffer the misfortune to encounter one, you will see your insides...out." Skuld's man pulled a cord, dropping the curtain separating the bird from the slipskins. Moshim waited in silence.

Immediately, the slipskins' guttural clicks rose in tone and frequency until seeming to contract beyond human awareness. One of Skuld's men clapped hands to his ears and backed away. The male slipskin stomped towards the bird, shrieking and clicking, while the female cowered in a corner, enveloping the infant. Claws scoured the wagon floor as the inside-out bird paced, head bobbing. The male charged. A claw flashed out and disembowelled it, and the crowd gasped. Blood poured between the wagon bars, pooling on the dry earth. Eluding its mother's grasp, the infant slipskin rushed the bird, flailing its limbs and emitting a rapid drumroll of squeaks. The bird shrieked and flapped stubby wings. It stepped back, bracing, then speared the infant through its neck, pinning its juddering body. Dipping its beak, it tore away the infant's ribcage in a fountain of gore.

The female pressed her hands to her temples and moaned, the noise rising to a shrill keening that wavered in and out of hearing. She fell to her knees and crawled to the bodies of her child and mate. Long, tapered fingers skimmed over what remained of her family, lingering over their faces and wounds, then she lay with them as the bird watched in silence, squatting in a corner. Moshim closed his eyes.

Skuld was impassive. Pops and crackles from the burning torches were the only sounds in the clearing.

Even in the famine, Canna had never witnessed such grief and despair, so viscerally expressed. But despite the clamminess of his hands and pounding of his heart, a part of his mind pulled away from the scene, viewed it with analytical detachment. Grief is a facet of love, he considered. But can a thing without a soul, love?

Jerking upright, the female produced rapid, low frequency clicks and approached the bird, grabbing at its claws and beak, trying to pull them to her. Skittering away, the bird bobbed and twirled to keep the slipskin in view. She stalked after it, swiping and clicking. Tiring of the dance and backed into a corner, the bird lashed out, opening her body from sternum to groin. Canna stared at the twitching corpse, a messy pile which moments before had been a bereft mother.

Poesha appeared and touched his elbow. "That was dark."

People murmured around them. Skuld gesticulated at someone, and the wagon was covered.

"I'd heard of slipskins, but never seen one before," Canna said.

"They don't leave their caves much; can't survive without that fungus they grow. They can be pretty vicious. Skuld lost a man capturing these."

"They were a family."

Canna walked away, Poesha staring after him. Over his shoulder, Canna said, "Tell your friend my answer is no."

# 2. TORPOR

*9th day of Morshugr, 893 AZ.*

Canna's mind was vacant as he held a nugget of red-stained glass poised in his tweezers. With clamp, lubricated blade and miniature hammer, he had released the piece from a larger section acquired from Riverbend market, exchanged for a decrepit pair of pliers. Despite the bridgewarden's insistence on the use of the Bryggnmark currency, bartering remained a popular means of exchange in most of the market villages.

Before final polishing, the glass was honed into a pleasing form with The Gobbler, a contraption of Canna's own invention, which consisted of a rotating sanding belt, powered by a foot pedal. An earlier iteration nearly relieved him of his fingers. A mirror secured to Canna's open door reflected morning sunshine onto the table; this was the only time of day when delicate work was feasible.

Using a thick mitten, he retrieved a steaming crucible from a stand over his hearth, caring nothing for the new injuries scorched onto the table's patina. He stirred the hot, sticky birch bark and transferred a gobbet of it to the flattened underside of the glass oval, then pressed the glass to the middle of a bronze pendant, hanging from a braided loop of leather. *Vitality, Perseverance, Humility* was inscribed around the pendant's circumference. Blowing away an invisible speck, he transferred the completed necklace to a display case on the table. At this point, as always, he imagined Poesha Jalana appraising his work through his eyes, cocking an eyebrow and smirking inside his mind. She approved, and he pictured her wearing it. With luck, the necklace and his other trinkets would sell at the market come Gallday.

Incomplete pieces lay scattered about on the table. With a curved arm he shovelled them into a wooden box, which he banged on the floor and shoved away with a foot. His stomach growled but he could not eat; the keening of the slipskin mother resurfaced in his thoughts, her clever hands dancing again over the remains of her family.

From another small chest, Canna withdrew a fossilised skull, a little smaller than his fist, and a few tools wrapped in cloth. The skull sat in profile, half-released from its incarceration. Using a stiff brush and a hard iron stylus, he teased away miniscule fragments of rock, removing dust with a damp rag. He noted the tiny incisors, and the relatively large eye-teeth in the short snout; tools for stabbing and securing prey. The upper eye-tooth was broken. Anchor points in the skull suggested large jaw muscles, and a powerful bite for the creature's size. Huge, forward-facing orbital lobes gaped under a domed skull. A suite of exquisite, harmonised features, suggestive of active hunting. A lifestyle similar to that of a precet, Canna thought, though the latter's skull was somewhat longer, and it used large upper incisors, rather than eye-teeth, to stab and anchor. Canna knew this well, as a ragged scar on his forearm attested.

Two animals with different means, then, to common, murderous ends. Did this little beast ever live? Its broken tooth suggested as much. *Twisted things that could not live,* Moshim had said, but perhaps Svangur allowed it a trial run, of sorts, watching it hunt, feed, seek a mate, before deciding to commit it to the earth with His other failures. Or was it truly a lifeless prototype, empty of vitality, its weapons never wielded? Wasted perfection.

#

Canna took a shortcut through Riverbend, avoiding the footbridge and leaping the Odel River at its narrowest point. Glancing around, he scaled a fence and crossed Faye's field, arriving near the Horn Tavern, where a few punters milled about for opening time. The eastern watchtower cast him in shadow, and he climbed the ladder. On the platform, a heavyset man sat facing away, wearing the yellow uniform of the drengr.

Canna peeped over the lip of the platform. "Watha Biorf!"

Biorf jerked and dropped his pipe. "Ruin, Canna, I nearly browned myself," he breathed, laughing with a palm on his chest.

"Riverbend's safe from northern heathens with you looking out for us, Biorf."

"You'll sleep better to know I've only two more nights on watch. This shit's soul destroying. Not doing my back much good either."

They stuffed their pipes with tobacco, lit them with a thin candle, and stood gazing eastwards, puffing smoke from the side of their mouths into the spring breeze.

"Got something for you," Biorf said. He pulled out a piece of slate, bearing a wobbly diagram of concentric spoked circles, rendered in chalk. "Spoke to Faye's sister, Koia, she knows a bit about Austeri stuff." Biorf waved smoke from his eyes. "So, the inner circle here is our sundial, divided into fourteen hours. The outer circle's the Austeri clock, divvied up into twenty hours, so our hours are longer than theirs, right? Both measure the time from midnight to midnight. Go to the sundial, check the hour and this slate'll show you the equivalent time for the stick on your little timepiece, so you can set it." Canna thanked him.

"Thank Koia," Biorf said, his voice hoarsened by a lungful of smoke. "The shit that woman knows is just weird." The two men were silent for a few moments, staring to the distant twin mountains, Vettr's Horns.

A voice called from below. "Cosy up there, boys?"

Biorf sucked his teeth, and glared down at a dumpy teenager grinning up at him. "Go shave your backfur Pieja, I could piss in your eye from here."

Canna laughed and they settled into silence again, puffing. A woman set out a few chairs and tables by the tavern.

"What was that, the other night? The slipskins," Canna asked.

"Don't know. Mad, wasn't it? I'm sure there was a lesson for us there, but I don't know what it was. Moshim's not given to stunts, usually. Not his style."

"I'm not sure it was his idea. I think this Skuld Heel was behind it, this sea captain. He wanted me to go on a journey to Eyra with him, to make notes on the wildlife."

"Moshim?"

"No, Skuld asked me, but Moshim's going too, believe it or not. To convert the natives, if there are any."

"Huh. You said no I suppose."

"How'd you know?"

"Just a guess."

Canna frowned, while Biorf braced his hands against the watchtower wall and groaned into a squat. "Got anything for a bad back? Killing me, it is. I'm not consulting that wretched butcher who calls himself a laknir, either. He'll tell me to pull out my eyes with a spoon and stuff them up my bum, or some such."

"Still giving you grief?" Canna said. "I can get some backwort for a paste, but it won't be ready today. Some exercises might help. Look."

Canna placed his pipe down with care, then dropped to all fours, tucked in his head and humped his back. Then, he pushed his hips down and looked ahead. A vein popped into visibility at his temple. Biorf puffed on his pipe, watching in silence as Canna adopted various contortions, thrusting and stretching, on the dusty platform.

"You know what Canna, you're pretty weird."

A few miles South of Riverbend, where the Odel River met the River Ara, stood the Three Bridges Inn. Erected at an intersection of trade routes of barge and cart, the isolated place had no local punters and inspired no affection or loyalty. It was, however, well patronised by a transient cast of traders, travellers to the towns of Silves and Ballekka, and those of no particular origin or destination.

Canna loitered outside the Inn, sweating and itchy in the dusty air. He pulled off his cotton shirt, tucking it into his waistband, and took a swig of weak beer from a leather bag. Carts, heaving under crates and barrels, were haphazardly stationed about the place, and Canna veered his eyes from the baleful suspicion of caravan guards.

A skinny man with an unkempt beard and wild hair stumbled from the Inn, and Canna stiffened as the man thrust skeletal knuckles towards him.

"A flap, a wave. Day bats and night birds, I would raise flowers in my sorrow, would they grow there. Hier shirtless man, listen." Wobbling, he peered at Canna and hissed, "It sleeps there, in the trees. It talks to me of a night."

Canna mumbled reassuring noises, and hurried away along the path, disappearing over the rise. Lunacy in the skinny man's face evaporated. He flattened his hair, waited a while, and followed.

Canna walked eastwards along the banks of the Ara, plucking isolated bushels of backwort, and stuffing them into a knapsack. More were needed to concoct a decent amount of anti-inflammation paste. Yfir partially obscured the Sun, creating a hazy glow near the ring's zenith. After a couple of miles, he welcomed the cooler air of Deliverance Gorge, but not the swarms of tiny flies which droned about his head. Foliage and moss spotted the sheer rock walls. A wooden walkway zigzagged a few metres above the shallow, rushing water, supported by a scaffold of planks.

A few times, he clambered down to gather more backwort, squeezing between wooden slats and soaking his ankles to reach the clusters of bulbous, lilac flowers. Emerging into the heat, he left the gorge and re-joined the main wagon trail towards Ballekka, winding through meadowland and floodplain. Backwort was more common here, and apothecary's bounty grew all about; he gathered wince-balm, yellow-belly flowers and mullein. His mother had smeared oil of the latter on his throat and chest when he awoke in the night, hacking and spluttering. Lungwort, she called it. In her final days, she ate the leaves, desperate for any meagre vitality, repudiating her body's failure.

The slipskin mother had accepted its fate, willed the inside-out bird to end it. Who decided these creatures have no souls? Did Zarat open one, look for a soul and find none? Perhaps by similar reasoning he concluded the souls of the torpid are unworthy, laying one side by side with that of a gauldr and finding it wanting by comparison. Ah, here is the issue. You see here, here and here, how the soul has become swollen and discoloured. It is good for nothing, Dregva take it.

Canna contemplated the vague path that branched off from the Ballekka trail, into the Horn Valley towards Bradden's farm, refuge of the torpid man and his wife.

#

A skinny heidrn ogled Canna as he approached the Bradden farmhouse. Thatch sagged with mould, and unhappy vegetables strained from a tiny patch of stony soil. Ivy weaved up the sides of the tottering building, inviting it back to the earth. Violent noise issued from within; a crash, a thump and a woman's beseeching voice. He called out but was not answered.

The door stood ajar and he poked his head in and saw Bradden Scar thrashing on the floor, jerking and foaming. Bradden Reed, his wife, bent over him, pulling at his arms and trying to stuff something in his mouth. Bradden was a shrivelled version of the prosperous farmer Canna remembered, a man of imperious presence with a retinue of underlings and an attractive wife half his age. Writhing before Canna was a lank-haired, wild-eyed wreck.

"Don't grab at him, don't do that," Canna said, banging the door open. "Here, just…stop him hurting his head." Canna tugged his shirt from his waistband and placed it under the man's head, scraping a chair aside to create space for the flailing. With a final, tortured arching of his spine, Bradden's torment subsided, and he lay prone, breathing heavily, eyes unfocussed. He had wet himself.

"Go outside now Bradden, clean yourself," Reed said. She helped him up and stripped him naked, while Canna averted his eyes. Bradden wandered outside. Bradden Reed scowled at Canna while she straightened her shift and secured her hair with a band. Canna stared. "Yeah, I do look like shit, Canna. Thank you for noticing." She dragged a chair and invited him to sit.

Canna winced. "Does this happen a lot?"

"Every couple of days, maybe. You can't be here, Canna, why are you here?"

"I saw something on Ostarnight. Slipskins."

"What?"

"Never mind. Some things the gauldr said, I got to wondering about torpor, what we think it's about. Your sister was there and she spoke about you, living here."

Bradden wandered back into the home, still naked. He snatched up a pair of trousers from a corner and after staring at them for some moments, flapped them in the air, shaking and whirling them faster and faster until the frenetic action seemed to distress him, and he emitted high-pitched sounds of panic.

"Bradden, hush now, hush." His wife stroked his hair, murmuring soothing entreaties, and he relaxed while she helped him into his clothes. He planted himself on the floor and she gave him a clutch of odds and ends; buttons, pieces of string, blocks of wood. "Here you go now Bradden, play with your things."

"Thank you," he whispered, eyes moist, then fiddled with bits of string, arranging them into complex, branching patterns on the floor.

Reed resumed her chair and offered Canna a sour smile. "You can thank Alina for her concern. Tell her I'll manage. Until I don't."

"Does he suffer a great deal?" Canna asked.

"The fits, as you've seen. Tremors. He soils himself sometimes. His thinking's muddled, his memory. How much he suffers, I don't know. Some days are better, and he can remember things, but I have to piece it together for him." She held herself, and wiped an eye with a quick wrist movement.

"Lavender grows nearby, doesn't it?" Canna said. "Listen, boil the leaves up in water, very hot, and get him to breathe the fumes. It may help him a little. With the tremors."

Reed nodded and moved to the hearth, chopped some wilted herbs and stirred them into a pot of steaming broth.

"Would you like some, Canna?" she asked, in a clipped tone. "It's almost done."

"Okay, yes please." Bradden was staring at him from the floor, his eyes and mouth wide circles of shock. "How did he...I never heard, really, what happened to him."

Words seemed to rush from her then, as if a barrier had given way. She busied herself about the home as she spoke, while her husband stared up at her, listening.

#

Bradden's old friend the broker, Klaid Sherlatha, had marshalled all his connections and Bradden's coin to scour southern Ibr and assemble two wagons of the region's finest commodities. Leathers, furs, tools, jewellery, tempered steel weapons, spices, dried fish.

A strange people, the Noror, obsessed with vast, overlapping networks of familial relationships and complex hierarchies. Their system of honorifics constituted a language of its own. Despite heretic beliefs, and a garbled variant of the Ibrian language, they were ultimately people of the Book. Widdith-adjacent, Bradden called them. Like people everywhere, they valued the acquisition of stuff. Bradden and Klaid would exploit these commonalities to establish and formalise a long-term trade agreement. Vast, untapped reserves of coal lay waiting, buried in the northern tundra, and a leaf of the warmer valleys made for a hot drink with addictive, stimulant effects.

They left Ballekka for the fortress-city of Murkka with three hand-picked drengrs, who were led by their hirdrengr. Kyr-driver Punain Paita, and Vermel Kamis, Klaid's ficksa, completed the delegation. Two kyrs pulled the wagons, a third brought as a gift for the Noror.

By the fourth night, rolling greenery gave way to frigid plains, pocked with hardy bushels. They camped in low, sprawling ruins, building a fire in the centre of what could have been a municipal square. When dawn broke, drengr Fioror Storr was gone, as were all three kyrs. One beast lay dead a short distance away, its eyes put out, belly ripped open. Bite marks. Klaid insisted the mission continue, so Vermel and Punain cannibalised a wagon, fabricating a hand-pulled cart to transport a manageable selection of supplies and commodities. Klaid, Bradden, Vermel and the hirdrengr Raor Skyta would take the cart north to complete a diminished trade mission to Murkka, expected to be a dozen days' round trip. Drengr Rougor Shemir and Punain would ensconce themselves in the ruins, with the two immobilised wagons and the bulk of the supplies.

Days later, the four men tugged the cart through a canyon, to avoid a steep climb. Raor protested that entering the canyon left them vulnerable, that they should take the higher ground, but he was overruled by his exhausted companions. They heaved the cart along the rocky bank of a stony, icy stream, grunts of exertion and shouted instructions producing strange echoes in the enclosed space.

Five Noror men waited for them at the canyon's end. More appeared behind. They approached, pulling down hoods to reveal their shaven heads. Smiling with empty palms raised outward, they clapped the southerners on the back and chattered in their wittering dialect.

The Noror poked and rummaged at the cart, one of them cracking open a case of jamweed and frowning at the leaves as he dumped them on the ground. Klaid's feeble attempt to negotiate was ignored, aside from bemused hilarity at his inept execution of their tongue. Rummaging escalated to ransacking and the Noror haggled with each other over belts, cloaks, jewels and daggers, exchanging laughs and good-natured blows. Raor barked a warning, hand on sword, and a Noror loosed an arrow into his gut. Raor staggered, and another man grabbed him from behind and slit his throat.

Klaid and Bradden stood frozen as Vermel yelled his outrage and rushed the northerners. Contemptuous blows left him crumpled and bleeding on the canyon floor, spitting teeth, nose broken. Ignoring the southerners, the Noror distributed the entire stock between themselves, even dragging away the cart itself. They left northwards, unhurried and laughing.

Klaid, Bradden and the bleeding Vermel retreated south, bracing for hardship until they could reach their wagons, consoling themselves that they were immunised from further attack by having nothing left to steal. Foodless days shrank them. They harvested cloudberries and brewed a thin, foul gruel from rock-scraped lichen. Klaid gorged on pale berries that left him doubled in pain and shitting water for a day.

A speck in the distance resolved into the shape of a man; Punain the kyr-driver was staggering north, alone, with a meagre bag of foodstuffs. The wagons had been torched in the night and the drengr Rougor was dead, his torso a burgled cavity. Half-mad with fear and hunger, the four men turned east, hoping to meet traders on the route between Ballekka and Goza, or failing that, to cross the mountain pass to the village of Luret. They at least had Rougor's sword.

After making camp in the foothills, Bradden shivered awake to the sound of cracking and tearing. Vermel was beside him, staring, his body rocking gently. Bradden sat up, blinked and rubbed his eyes. Fioror, the disappeared drengr, squatted over Vermel's lifeless body, feeding in the dim light of fire's embers. Fioror's mouth was unnaturally huge, as if his jaw was untethered from his skull, and with it he ripped chunks of flesh from his victim, swallowing them whole. Daggers of bone extended from his wrists, longer than his fingers. Fioror turned his blood-soaked gape to Bradden, who screamed, waking Klaid and Punain. They fought the creature they had known as Fioror, Punain gouging it in the calf, and it fled hobbling into the darkness, roaring. Klaid was on his knees, whimpering, blind and leaking; the creature had spat some caustic substance into his eyes and stabbed his belly with a wrist spike.

Klaid took a day to die and Bradden and Punain stood arguing by the corpse, starving and demented. With little ado, Punain hacked flesh from Klaid's buttocks and thigh and ate the stuff raw. He retched, but kept it down, sitting with hands folded over his gut like a man after a hearty plate of steak and vegetables. Blood drying around his mouth, he bagged hunks of Klaid for the trek through the mountains. Horrified, Bradden would not abase himself so, but fearing Punain may kill him, swore to never speak of it.

Bradden deteriorated over the next couple of days, growing weaker and slipping into torpor. Punain grew stronger and left his companion to wander and die.

After weeks of shambling, droopy-eyed and dribbling, the torpid Bradden was intercepted by a travelling party of Noror from Goza, the only town in Ibr with significant populations of Austeri, Widdith and Noror. In their heathen interpretation of the Book of Zarat, the Noror believed torpor a casting away of the burden of selfhood, allowing communion with God. They revived Bradden, hoping, perhaps, he would share some sacred insight, but Bradden's mind was fractured. Between bouts of crying and shaking, he imparted a disjointed account of his story and managed to communicate his origin. They resolved to bring him home.

A woman visited Reed at her home in Riverbend one night, hooded to hide her baldness. The visitor told her Bradden was recuperating at the abandoned farmstead in the Horn Valley. By decree of the Overdrengr, her husband would be forever shunned, unable to trade, worship, or interact with Widdith people in any way. She could abandon him to death and suffer the ignominy of spousal disloyalty, or join him in his renouncement. With her sister's help, she loaded as much belongings as could fit on a small kyr-drawn cart, and went to her husband.

#

"Do you believe it?" Canna asked. "That this Fioror was a…"

Reed paused ladling out the broth. "I don't know Canna, but his story's consistent. He's incapable of fanciful invention." She thumped the bowls down on the table and helped her husband up into a chair. "He chose starvation over barbarism. I'd say his soul passed a test, not failed it. Wouldn't you?"

He had no answer, and was quiet for a moment."What happened to Punain?"

"How would I know?"

"Of course. I'm sorry, Reed." Glancing down, his eyes widened at the nascent swelling at her belly.

She saw his shock. "You always were observant, Canna, even as a boy. The sickness has passed. I'll manage."

Bradden slurped at his broth, and Reed wiped his mouth with a rag. He smiled at Canna, appearing to see him for the first time. "It was an animal, Canna," he slurred. "You like animals, don't you?"

Later, from the shadows of a hillside copse, the skinny man watched Canna leave.

# 3. ORDER AND SURVIVAL

*10th day of Morshugr, 893 AZ.*

The shelled, tentacled thing lay on a rock, drying in the Sun and extremely dead.

"Don't see them often, this far upriver," Canna said. "Good condition, mind. May've got caught in the watermill. It's called a whip sailor."

Canna and Taffa sat by the Odel River, their trousers damp from kneeling on stepping stones with their nets poised. Canna poked his iron stylus at the mess of unhappy tentacles sagging from a striped, curved shell. An arrowhead carapace shielded the part that did the creature's thinking.

"See the eye here? They're on the sides so's it can see all around itself. The eye's just a gap filled with seawater really, that lets in light. It wouldn't be able to see much, just shades of light and dark, vague shapes. Enough to tell something bigger's coming to eat it, so it can scarper."

Taffa picked his nose and stared at the thing. "It stinks."

"You stink. You know, if I pulled your eye out your head, Taffa, and poked around in it, it would look a lot more complicated." The boy made a face and Canna supressed a smile. "It's filled with special jelly, and has a see-through covering. The coloured bit expands or contracts to let more or less light in. Where the whip sailor's just got a gap, you've got a special, muscular hole." A passer-by gave Canna a look.

Taffa leant back, propping himself with elbows locked. "Why's its eyes so shit, then? Why not have good eyes like what we do?"

"Good question Taffa." Natural inquisitiveness found scant outlet in the boy's restricted little life. His father was a blacksmith, so he

26

would be a blacksmith also, until he stepped onto the Bridge. If he could enrich his existence with a little wonder, and appreciate that the world extended past the boundaries of his workshop, so much the better. Or maybe not.

"Svangur gave every animal just what it needs to get by, I suppose," Canna said, mirroring the boy's posture. "Or it'd be a waste of stuff. The animals that eat this thing were given just enough to get by as well, to hunt. Something doesn't have to be perfect to be useful. Having two fingers would be better than having none."

"But what's it all for?"

"What do you mean?"

"Why not just make everything perfect, so everything's happy? S'like putting on a show at the bottom of the sea that no one'll see." Canna had no answer and knotted his brow while Taffa peered closer at the whip sailor. "Life's a real mess, isn't it?"

"No, it's the opposite, Taffa. This jumble of stones here on the bank, it's just a jumble of stones, right? Disorganised. But you've been to Vitgut Lake, haven't you? On the eastern shore there, pebbles closest to the water are small, but the farther you get from the water, the pebbles get bigger. Things that aren't alive can organise themselves sometimes, but only in a simple way. Everything is made of stuff; you, me, this thing," He raised a saggy tentacle with his stylus. "Pebbles. But with things that are alive, the stuff's arranged in such a complicated way that it can do amazing things, like fart and talk and build statues. That's Svangur's craftsmanship."

Biorf and another drengr approached, faces grim. "Canna, the bridgewarden needs to see you."

"Watha Biorf. Um, alright." He held the whip sailor aloft by the shell, hand hovering with indecision, then threw it in the river. "I need to fetch some leather strips from Faye but I'll be there in a bit. What's he want me for?"

"Now, Canna."

#

Poesha met Canna and the drengrs by the Nameless Stone, the great wedge of rock placed in the earth before the village was a village. It was significant for its lack of cultural and spiritual significance. It was simply there.

Poesha dismissed the drengrs, then pulled Canna close and hissed. "Ruin, Canna. What have you done?"

A fleck of saliva landed on Canna's face and his stomach rose into his chest, as if he were hurtling to the ground. "What's going on?"

"You helped Bradden, you fool. Let me do the talking. Appeal to his mercy and forgiveness, and for God's sake, only speak when asked a direct question." Poesha pinched his lower lip in a thumb and forefinger, pulling it downwards and showing a row of neat, clean teeth.

By a distance the largest building in the village, the wardenhouse was a two-storied right-angle, surrounded by a low, dry-stone wall.

Javic Silver, the warden's son, greeted them on the decked platform by the entrance. "He's ready for you in the heimver. What's this about, Poesha?"

"Nothing to worry about, Silver, thank you."

#

Javic Tor glowered behind an ornate desk, wearing his ceremonial chain over a black tunic and purple cloak. A large sword hung on the wall to his left, lamps burned in each corner and a chair sat opposite the bridgewarden. Nothing else. Where he shrank on stage, Javic filled this space. Canna lowered himself halfway to the chair.

"I did not tell you to sit."

"Sorry," said Canna, dithering in a weird, momentary dance, then scraping the chair to the side. Poesha grimaced at the bridgewarden's left.

Javic waited, glaring at Canna, then turned to Poesha. "Is he simple? I was not told he was simple."

"Ah. No, warden. Canna, you will respond to the warden by his title," Poesha said.

"I'm sorry, Hier warden," said Canna. His chin sunk towards his chest, as if a weight hung from it. Ears burning, he looked up with an effort to find the warden's glare boring into him, so he defocussed his vision. The blurry shape continued talking.

"Uncross your eyes, what the fuck is wrong with you? The only reason you're not already facing trial by five decent men is your friendship with my ficksa here. He begged me to hold this," Javic weaved a pattern in the air with his fingers, "friendly chat, before letting justice take its course. I am breaking a decree of the Overdrengr; His Vitality never reversed his late father's decision. I hope you appreciate Poesha's friendship." Canna remained silent. Poesha raised his eyebrows and nodded to Canna.

"I do, warden. And thank you."

"God's ribs, a sensible answer. Did you visit the home of Bradden Scar and his wife?"

"Yes, warden."

"You spoke with them?"

"With Reed, yes, warden."

"You helped them in any way?"

"Yes, warden."

"Do you understand, Canna, that Bradden Scar was renounced? That torpor proved his soul weak and unworthy in the eyes of Svangur?"

Canna paused. Again, the slipskin mother keened its plea for release, grief buckling its knees. Except now it bore the dead, bulging eyes of a whip sailor, and a mess of tentacles hung from its chin like a slimy beard.

"I do, warden."

Javic narrowed his small eyes, to the point that Canna wondered if he could still see. The warden's speech slowed, and he enunciated each word. "Think carefully before you answer now, Canna. Did you knowingly give succour to Bradden Scar and his wife, Bradden Reed, who chose to join her husband in his renouncement?"

He did not think carefully before he answered. "Yes, warden."

Poesha closed his eyes and bent his head. Javic exhaled, sat back and scratched his beard. He glanced at Poesha then back at Canna.

"You will have the box. Do you know what that means? I see little choice, here. Decent men will find you ruinous to the principles of Widdernity and you will be held in a small room with no windows. You will be starved until either you die a fool, but a fool ready to fight for Svangur, or you will enter torpor like your friend in the valley, and be tossed to the fishes." Pausing, he glared at Canna. "I asked you a question."

"I...I understand, warden," said Canna. His thoughts were a drunk man running full tilt, downhill through a forest. "I didn't know there was a box in Riverbend."

"What? The box itself is hardly the point, man. It's a room, any room. God's ribs." Turning to Poesha, he said, "He *is* simple."

Hurtling faster, arms wheeling, the drunk man felt branches whipping his face. He didn't know where he was running to.

Javic pinched the bridge of his nose with a thumb and forefinger, and spoke to his desk. "You're well liked, Canna. You're a grafter and you help people. Talk to me, tell me your side."

Prostrate on the forest floor, dazed and bloodied, the drunken man gathered himself, brushing leaves and sticks from his hair and clothes.

"I don't know why I went there, warden. I told Reed that lavender might ease his tremors. I stopped him hurting himself when he seized on the floor. They're living pitifully. Like a child, he is, now." Canna's eyes wandered to Poesha, who stood impassive.

"Talk to *me*, Canna."

"She told me what happened to him, warden. How he went into torpor. He was on a trade mission but one of them was a...a monster of some kind, that only looked like a man. It attacked them. Ate them. Noror bandits robbed them as well and left them with nothing."

"What are you blathering about, man? Monsters?"

"I believed him, warden. Believed her, I mean, and she believed him. I think. If it's true, there's more of them. Must be." Javic squinted at Canna, shaking his head, and Canna blundered on. "There were only two survivors. The other man resorted to cannibalism."

"This monster?"

"No," said Canna, formality forgotten. "Another man, a normal man. But Bradden refused to eat his friend." The words struck Canna as surreal and absurd, even as he said them, but the drunken man had clambered to the top of the hill, only to hurtle down once more. "Bradden starved, went into torpor and the other man abandoned him. Torpor kept him alive, somehow, I think. He was there a long time. I know what torpor is, what it means, but Bradden passed a test didn't he? He didn't fail one. I don't know much about souls but, it's just like the machinery of his mind is broken. Just because everyone thinks something is true, doesn't mean it is, does it? Bradden's woman is with child."

Javic's mouth dropped open and he turned to Poesha. "G'ribs. What now, ficksa?"

"Well, warden—"

"Drop the courtesy, just give me something."

Poesha's body loosened. "Javic. Canna's a good man. Naïve and weird, but he does a lot for people here. He helped your son with his rashes, you remember? Walked halfway to Qeren to gather the plants. He's a dreamer, talks nonsense sometimes but he's harmless and a good Widdith." Poesha took a breath, then slowed his voice. "Few people know what's happened. I gave the drengrs no information and the witness is...pliable." Implication hung in the air.

Javic said, "Go home, Canna. I need to think on this further. Don't consider running. You will be collected at first light."

# 4. THE GIFT

*10th day of Morshugr, 893 AZ.*

A young man and a young woman walked across the moor, and the young man knew that soon, one or both of them would die.

She took his arm and leaned into him as they picked their way along a fractured path through yellow gorse and bruise-purple heather. Neither spoke, each lost in thoughts of the other, but theirs was not the silence of dumbfounded, romantic inertia; it was a shared confidence that each would fulfil their role in an unspoken agreement. A glow above the Arada hills marked the Sun's passing.

"Better go back, hadn't we?" he said. "Your folks'll worry."

"I'm a child no more, Abal. They trust you, anyway. They're sad you're leaving, I think." They shared a different silence, then, and she chewed her lip. "You wanted to see the ruins, did y'not? We could sit there a little while, undisturbed like." No reply came but she caught the smile as he averted his face.

He had arrived at the farmstead door, shivering, dripping wet and favouring one leg, seeking a bed for a few nights in exchange for work of any kind. Over her father's broad shoulder, he craned his neck for a better look at her. His jaw dropped and his expression mirrored her own; she stared from the table with a soup spoon poised halfway towards her open mouth.

"Sorry to disturb you, Frei," he'd said, though she was barely old enough for the honorific; she remembered the shedding of her backfur well enough.

Word was sent to his family in Teoton, he said, voice cracking, of the drowning of his uncle, a fisherman of Gallr village. To Gallr his parents sent him, with a handful of coin and a knapsack of meagre victuals, to support his poor aunt and become a fisherman himself. On the first evening of his journey, the ferryman at the Teo Delta relieved him of his Bryggnmarks before granting debarkation, on pain of a beating, leaving him broke and weeping in the darkness. He learned, later, the ferry ran only in daylight, and that his accursed "ferryman" was a criminal chancer with a boat of his own.

Despite needing to merely follow the Teo southwards, he contrived to lose his bearings more than once, and sprained his ankle scrambling over a fence, an irate farm boy yelling imprecations after him. The injury was worsened by walking and needed rest. If he could but impose on their goodwill for a few nights, he said, pushing wet hair from his eyes, he would be in their debt.

Her mother held her tongue, arms folded, mouth a thin line of disapproval. Her father immediately ushered the waif inside. His coarse belligerence was tempered by a weakness for lost and broken things.

"Uncrease y'sour face, wife," her father said. "Another bowl for the boy now. And prepare the spare cot." He grinned at the dripping stranger. "I welcome you, lad, but I'll have no wastrels under this roof. You'll need no ankles to milk kyrs or churn butter."

A perrit burst from its hiding place beneath the gorse, and dashed away up the gentle incline ahead of them, its sleek body weaving through the foliage. She snickered as he started in alarm.

A breeze picked up over the moor, and she pushed stray hairs from her eyes. *What does he see now?* She wondered. *The woman I wish to be? Or the child within who intrudes upon the world, who speaks daftness unbidden?* She sighed and sucked her teeth. *Mayhap he sees that I stage myself for him, and appreciates my doing so, anyways.*

Stopping, he turned to face her and rubbed his arms with vigour. Her heartbeat quickened.

"Everything about you is lovely, Gipta," he said, emphasising the first word as if responding to her thoughts. Responses battled for dominion of her mouth and her words came out in a jumble. She was thankful for his interruption. "I brought you a gift."

From his hip-bag he withdrew a small, blue glass vial and presented it to her with a mock flourish. "It's ruca tree oil. Softens the skin and it has healing properties. They reckon, anyway. The Austeri swear by it."

She jabbed a finger in his chest. "You think me a crone then, Abal? Need potions to look beautiful, do I? Ah, don't look hurt, I'm teasing. Thank you." On tiptoe, she kissed his cheek. Moths fluttered about the moor, navigating by uncanny triangulation of Yfir and the Moon. Facing Gipta, Abal eased the vial from her fingers, opened it, and rubbed some of the oily, aromatic liquid into her throat and cheeks. He took his time. It tingled her skin and she smiled at him. The stuff smelt odd; not entirely pleasant, spicy and exotic. He raised his hand towards her cheek and she drank in the sight of his parted mouth.

An abrupt slackening of his facial muscles made her gasp; the cold vacancy there.

A spike of bone erupted from his wrist. It was the length of his hand, pointed, pale and wet. He stabbed her with it several times in the upper chest. Then he reached into the wounds and grasped her around the collar bone.

#

After blinding it with caustic stuff spewed from his belly, he had secured the human by snapping its wrists and an ankle. It mewled, "Abal, Abal," while he dragged it along, as if expecting him to help. Abal was not his name. He didn't need one.

He closed his eyes and sniffed. The female's spoor tormented his nostrils. Close now. Shallow, juddering breaths escaped a tightening of his throat, his eyelids fluttered and his tongue was thick and dry. He stopped, grasped the human's hair and brought his face close to its throat, teeth bared, jaw shaking. With an effort, he stilled himself, and shoved the gift up the hill before him.

Ruins loomed; a grassy mound, topped by wrecked stone columns of triangular cross section, a broken minaret and a jumble of crenelated walls; abandoned playthings of some giant, petulant infant. Moon and Bridgelight competed to form eccentric patterns of shadow that confounded his vision, disorienting him, but his nose was faithful to his purpose. Even the keening human seemed able now to detect the female's scent. It whimpered and pissed itself, and he dragged it through a black entranceway into the belly of the ruins.

His eyes adjusted to the darkness and he crept through dank, low-ceilinged passages and rooms of pale, lichen-covered stone. He closed his eyes and inhaled. No small animals dwelled here, nor had they for some time. They knew better.

A wet growl bounced around the walls, and he gasped, stopped. She knows I'm here, he thought, could sense me before I entered. His legs felt controlled by someone else as they shambled him forward, his hands insubstantial. The human whimpered again, calling for its mother, and he smiled in the darkness. The gift was plump and healthy, its wails and fear-stink his courtship. But if the female was underwhelmed, she would end him for wasting her time. If she felt insulted, his end would be a lingering one. Wiping sweat from his eyes, and licking his lips, he ducked under a low entrance and pulled the squealing human over a pile of rubble.

Stillness and silence weighed heavy in a small, rectangular room. Gnawed bones and hunks of flesh lay strewn, illuminated by the embers of a fire. From shadow, the female unfurled herself. Firelight caught the wetness of her teeth and the deep yellow of her eyes as she sat, regarding him. She was magnificent and his thoughts trembled at the edge of dissolution. Blood flooded to his groin and his teeth rattled. He froze and sweltered. Bowing his head, he ventured only fleeting glances. Of his species but not like him, she was bigger, stronger, her lethality unfettered by any need to pass for human. One of her wrist-spikes was the length of both of his combined.

She hissed, displaying her teeth, instructing him. He removed his clothes, fumbling at his belt buckle, and tore away the human's blood-stained shift. He crept forward with his eyes averted, pushing the human before him. The female licked her lips, appraising the gift, then pulled it to her. It struggled and wailed, and he supposed its mind had deserted it by now. A cuff to the temple silenced it, and it crumpled to the ground.

The female braced the length of herself over the prone human, dwarfing it, breathing it deep and lingering at its throat. Rising to a squat and bracing a rear leg on the human's spine, the female tore away an arm. She bit a few huge chunks from the wet end, and swallowed without chewing, her eyes fixed on his. She tossed the arm from her and sniffed, wiping her mouth with a forearm while the human bled and jerked. He met her eyes for a moment; a calculated challenge.

She leered and growled; a throaty rumble. A new smell came to him then, almost buried under the miasma of her powerful aroma, the human's stink, and the scented oil. He wilted as fear coursed through him. Another male.

It had been here, with her.

# 5. JUDGEMENT

*10$^{th}$ – 11$^{th}$ days of Morshugr, 893 AZ.*

His home was neat and swept clean. A small pile of clothes lay folded in the corner, with his shaving knife and soap. Jewellery-making tools were wrapped in a cloth packet on his table, and tied with cord. Leather straps, coloured glass baubles, beads and the like were sorted into separate partitions of a wooden case. Ashes from the open hearth had been gathered and discarded. Distillates and solutions in tiny glass bottles, and drawstring bags of dried herbs stood labelled and arranged on the dwelling's single shelf. Canna was washed and shaved, and his reflection regarded him from his warped and clouded mirror.

"I am afraid of dying," the reflection said. It paused, lower lip trembling, and then said, "I'm afraid of being dead."

The Noror would ask favours of Svangur, Canna knew, as if He had no troubles of His own and would intercede in their petty concerns. Such demands, prayers they called them, were couched in murmured, reverential tones, whispered from bowed heads. But demands they were. He could see the appeal, but the absurdity and gall of it were too blatant to countenance.

Sitting to face a blank wall, he set to examining his selfhood, his mind a fossil to be unveiled through delicate brushing and scraping. Memories resisted order, chronologically or in relation to each other; he lacked a coherent story of his own life. Scenes he had lived were only half-remembered, uncentered. Even the common factor uniting them, himself, seemed transitory, a thing unrelated to the observer in the present. Perhaps this incoherence informed his submissiveness, his lack of self-regard. But, by allowing him to withdraw from himself, perhaps it helped him to assess with clarity the certainties that others took for granted, clouded by the need to centre themselves in the uncaring business of the world.

Some years ago, he milled about the crowded market at Keth. Why he was there, or with whom, he had forgotten. He was young but not very. A woman dropped a purse and he watched it fall to the ground, dusted by busy feet. Reaching down, he felt the weight of the marks there, and saw the woman move away through the crowd. She wore a distinctive, feathered hat and a red shawl. He could have followed her but stood paralysed, purse in hand, as moral and economic calculations unspooled. Pocketing the purse, he bolted.

For days, he reasoned that his need for the coin was greater. An orphan of the famine (twiggers, they called, them, for their twig-like limbs) he relied on the mercy of the good family Poesha, his days spent labouring on Faye's farm. But his justifications lacked foundation, and crumbled under scrutiny. Even now, recalling the act provoked a physical shame-response, as if his trousers had suddenly fallen down in temple. Reliving his encounter with the Braddens provoked no such feeling, only a satisfaction that his knowledge helped ease the torment of a broken man.

Disconcerted, it occurred to him now that his moral sense was, to a degree, predicated by ad-hoc risk/reward calculations, and post-hoc justifications. So, was his absence of shame regarding Bradden simply his mind convincing itself that it deserved to endure? Perhaps, in time, he would cringe in embarrassment at the remembrance of helping Bradden. On balance, he thought not, though he could not be certain. Shame at his theft bloomed almost from the moment of the act, an ember flaring into a conflagration which reduced his meagre rationalisations to ashes, ruinous yet cleansing.

So, shame for a genuine crime that would be punishable by, what, ten lashes of Mother's Ruin? And no shame for an act punishable by slow torture and death. He thought, there is something wrong with me, or there is something wrong with the world. Which is it? Herding unruly memories of social exchanges, childish conflicts, he observed his responses, and others' responses to him, as he had observed the complex dance of luminescent clown beetles during his overcoming. Something set him apart from his people, he concluded, a certain oddness, but he found no great failings or major flaws. What of the world? The late Overdrengr's drastic measures during the famine to "Preserve Widdith vitality," were a mark against the world, surely, as was the gauldr's perverse sacrifice.

Canna exhaled and his heart slowed. His fossils and animal specimens were either packed in wooden boxes or had been thrown away, but the little hunter's skull lingered on his table, as if waiting there to intrude on his thoughts. Its final ambush.

"Curiosity's done for me. Was it so for you, Liyo?" He had named the erstwhile killer after the wily, patient hunter sent by Dregva to hunt Svangur, after the crazed Vettr's ignominious failure. It stared back at him in broken-toothed goofiness. You lived, Canna thought. I know it. You embraced your stillness, waiting for the vigilance of scurrying things to waver, then you pounced, assured of your prowess. You railed against death.

Canna wondered why he had not simply fled, why he knew he would not. Perhaps there was something wrong with him, after all. He was neither the slipskin child, defying mortality, nor the mother, embracing its fate. They all went quick. There was that, at least. Every beast he had studied was given tools by Svangur to stay alive, the means to struggle, and advocate its existence. Even a worm on a hook wriggles and wriggling is the right thing to do. He should at least concoct a defence for the five decent men. Wriggle a bit.

Perhaps Svangur favoured brutality and abhorred weaklings such as he, His fetish for humility notwithstanding. According to his Book, Zarat raised a hand to end a mosquito that fed upon his arm, in the jail of the warlord Satheen. Svangur stayed his hand. He told him he had breathed perseverance and vitality into all His creations that moved on the surface of the world, but humility was man's gift alone. And what, now, was the course of greatest humility? Accept or resist?

According to Poesha, the Austeri had discovered a great law, which in its simplicity and power, explained the movement of the Moon about the Earth and why objects fall when let go. Would that there was some other unifying principle, to explain the grief of a slipskin mother as its child is ripped apart, the wriggling of a worm on a hook, a man reduced to a gibbering wreck by torpor, his own fear and shame. Canna took the Austeri timepiece from his pocket. Its ticking had slowed. Which would be worse, starving or drowning?

He could not bring himself to pray, Noror-style, but the Austeri pursued a more compelling practice. Dying Austeri bequeathed to their relatives short, written accounts, known as *qil a'jhira*, translating to something like: clarity of the end. The dying set out with brevity their wisdom accrued through life, and advice for those left behind. They were prized by Austeri families, passed down through the generations in swirling, framed calligraphy. They were windows into a former world, into the adaptations its people devised to mitigate the pressures they faced. Enormous political significance was attached to the *qil a'jhira* of the ruling Fathers. A good tradition, Canna thought. He took a sheaf of his most expensive parchment, and wrote:

*Our religion is unsupported by observable facts and is therefore not a useful framework by which to understand the world. New frameworks should be drawn up, derived from carefully recorded facts. They should be tested routinely against new facts which come to light, and modified as needed. The establishment and testing of explanatory frameworks should be unfettered by concerns of virtue and sin. Knowledge and explanatory frameworks should be exploited to reduce suffering.*

With a petulant flourish, he scrawled *The Book of Canna* across the top, before folding the paper precisely in half. Before sleeping, he masturbated while thinking of Poesha Jalana, and wept.

#

Canna plodded after Poesha along the riverbank, towards the wardenhouse. His hair was slicked and he wore a clean, white cotton shirt, tucked into rarely worn, formal trousers.

A grizzled man lounged on a small platform on the bank, whittling and smoking a pipe, paying little attention to his stationary fishing rod. He waved, and Canna moved his face to produce something like a smile in return.

"Caught anything, Mazof?" Poesha asked. Without waiting for a reply, his expression returned to grimness.

To Canna, all things seemed rendered in extra detail, hyperreal; the tumbling and eddies of the water through the mill, the grain of the wood on a passing haycart. His ability to focus his auditory attention had failed. The normal hubbub of village life was muffled, yet some sounds burst into his awareness with unnatural loudness. He was struck by how an emotional state could influence his body's ability to interpret its surroundings, but he could not define the emotional state itself. Was he panicking? He considered the rhythm of his gait, the way the swing of his arms counterbalanced the momentum of his legs. For a moment, he tried walking so that left arm synced with left leg, right arm with right leg. It felt unnatural, his torso destabilised. Running his tongue slowly around his mouth, he was unsure whether his teeth could transmit sensation, and wondered how this could be determined for certain. He swallowed a few times, listening to the weird little noises his throat made. Poesha was talking to him.

"Sorry Poesha, what?"

"I said it's a good sign he sent me for you. That means he hasn't chosen, yet, to put you before the five decent men. Or he'd have sent drengrs to announce the charges. We may un-screw you yet."

"Who are these five decent men, anyway?"

"You've a talent for pointless questions. They're whichever men will deliver the result the warden desires."

Canna dug in his knapsack and pulled out a folded piece of parchment. "I wrote you something," he said, handing it over.

"What's this, love letter for my sister?" Poesha replied, and Canna felt his cheeks flush. Opening the paper, Poesha squinted at it and crinkled his nose. Then he handed it back to Canna in silence. For a while, they just walked.

Poesha said to the air ahead of them, "The Book of Canna. Bit arrogant, don't you think?"

"How do you mean?"

"You've committed a crime, Canna, and you react by blaming the whole world. Perhaps you lack self-reflection."

Canna was surprised by his own rush of anger and clenched his teeth. "I don't blame the whole world, Poesha, just our shitty corner of it. We're here on our peninsula, eating and shitting, dying in droves because we don't even know why people get sick, and we think we've got it all sewn up, how the world works. G'ribs, Faye's daughter's had three still-births, and a fourth was drowned because of an extra finger. Svangur didn't want that for us, surely." Embarrassed, Canna struggled to tame his breathing.

"Look, Canna," Poesha said, "there are two types of idea in the world. Ideas that are true, and ideas that are useful." He pointed to Yfir, peeking from glowering clouds. "The idea that there's a great ring surrounding the world is true. Sailors and the seidhr worked that out years ago. But the idea that the thing in the sky's a bridge, linking the world to heaven? It doesn't even make sense, but the idea's useful. You see? Useful ideas are useful because they achieve things, doesn't matter if they're true. Holding people together. Getting them to do what you want."

They reached the western footbridge. "Stop a moment, Canna." Poesha motioned for Canna to sit on the long bench that ran along the bridge. He dumped himself down with his elbows on his knees, staring at the space between his feet. "Remember what my old man used to say about arguing with mum? He said clearing the air is overrated. He said, rather than blurt something you'll regret, take yourself off somewhere quiet, write down what you wanted to say on a piece of paper. Then, screw up that piece of paper very, very tightly, and pop it up your bum."

"Sounds like your dad, very much so."

An old man was swimming downriver towards their bridge, naked. He moved in a languid backstroke, and had a vit pup balanced on his belly. The pup munched a carrot, decorating the old man's chest hair with orange crumbs.

As he approached, Poesha called out to him with a laugh. "Watha Arfa, nice morning for it!"

"Good morning gentlemen," Arfa returned, "I detect a note of mockery, but I believe you will find…" He disappeared under the bridge, Poesha and Canna turning to follow his progress, then reappeared on the other side. "That this is the most efficient method of traversal from one end of the village to the other."

Poesha called after the bobbing head, "Mazof's fishing downstream, Arfa. Don't snag your balls on his hook."

Poesha and Canna resumed their place, facing westwards to where the river disappeared under an arched section of the village wall.

"I'm thankful for your help, Poesha. For everything, really. Forget the note. I was in a state last night."

Poesha nodded, then frowned at Canna. "Bradden's talk of a monster…do you believe it? This something I need to worry about?"

"I believe it. Reed convinced me. There's a lot we don't know, Poesha. If it's true, there'll be more of them."

Poesha rose. "I'll think on it. Speaking of monsters, let's not keep Javic waiting."

Canna nodded, and sighed with his eyes downcast. "There's something else I need to tell you. I might be approaching my end, Poesha. I have to unburden myself and you're my oldest friend."

Poesha's brow furrowed in concern. "What is it?"

"I'd love to hump your sister."

Poesha laughed and dug him in the ribs. "You're demented. Come on."

Stepping from the footbridge, they passed the temple of Svangur and the kneeling statue of Zarat, an arm outstretched in supplication and despair.

#

Javic Silver attended the heimver with his father, prompting a querulous glance between Poesha and Canna. Poesha again stood erect at the warden's right, the younger Javic to his father's left, arms folded, leaning with one foot on the wall behind him. The bridgewarden had shaved and his fingernails were clipped, and Canna wondered if this were a sign.

"I struggled with what to do with you, so I consulted my son," Javic said. "Unlike you, he is wise beyond his years and you will agree, I think, that you owe him a debt. Silver, summarise your arguments please."

Silver pushed himself from the wall and nodded at his father. He addressed Javic while fixing Canna with a look of cool appraisal. "Thank you, father. Poesha's defence of Canna's character, as you related to me last night, is probably accurate, but irrelevant. Laws exist for the benefit of communities, for the people as a whole, and crimes are regarded as such because they damage Widdernity. Our decision, excuse me, *your* decision, father, should be geared to reaching the outcome of least damage. Subjective assessments of character are a distraction."

The warden smiled and nodded with an air of regal indulgence. Poesha pursed his lips.

Silver continued, "Canna has committed an offense against God, and potentially damaged the vitality of the people. It is fortunate, for him, that his crime is known only to a few. I'm assured that the witness who brought this to our attention is a man of wisdom and discretion. Canna is useful, as he's demonstrated on many occasions. His knowledge of healing remedies is unrivalled in the community, and his trinkets have a reputation for beauty and craftsmanship, which reflects well on Riverbend.

"So, we must balance the impact of his offences with both his past and potential future usefulness. I argue that his offence outweighs his past usefulness, and can only be ameliorated by substantial effort." Silver paused, and turned to his father for the first time. "Captain Skuld Heel is embarking on a voyage of discovery to Eyra. As I understand it, he already requested Canna's inclusion, on your ficksa's recommendation, as a naturalist observer. Skuld is experienced in nurturing the potential of weaker men, even if they do not see it themselves. Canna refused in cowardice. Gauldr Moshim, a man twice Canna's age, has confirmed his own inclusion. I propose that Canna joins the expedition. If he comports himself with perseverance and humility, and contributes to its success, his debt to Riverbend and the Widdith people will be paid."

The Bridgewarden's face unknotted, and he smiled at his son as Canna's heart pounded. "It is decided. You leave in five days, Canna. Get your affairs in order." Canna spluttered a protest and the warden levelled a gaze at him. "The box is still an option, if you prefer."

# 6. THE IMPROBABLE

*A Naturalist's Diary. 30$^{th}$ day of Morshugr, 893 AZ.*

Dedication of this Diary to His Vitality Fan Parley: Overdrengr of Ibr, Bridgewarden of Silves, First Speaker of the Bryggn.

In belief of the good reception and honours that Your Vitality bestows on all sort of books, as a First Speaker so inclined to favour works of artistry and natural philosophy, chiefly those which by their nobleness do not submit to the service of the corrupt and ruinous, I have determined bringing to light this humble Diary.

Of sound mind, I engage in this journey of my own will, and proffer my gratitude to Your Vitality for the wisdom, designs and means that have enabled this great enterprise to transpire; not least the precious material to which I commit these words. With perseverance, humility and what meagre vitality with which I am bestowed, I seek to bring illumination to Svangur's works, that others of greater mastery and accomplishment may chance upon what dim glow my discoveries provide, and reveal the full radiance of His whole creation and our souls.

I entreat Your Vitality to receive this humble work under your protection, that you will not, despite its regrettable dearth of erudition and elegance, disdain what little service it may provide yourself, the Widdith People, and the Intention of Svangur.

#

Canna's eyes boggled at what he had written. Skuld clapped him on the back.

"That's the stuff, Canna. His sweatiness will be most pleased with such a floral tribute." The two of them were crowded in the tiny cabin, which was little longer than Canna himself. One end was filled by a functional desk with one drawer, and a fold-down sleeping platform was attached to a bulkhead by chains. The remaining space was given over to wooden containers of writing materials, shaving supplies and clothing.

"I'm not sure it even makes any sense," said Canna, "But thank you for your assistance, captain. This is all so novel to me." Canna gave the captain a pathetic, grateful smile.

"You're welcome my young friend," Skuld replied. His sonorous voice reverberated around the cabin. He is a man, Canna thought, whose vitality would pervade any space, and not simply because of his imposing frame. In this cramped box, the captain's presence seemed rather absurd. He chewed methodically, and spat dark liquid into a tin pot he produced as if from nowhere. "The chances of him actually reading the thing are slim, at best, but it must be done. Now," he gave an exaggerated bow, and his voice boomed, "I entreat you, in turn, O Most Vital Illuminator of Arseholes, to commit to history your discoveries in whatever manner most pleases your will."

#

By way of introduction to this record (belatedly I admit, given we are 6 days into the journey. But then, my stomach has only of late allowed me even a modicum of peace), I should set out something of our plan, our vessel, our men, and my particular purpose. Presumably, our good Captain Skuld also keeps a log or diary of some type (not for the first or last time, I betray my ignorance of nautical ways) so I hope there arises no great contradiction between these two records. If there does, the fault will assuredly be my own.

While I think of it, I must note that Yfir has changed shape just a little, being somewhat broader and taller. Our capable navigator, Ulter Wan, employs the ring as a navigation aid, along with the tiny moons that sweep along its dark bands. He also utilises the stars and the Red Wanderer, which he tells me is another world like our own. It is a wondrous thing that, along with multitudes of written tables and mysterious little devices, the tools of his trade include a structure that encircles the entirety of the Earth. Ulter explained to me with patience and clarity some of the methods of his work, but regretfully, the seeds of his knowledge were sown upon stony, infertile ground. I simply could not follow. Regardless, I eagerly anticipate more conversations with the man; the breadth of his knowledge is matched only by the mildness of his temperament.

Already my Diary has veered into tangent, its hull creaking and groaning. Ah, as the captain would say, "Onward!"

Given that I have no animals to study at present (I will not refer to the men as such!) I instead turn my anatomical eye to the vessel itself, upon which our lives depend. Rather like an animal, its designer created it so that its structures complement its functions. A ship, like a human, must be named and ours is named *Improbable*. The captain tells me the name arose from the wit of the ship's creator, a master shipbuilder by name of Knuld Calldr, who is on the journey with us. Supposedly wiser heads in the dusty College of Silves advised Knuld that his innovations would compromise the structure of the whole, and were doomed to failure. And yet, here we are, in it. Perhaps Dregva was similarly scornful of Svangur's creation.

The vessel is based upon that of a standard ravel-type ship, I am told, which means that its triangular sails (are they called lantern sails?) lend it speed, manoeuvrability and the ability to move in defiance of the wind. Its overall shape allows it to travel relatively distantly upriver, which is convenient to our purpose. As to the more detailed aspects of the vessel's structure, I will avoid excessive detail for the sake of the reader's patience. Suffice to say there is a main deck, with the mainmast upon it. Beneath that, there is the lower deck where the bulk of the men lay their heads, and cabins for the officers and others of various purpose. One such cabin houses a small, timid but inquisitive animal, ill-suited to voyages at sea (me).

Beneath the lower deck lies the hold, full of barrels and cases, stacked with great strategy and care. Upon the main deck is the forecastle deck, from which erupts the foremast. Within the galley our cook concocts his works. Aft is the quarter deck, with the aft mast and stern, under which are Skuld's cabin and our general office of sorts, where the captain gathers his officers to delegate his wishes. We also have two rowboats attached to the ship, which were used to tow the *Improbable* away from the Silves docks as women and children waved from the Ara Bridge.

Knuld has implemented a number of what I am told are innovative features in his creation. Most notably, these include a pumping and fire-quelling system. With men pumping a great double handle down in the hold, water can be expunged from the vessel, or redirected to quell fires in the lower deck. Fire is the great dread of sea-faring men, and unsurprisingly so; they are almost always disastrous. *Improbable's* fire-quelling system works by means of water pumped under pressure with a small amount of air, and forced through very tiny nozzles. This creates a fine mist, which, because it is made up of such fine droplets of water, converts fire to steam most efficiently, as well as dampening the fire's fuel. At least, so goes the theory.

Knuld's other great innovation is the boxy structure on the main deck. Interleaved vertically placed flanges, one extending up above, one opening underneath, allow cool air into the lower deck, while also preventing the ingress of water, which is instead sluiced away by means of various small holes.

I have mentioned some senior members of the expedition already: our Captain Skuld Heel; Navigator Ulter Wan; and Master Shipbuilder Knuld Calldr. Making up the roster of esteemed officers are Hal Revener, laknir and barber; our First Hand, Dalind Bark, who leads the ordinary sailors (known as hands); and finally, Noron Valis, Ship's Cook and Quartermaster.

It would be wrong for me, in my subjectivity, to submit to parchment ignorant appraisals of my co-travellers, other than to note their obvious virtues. However…however. Noron Valis is a man of such disagreeableness and volcanic temper that I cannot help but pass comment. His vituperation is matched by his physical presence; somehow his muscles yearn to burst from his skin. Cook's Boy, Arjier Stender, does his bidding, and his treatment of the fellow is reprehensible. Poor Arjier is a stout boy, a fact of which Noron likes to remind him often, and in no uncertain terms.

Yesterday afternoon, as I stood on the main deck, willing the spasms of my stomach to quell, Arjier staggered from the forecastle, wild panic in his eyes, followed by his master. Noron beat the boy about the body and backside with a ladle, roaring at him, "Did your father — in your mother's milk, you fat, miserable — stain?"

According to the captain, Elder Arjier is a wealthy Lepe merchant who sent his boy on this voyage to "Straighten his back and put some hair on his balls." Well, Noron's tutelage will surely either do so, or destroy him.

Our first hand has seven good hands to do his bidding, one of whom is a mere boy by the name of Millitre Lon. A handsome, agile and intelligent lad, he shows no signs of being browbeaten by either his colleagues or the officers. Despite being a keen student of the art of obscene mockery, he is well liked, because he laughs at himself as much as at others, and his verbal barbs lack malice. I suspect he will thrive much more successfully than the other boy, Arjier. We also have on board three highly capable drengrs, led by Hirdrengr Tove Kyrhorn. I am told that while it is usual to have fighting men aboard such a voyage, we are fortunate to have an elite unit with us, hand-picked by the Overdrengr himself.

Three others make up our full roster of men, occupying special positions as it were, as they are neither officers, hands or drengrs. One of these is me. Gauldr Moshim Vitchum is with us, providing spiritual guidance. He will, of course, come into his own in the event that we encounter unlearned peoples. Finally, we have a bard, Slatre Run, whose purpose, as far as I can tell, is to simply entertain the men by telling witty stories, playing music and indulging in general mummery. I had no inkling that voyages included such a role, but I suppose he serves an important function and I am glad he is here. His acrobatics, high among the rigging, are most alarming, though impressive and entertaining, drawing gasps of worry and approval from the men below. Moshim and myself have the privilege of inclusion in officers' meetings, whereas the bard does not.

I should say something of our mission. We are sailing south, maintaining a close distance from Eyra's western coast. We are to visit the Orn Islands, to re-supply with fresh meat, vegetation and game. We then venture forth into uncharted waters, until, in Ulter's words, "The ring appears nothing more than a thin line in the sky," and we will seek ingress into the great continent by means of the most viable inlet.

We hope to discover resources advantageous to Widdernity, and perhaps to initiate trade arrangements with people of sufficient civilisation. The prospect of discovering unlearned peoples is most exciting to me, and the Gauldr College of Silves has produced rather beautiful pictorial versions of the Book of Zarat (which I have perused), that they may be comprehensible by illiterates. I am not wholly naïve. I understand, of course, that spreading the teachings of the Book means in turn disseminating the influence of the Overdrengr and his Bryggn.

My part is somewhat secondary, though complementary to the overall objectives. Namely, to record my observations of plant and animal life that we may encounter, particularly any that promise future usefulness. Of course, there is a joy to be found in the simple act of discovery, and I confess to being impatient to begin.

My approach to the discovery and analysis of organisms has formerly led me into territory and conclusions which could be deemed blasphemous, but I am confident that any future revelations will ultimately lead to a greater understanding of His work. Skuld assures that my lack of systematised learning will prove a strength in approaching novel discovery, rather than a drawback. But I admit to being most intimidated by the wealth of knowledge in the world, and of the world, that is currently beyond me. I have therefore hit upon a principle which I call Graded Simplification, to which I shall cling when my ignorance threatens to overwhelm me.

The principle, such as it is, has three parts:
1: The origins and workings, of any particular phenomenon, can be understood to have grades of greater and lesser complexity.
2: A complete understanding of any phenomenon, requires a complete understanding of its origins and workings at every grade of complexity.
3: In order to meaningfully increase our knowledge of a phenomenon, it is only necessary to discover its origins and workings that are of one grade more complex, than our pre-existing knowledge.

For example, let us say we are trying to understand the working of my Austeri timepiece. We already understand it on one grade of complexity; that its hand and numbers indicate the time, by dividing the day into twenty hours. To understand it to its very fullest, we would need to know how the history of the Austeri people led to its need, their methods of smelting and mining, why brass appears a yellow colour to the human eye, why springs extend violently when compressed. This is Parts 1 and 2. Part 3 of the principle says, however, that to meaningfully increase our knowledge of the timepiece, we merely need to dismantle the thing, and analyse how the little gears and springs interact to make the hand turn at a set rate. There is some comfort to be had in the principle for an ignorant but inquisitive man.

I fear my Diary's structure is now so compromised that its hull is springing leaks and water is rising alarmingly, any coherent thread lost overboard. For I turn now from matters of epistemology to a trivial but engrossing diversion, much enjoyed by the men. When not on shift, the men indulge in a game known as Garor, or sometimes called Defend the Keep. I mention it because the men invited me to join them for a session, and while my ineptitude was a cause of great embarrassment to me, and hilarity to my competitors, it seemed to further my acceptance. God knows I have felt a complete imposter among such useful, capable individuals. Also, I find the game itself intriguing, though complex and baffling.

The only equipment required are something to keep a record of the score; the men use slate and chalk, and a dice. Really, it largely exists in the players' imaginations. Players each have a castle, or keep, to defend. Each has one hundred vitality points. They also have a set number of perseverance points, which, at the start of the game they distribute as they see fit across various attributes. Attributes include things like wall height, moat size, fighting ability, longbow range, rate of food production, resistance to disease, and more. One player, or rather, non-player, assumes the role of an Austeri-style, capricious god. After players have distributed their perseverance points, the god-figure rolls the dice to initiate a set of conditions, such as attacks of various types, disease prevalence, weather conditions and more. Round by round, the god-figure rolls the dice to tweak these conditions. So, for example, the weather can become colder or warmer.

In each round, players lose vitality points at a rate dependant on how their perseverance points are distributed. So, players with low disease resistance points will suffer if disease becomes more prevalent, for example, but will be less vulnerable to siege if they have a wide moat. After each round, players can, in a limited way, redistribute points between attributes, bolstering disease resistance, or increasing wall height for instance. Conditions generally change gradually, but can occasionally swing wildly. So, a player who has heavily invested, as it were, in armed defence, can suddenly fall victim to catastrophic weather conditions.

Winning the game essentially means surviving longer than the rest of the players. While luck plays a considerable part, there is a degree of skill involved. Young Millitre excels at the game, serenely disdaining anything the game throws at him. He would surely rival the Overdrengr's finest advisers for strategic prowess and I cannot but help wonder if his aptitude relates to the difficulty of his real-world existence.

I have not done full justice here to the complexity of the game; the men lost me quickly as they argued good-naturedly over the minutiae of the rules. Some versions of the game set players actively against one another, whereby they steal the other's points, and inflict ruin upon them. There is something primal, and somehow profound lurking in the principles of the game.

My eyes are straining in the candlelight, (this Diary may render me blind, at this rate) and I am due to meet the captain. Skuld and I have enjoyed setting the world straight through regular, meandering, conversations in his cabin, over wine and the jamweed he chews prodigiously. The leaf is, apparently, a product of the east, and has mildly addictive and relaxing properties.

Skuld enjoys the role of jocular, caring father of the men, I think. He shows genuine concern for those serving him, asking after their families and needs. But he confessed that part of my purpose here is to act as his interlocutor, so I feel pathetically grateful for holding a special place in his heart; he tries ideas on me like a woman testing clothing designs on a wooden dummy. Despite his gregariousness, he is prone to self-reflection and highly intelligent. His insights apparently led to great revolutions in the ability of sea-faring men to predict and analyse the weather.

I have yet to summon the courage to probe Skuld's motivation for the slaughter of the slipskins in Riverbend, an episode which haunts my sleep. In my cowardice, I fear that to do so would be to run our burgeoning friendship aground. Ah, he is calling me. His authority in this little world is absolute, so if he calls, I come.

# 7. THE ZEALOT

*6th day of Poori, 893 AZ.*

Moshim Vitchum gazed over the gunwale towards Yfir, pale and diffuse against the cloudless blue. His imagination laboured to contrive some profundity from the ocean's immensity, but casting ideas aside, gave up. It was simply a lot of water, all in one place. Spray cooled his well-lined face and he closed his eyes and flexed his neck, turning his head all about, wincing at the little crunchy noises.

Despite a life of preaching and study, he had always been physically powerful. At gauldr college he dominated his peers in the annual wrestling tournament, year after year, even giving the beast-like instructor, Gauldr Drak, something to think on. But now a nascent paunch crept over his trouser waist, his chest muscles were degrading into sagging bags of fat, and his back hurt, always. Unloading barges or helping Faye stack his haybales left his biceps quivering with fatigue for days. Riverbend people were kind, and showed their appreciation of his counsel through gifts of food; cupcakes, kyr-cheese and biscuits.

Moshim frowned at a trace of black mould in the join between gunwale and deck. A living thing, mould. Like all of Dregva's creations it was amateurish and ugly, yet ubiquitous and destructive. Bees were the special exception.

"'Scuse us, gauldr." The giant, Werdom Vein, dwarfed a swabbing brush in his paws, and offered Moshim a shy, goofy smile; a grin scrawled on a boulder. Moshim smiled, stepping aside to allow him to swab. The mould disappeared.

"Sorry Werdom. You're doing God's work there. Are you well?" What a specimen, thought Moshim. No fears of decline for him. Svangur did not bless the man with wit, to say the least, but ruin, he could probably rip the mainmast from its mooring and scratch his back with it, if he were so inclined.

"Yes, gauldr, Karelud gave me some of his biscuit and I ate it. He's my friend. I need more food than he does, 'cause he's only little. And he's teaching me to whistle. Listen." Agonised tootling issued from his pursed lips and he laughed, a remarkably girlish sound for one so massive.

Moshim craned up his neck. "It's good to have friends, Werdom. To help each other. Get on now, I shouldn't keep you from your work." Werdom moved away, hunching over the swabbing brush. Such a contrast to the apparition haunting Moshim's cabin earlier, the twitchy and nervous Ekkero Ashen. Incapable of repose as he stood in the doorway, his fingers worried at his hair, feet shuffling, eyes darting everywhere but at Moshim's. His speech, like his physical presence, was hurried and uncentred.

"I do five hundred sit ups now gauldr, I could used only to do thrice a hundred, but practice. This must please God, must it not? I persevere in all things, where I can, with what tools God give me. My father never did that many." For the first time he stilled, a far-off look about him. "A weak man. He had a deformity of the face."

Moshim nodded, ushered Ekkero inside to sit upon the cabin's sole chair. In the humble convention of his role, he sat himself on the floor, gazing upwards.

"Thank you gauldr. I hanker to speak to you of some things. Gauge your opinion." His knee bounced up and down and his mouth moved in silence, before words rushed from it. "Some of the men. I wonder at their want of virtue and their contribution to our purpose and Svangur's Intention. Qed, the Austeri exile. I've nay qualms of the man's labour but his beliefs are profane. Makes demands of his gods, he does. Idolatry, fiddling with little clay figurines. Should I stake my soul upon reliance of his? Others, too. The bard Slatre, and the other man, Hunvir. They revel in trivialities, gauldr. Hedonism. Sloth. Fester, it does. My fear."

Moshim considered, allowing a pause to decelerate the conversation and Ekkero's thoughts. "Still yourself. Breathe slowly." Ekkero did so, with an effort, and Moshim was surprised to see tears in the man's eyes. "I've not known you long, Ekkero, you're a man of vitality and perseverance, I see this. A servant of His Intention. But humility is the bridge uniting those virtues, son. Remember Zarat's words. 'Though we live abreast with men who insult our disposition, their aspect is to us a precious stone, buried in the mud of a clouded lake. Abide, as he abides.' Do you know what that means?"

Ekkero, struggling to compose himself, shook his head.

"It means other people might have virtues that you don't know about. Don't assume they have no virtue, just because you are unaware of them. Svangur tolerated Dregva's abuses, and he tolerates the frailties of men. He himself is imperfect, as are we. Tolerance and humility are not acts of the muscles, but of the heart. Train your heart in stillness, through repose, as you train your muscles through movement."

Ekkero nodded, and the nod became a rocking from the waist up. Then he stilled, and met Moshim's eyes. "My wife, or I, have something wrong about us, I fear. We've tried for a baby. Many times, but something…it doesn't take." His lip quivered then his mouth tightened in defiance. "She is a good woman, gauldr. I pulled her from the misfortune in which she found herself. She worked at the Lepe docks, you see."

Moshim jabbed a finger at him, and injected authority into his tone. "It is not your duty to succeed, Ekkero. It is your duty to try. In all things. If and when our mission brings us to uncivil people, you will be my right hand. There will be much to do, and I will need your vitality. I am not the young man I was."

Watching Werdom's hulking form lumbering about the deck, Moshim wondered if he should have imparted to Ekkero the value of delight in simple things. Or perhaps the man should follow the captain's example and chew jamweed, though no doubt the staining of his teeth would mortify him. Moshim fingered a plain circular locket that hung from a leather cord about his neck. Closing his eyes, he raised and kissed the locket, before letting it fall to his chest.

First Hand Dalind Bark approached. "Um, gauldr, officer's muster. Best not keep the captain waiting."

#

The captain surveyed the men who stood around the long table before him. Knuld and Ulter were engaged in the impenetrable lexicon of formulae, stress tolerances and corrosion rates. Laknir Hal spoke to Hirdrengr Tove of the treatment of bone fractures and means of stemming blood loss. Noron, the cook, unloaded innumerable complaints upon Dalind who bore them with fortitude, occasionally trying and failing to interject. Moshim was silent, chin lowered to his chest, appearing asleep. Skuld smiled; like himself, Canna was simply observing the others. Their eyes met and Skuld winked at him, then cleared his throat. Chatter withered away and they turned to him, expectant.

"Seat yourselves, gentleman," said Skuld, adopting his best captain tone. He remained standing and fetched bowls of fruits and nuts from a high cupboard, and shoved them around the table. "Help yourself. Thank you for joining me, everyone." Skuld sat, shuffled his chair away from the table, and leaned back, resting ankle on thigh. He weaved his fingers together and flexed them away from himself, knuckles popping. "Let's begin. Blessed with clement conditions, we are, my friends. The silver-water in my air-pressure gauge, a device of my own invention, lest you forget, suggests this will continue for the foreseeable. We will reach the Orn Islands in…ten days, perhaps, Hier Ulter?"

"I'd say so, sir," said Ulter, nodding. All the men leaned to the navigator as he spoke with the gentle querulous inflection of Qeren town. "Could be nine if this south-westerly remains at our backs."

"Excellent. As you know, gentlemen, the Orn Islands already bask in the invigorating glow of the Overdrengr's influence. To put it another way, somewhere on each island lies a rotting, wooden model of the Bridge, left by my brave but inferior predecessors. Nobody lives there, nor ever has by my reckoning. We'll visit the two largest islands, Hrno and Irna, largely for the sheer joy of exploration and discovery, but also to provide our inexperienced naturalist a gentle introduction to the wilder realms of Earth." Canna felt his cheeks flush. "Hier Knuld, will a careening be necessary?"

Knuld's expression was of grizzled indigestion as he rubbed the wispy hairs on his chin. He made a *maybe, maybe not* gesture and Canna wondered how a face could become so weathered.

"It's worth doing. We've lost a smidgen of pace; barnacles on the hull, what have you. Stink Bay on eastern Hrno's the perfect spot for it, glassy calm at high tide. If we roll my girl over and have a look at her belly, it's all to the good."

"Stink Bay?" Canna blurted, laughing. Wincing embarrassment around the table.

Skuld smiled at Canna with paternal indulgence. "Forgive him, gentlemen. He knows not our ways. Now Canna, during officer's muster, dialogue is mediated by the most senior officer. In other words, speak when you're spoken to. But your query is valid and insightful. On occasion, uncountable jellyfish expire on the shore, to rot in the sun. The stench will clear your sinuses, let me tell you."

Skuld turned back to his master shipbuilder. "Anything else, Knuld?"

"Just a plea for our first hand, if you're minded, captain, for scrubbing and swabbing to be undertook with naught complacency. The mirkwood, you see. Light and stiff, a beautiful wood for the purpose, but if not scrubbed sufficiently with a pumice after swabbing, it's prone to mould."

Skuld turned to his first hand. "Relay that to the men, Hier Dalind. I see a speck of mould on my deck and I will unleash my disappointment upon your scrotum. I can smell it from twenty paces. Mould, that is, not your scrotum. Your hygiene is beyond reproach. And keep up the fire drills. Every man is to be capable of working those pumps, even if blind, with a lungful of smoke and cock aflame. Morale?"

Dalind's hand stopped in the process of transferring a dried verell to his mouth. He started returning it to the bowl, but thought better of it and placed it on the table in front of him. "Um, morale's good, sir. The bard entertains us, the hands, I mean. Uncanny impressions of some of the officers." Faces around the table were impassive and Dalind hurried on. "Compliments to you Hier Knuld, the lower deck is blessedly cooled by your innovations. One thing, captain. Some men have reported thefts. Personal items. Karelud's had one of his agitator pamphlets taken, and Qed, one his little figurines."

Skuld's knuckles whitened. He glowered at Dalind, but his voice was gentle. "Only now, you report this to me, Dalind? My first hand? My sweet FH?" Men studied the table as the air closed about them. Dalind shrank while the captain's will swelled into every corner.

The first hand was a drowning man flailing for driftwood. "I'm sorry captain, I—"

A raised finger silenced him. "Mistrust is as lethal to a ship as fire and storm. Any further incidents of theft will be reported to me immediately, Dalind. But experience whispers to me that confronting the men at this stage will compound the enmity between them. I will impress upon the bard the need to foster good spirit, and this applies to you all. Men do not steal from those they regard as brothers. However, if the thief is identified with certainty, I will flog the bastard."

Skuld's posture relaxed and he smiled. "Noron, gracious culinary conjurer and master of stores. Report, if you would."

Noron pouted and arched his fingers, a remarkably feminine gesture for a pile of boulders, held together by clothing. "All good, captain, stores are in good shape, full rations to continue. Could do with a hand treating the barrels. The boy though, sir, if I may say so, is a fucking wanker." His voice rose, his fists clenched and he bared his teeth, as if goaded by some remorseless, invisible tormentor. "Fat fucking wanker. Fucked up the rotation, would have cost us a day's meat. Doesn't listen, to me or my ladle. I put the bastard on half rations."

Skuld closed his eyes and took a moment. "Is that wise, Noron? The boy simply lacks experience."

Noron bellowed, "He lacks brains and balls! I'll ruin the bastard if I see fit."

Skuld banged the table and roared, "Remember who the boy's father is, for ruin's sake! Keep your sadism under control, you lunatic."

Rising into a crouch, his chair hurtling backwards and thumping on the bulkhead, Noron countered with even greater ferocity. A finger jabbed and spittle flew. "I'll run my fucking galley as I see fit and I wouldn't give a shit if the boy was the Overdrengr's fuck hole!"

The captain spluttered a laugh. "Very well, Noron. I thank you, as always, for your honesty and eloquence. Anything else?"

Noron retook his seat in a pose of regal detachment. "No, captain."

"Then let us hear from our pioneers of science. Hal, Canna?"

Canna blinked and glanced sidelong at the other men, wondering if he had imagined the tirade.

Hal spoke. "No major issues, captain. Hand Hunvir clonked his head on the main boom, the silly sausage. He'll be fine. The big man though, Werdom, picks at his cuticles to a damaging degree which I am treating with an ointment. It sounds trivial but he lacks the sense to desist, I fear, and risks befoulment. And our bard seems unwell. Clasps his stomach when he thinks others are not watching and his features are drawn. With some reluctance he allowed me to examine him."

"Is it the twitches?"

"Unlikely at this stage, sir. If I didn't know better, I'd say he lacks nourishment." Noron bristled and the laknir grinned. "I'll monitor him, captain, and I don't wish to exaggerate. He functions well enough. It's his first time at sea and some men react badly to the sea air and stored water."

Skuld nodded at Canna.

"Um, nothing to report at the moment, captain. My diary has started, as you know. I'm using graded simplification to, um, figure out how the complexity of things...no, I mean, I'm looking at things at different layers of how complicated they are and—"

"Excellent, Canna, sounds very clever. Let us hear from the loyal fist of the Overdrengr. Hirdrengr Tove?"

A polite smile. The hirdrengr's presence rivalled that of the captain; less theatrical, but more menacing. Each syllable was enunciated while his torso, arms and hands remained still.

"Thank you, captain," he said. "All is well with my three drengrs, Nijal and the twins. They are experienced and disciplined. I occupy them with drills and maintenance of their weapons and equipment. As you know, our purpose is to provide military support to the mission's aims. However, please consider us at your service."

"Tove," said the captain, "I thank you for your generous offer, but if your men are bored, just say as much." Tove did not react and the captain spread his arms in welcome. "I see no reason for your drengrs not to mix with the men a little more. Remind them, please, that on the *Improbable*, the drengr-civilian relationship does not apply. The men are not villagers to be presided over."

Tove nodded. "Very good, captain."

"It is good," Skuld boomed. "Most good. Blessed am I, with the finest cadre of officers ever to set sail and I thank you all for your duty and labour. I bid you good day and God hone your blades. Canna, Moshim, tarry a moment." Each man gave a curt bow as he shuffled out. Noron curtseyed extravagantly and Skuld threw a nut at him.

When the three were alone, Skuld sucked his teeth, pushed his chair back against the bulkhead and lay his feet on the table with his fingers laced behind his head. "Thank you, both. You may speak freely." He grinned at Canna. "That means, Philos, you may blurt out whatever enters your clever head without waiting for me to talk." Canna smiled in abashment at the mention of the nickname the crew had given him, Philosopher. Whether it was meant in affection or mockery, he was unsure. Perhaps both.

"Captain," Canna said, assembling his words with caution, "if I may say so, I was taken aback by your exchange with Noron. Is he always so…combative?"

"Oh yes, Canna, he is. And the only viable response is to reciprocate his fury ten-fold. It's the only means by which he can assimilate information. His ears literally do not hear words spoken at normal volume. You witnessed mere polite banter by our standards. Behold the wonkiness of my nose." Skuld leaned forward and waggled his nose with thumb and forefinger. "The bastard headbutted me once. I dangled him over the gunwale by his ankles for that. But there's no finer ship's cook or quartermaster to be found, I assure you."

Skuld pulled dark leaves from a small tin and popped them in his mouth. His wonky nose bobbed as he chewed. From somewhere he fetched two clay bottles with cork stoppers.

"Beer, gentlemen. Drink, I insist."

Canna sipped. Moshim took a hearty swig and let out a satisfied breath.

"Thank you, captain," the gauldr said, raising the bottle in toast.

Skuld nodded and sighed. "Enough preamble. Listen. Tensions, rivalries and affections between seafaring men are to me as clear as if they were coloured strings, linking them by hand and foot. The frigidity between the two of you pains me, in my love for you both. I am here to thaw it. Canna, this is about the slaughter of the slipskins, yes? A lamentable, though spectacular episode for which I bear as much guilt as the gauldr. I apologise for my part in it."

Canna straightened his back. "If we are speaking frankly, captain, inflicting such misery was cruel and pointless."

Moshim fingered the locket at his chest and spoke. "I apologise also, Canna. The creatures suffered greatly, unnecessarily so. I offer no excuse, only an explanation. The Book teaches that the agony of soulless beasts carries no weight, it has no bearing, whereas a man's suffering tempers his soul for the ultimate battle with Dregva. This is what I wished to convey in my sermon. However, searching my heart I admit that with the captain's help, I desired to give the people bloody entertainment, to further my own standing. This was the opposite of the humility which I preach to others, and it is to my shame. Suffering is suffering, regardless of spiritual implications, and I am unsurprised by your reaction. You're a man of decency and your concern does you credit."

Canna blinked, surprised at the lump rising in his throat. "Thank you, Moshim."

"I'm aware of your reason for being here, Canna. The real reason. As is the captain, of course. Bradden."

Canna's heartbeat quickened as Skuld cast him an ambiguous expression.

Moshim spoke again. "The Book offers no justification for punishing acts of kindness, regardless of the recipient of that kindness. Renunciation of the torpid was an economic, political strategy of the late Overdrengr, in the guise of a spiritual imperative. Giving succour to Bradden was an act of humility, in your knowledge that he could not join you in your final battle at Svangur's side. Northerners believe Zarat himself entered torpor, lending him the clarity to commune with God."

Skuld clapped his hands and gave an exaggerated wink. "Don't worry Canna, your secret's safe with us. I am pleased this has been resolved and I am nourished by discussions of life and of the spirit." Chewing in contemplation, he seemed to forget he was not alone and spoke to the overhead. "Travelled far, I have, and seen many sad and wonderful things. Everything is connected, is it not? Every tiny plant and crawling thing has its little corner of existence exquisitely crafted for it, and each fulfils its part in a web of mutual reliance. The tiny veins within a leaf resemble the blood system of a man; such balance within nature fascinates me.

"I met a farmer, once, who for some reason known only to himself, mated a vit with a precet. The kitten, pup? had the hunting instinct of a precet, pouncing at string, but the scampering legs of a vit. Remarkable little creature."

Skuld frowned, shook his head and turned back to the men before him. "Canna, you illuminate the workings of God's creation, and Moshim, you give it meaning. I thank you both. Go now."

# 8. OVERCOMING

*8<sup>th</sup> day of Poori, 893 AZ.*

Karelud Darkener tottered the heavy parcel on one thigh, freeing a hand to rap on the door of the captain's cabin. Greeted with silence, he muttered an oath. The old bastard was making him wait. It was too hot, his arms ached and he did not need this shit.

As he was about to knock again, Skuld's voice called out. "Enter."

Gritting his teeth, Karelud entered, arms straining under the load. "Your linens and whatnot, sir."

Skuld and his navigator, Ulter, conversed over a chart laid out on the table before them, ignoring him. Tove sat aloof, smoking a pipe, and studied Karelud through a cloud of smoke. A sour twist to his mouth, Karelud glanced around the cabin; bottles of Lepe wine, arranged in a wooden frame; a thick, ornate Gozan rug beside the four-posted bed. The space.

Skuld waved a hand towards the bulkhead opposite the door. "Down there."

Karelud shambled to the far end of the cabin, deposited his burden and stood to attention. "Will that be all, Captain?" he asked.

Skuld produced a small earthenware pot, which featured an elegant rendering of the Bryggn crest, in gold. It was filled with a stinking brown liquid, and its outside was tarnished by old stains of the same stuff: the captain's jamweed expectorations.

"Get rid of this, please. Ask the cook's boy to scrub it. Thank you Karemund."

Karelud's shoulders sagged as he gazed at the pot. Traded at Arada, it would feed him for a month, and he imagined pouring its contents over the captain.

"Yes, sir."

He left, and hurled the contents of the pot overboard. "Fancy twats."

Atop the forecastle deck, the bard entertained a group of hands with a bawdy song, accompanied by delicate plucking of a tagelharp and rude blasts on a massive horn. Karelud felt a thump through his tattered shoes, from the cargo hatch upon which he stood. Someone desired egress. He twirled the clay pot in his fingers and gazed at the horizon, feeling cool air unknot his brow. The thumps beneath him increased in urgency. He stepped aside, the hatch immediately bursting open to reveal an intractable mass of tarry rope. Karelud stared at it in confusion, and fought off a smirk as Canna's sweaty face pushed its way through the tangle.

"Philos! Sorry brohir, I didn't realise you were there. Daydreaming again, I was. Here, let me." Plunging his hands into the stuff, he helped Canna heave it through the hatch and dump it on deck. "Mucking in with us lowlifes, eh?" Canna nodded, taking the arm Karelud offered as he laboured through the hatch.

Thin fibres covered his upper body and he brushed at them to no effect. "Thank you. Ruin, that itches. Yes, I've been unpicking old rope for oakum."

"Not the most diverting task, is it?"

Canna wiped sweat from his brow and shook his head. "No, but it occupies my hands while I think." Karelud replied with a cursory smile.

Applause broke out at the conclusion of the bard's song. He bowed deep and flapped a hand at Canna and Karelud. "Lads, come up. Sit." Men sat in a rough circle, some on coils of rope or boxes, and made way for the newcomers. Werdom picked at his nails, his bulk hunched over crossed legs. His slack mouth broke into a smile as Karelud got comfortable next to him.

Slatre cocked a querulous eyebrow at the pot Karelud still clutched. "I like your new pot. Put your ear to it, you might hear the sea." Canna squeezed between the boy, Millitre, and Yavilad, who nodded a greeting. Hunvir sat propped on his elbows with his legs splayed, advertising his stoutness, and grinned. "Now gentlemen," Slatre began, "the captain believes morale among the men is not what it could be, and there's nothing like an enforced exercise in jollity to cheer a man's spirits, so here we are."

Karelud spoke up. "Slatre, did you ask Skuld about the contract amendments? He's expecting us to explore and whatnot. Our standard articles don't cover that shit."

"Yeah. Don't cover that shit," Werdom said.

Slatre shrugged. "Of course I've relayed your concerns. Alas, the captain and his henchmen are to us as the ancient, nameless gods of the Earth. Distant and implacable, disdainful of the trivial suffering of worms such as we. Anyway, you should talk to Dalind, he's your first hand." He indicated the quarterdeck deck, on which the man in question held the ship's wheel with a casual hand.

Ekkero turned his palms to Karelud in supplication, pained disapproval creasing his sharp features. "Karelud, our place is not to seek reward for our labours, that is vanity and sloth. We must humiliate our muscles in stillness and exert our vitality in the service of God's Intention."

Hunvir chuckled and spluttered.

Karelud scowled and pointed to his forehead. "God's ribs, spare me. I had it up to here with your sort in the gauldrhaven. Fucking hole. Stick your Widdith shit up your arse."

Ekkero's body jiggled as if at the mercy of his own personal earthquake.

Karelud turned back to the bard. "Anyway, fuck Dalind, he's useless. How come you aren't FH, Yav? You'd be better than that kettle of piss and you do half his work anyway."

Yavilad shrugged. His voice was slow and quiet but its musicality commanded the men's attention. "Yeah. I'd rather not be from home that long. You know my daughter's problems, her thwartism. A lot of help, she needs. I like to spend time with her."

Ekkero looked shocked. "She's hang faced? And you let her live? Yav, the Book says 'Relieve an ill-formed child's life.' What use is she to God?"

Hunvir's eyes widened and he breathed, "Prick."

Yavilad's expression was mild and he picked something from his teeth. "Mm. There's debate on that, Ekkero. Zarat was a Nagrellian tribesman, as you know. His writings on fertility found their way to Magnate Arslan, who made him his laknir. But Arslan tried to force a unified belief system on the north Eyran tribes, a mish-mash of People of the Body stuff and low-Austeri animism. Zarat objected and fled across the Aran Sea to Southern Ibr."

Yavilad swigged from a leather flask, wiped his mouth, and continued. "The point is, Zarat's written scraps were in Nagrellian, and were only translated into Ibrian years later. By that time, the Eyran tribes and the Nagrellian language were all gone. 'Relieve' in the Book is probably translated from the Nagrellian word, 'ghwuire' which meant 'provide succour,' not 'take away.' It was a mistranslation. Zarat meant the lives of ill-formed children should be made comfortable, not that they should be murdered. The latter interpretation makes no sense when you consider the next line, 'Lend them vitality as they lend you humility.' Perhaps you can see, Ekkero, how the Book can be exploited to justify the foulest actions," a pause, "to men of lesser wit."

Ekkero blinked, and his knee juddered, as if it wished to tear itself loose.

The boy Millitre let out a high-pitched giggle, pointed at Ekkero and slapped his thigh. "We got a scholar! Laknir, come quick! This man has a new arsehole which needs sewing up!"

Yavilad said, his voice controlled, "If it makes you feel better, Ekkero, my daughter's unlikely to see adulthood."

The bard clapped his hands. "Heart-warming stuff. I hope you could follow all that, Werdom."

Under the big man's scrunched forehead, kindled a vague awareness that he was being mocked. "What you say?" With surprising grace and swiftness, he uncoiled to his feet, fists clenched, eyes mad. Karelud calmed him with a gesture and he sat.

"Ruin, Kare, keep your troll under control," said Hunvir, looking Werdom up and down. "Where'd you find him anyway?"

Werdom's face resumed its usual placidity. On the main deck, Tove and his three drengrs clanked swords, thrusting and parrying with stylised, languid movements.

Canna noted with interest that the Bard had not flinched at Werdom's anger.

Slatre spoke again. "Werdom, my sweet one, I made mock, and apologise. Forgive me." Turning to the rest of them, he said, "In the spirit of resignation to our enforced proximity, let us learn something of each other, by sharing tales of our overcoming."

Millitre piped up with a grin. "This trip's my overcoming."

Yavilad raised his eyebrows. "God's ribs, that's harsh. I just wrote a poem. Shite, it was."

"Ekkero," Slatre said, "why don't you tell us how you came to leave childhood things behind. Show us you are more than a remorseless weapon of the Lord."

Ekkero's hands scurried over himself, scratching his nose, running through his hair. "Um, it was odd, as regards intentions and outcome achieved. The dichotomy therein. I was thirteen. Resolved, I was, to run the distance from West End, in Lepe, along the coast and up to Keth, then loop back through Nifl Forest. Through the south west side of it cuts an old road."

"That must be, what, fifty miles?" said Millitre.

"Well, that was the intention, but for me Svangur required other work. On Lepe outskirts, around Fisheye Lane, a building was afire. If you've been there, you know what a nest of a place it is. I pulled some kids out and I was coughing, spewing up and that, but they were alright. Gauldr deemed that my overcoming."

Hunvir said, "Impressive. And you avoided cock-rot running through the docks?" Titters and giggles among the men. Hunvir held his belly and roared laughter. Ekkero stopped twitching and turned a cold eye on Hunvir.

As one, the men turned towards a wail from the main deck. Arjier, the cook's boy, staggered from the galley with blood pouring from his head. Chubby arms failed to slow the assaults which Noron rained upon him with an iron skillet. Canna winced while the men watched with interest.

Noron desisted momentarily and folded his arms, panting. "Just gonna take it? Take a swing, rich boy. Come on." Arjier wept, his face a child's painting of blood and snot. A chorus of gasps escaped the men on the quarterdeck, as the cook delivered an almighty kick to Arjier's balls. The boy crumpled. Tove and his drengrs had turned to watch and one of them laughed.

Slatre called down, "Noron, leave the boy alone, for the love of God. Someone'll have to clean up that blood." Arjier, leaking on hands and knees, raised his battered head to the quarterdeck.

Noron turned to Slatre like a man waking in confusion from a dream. "Wha'd you say?"

Slatre swallowed and winked at Canna. "We were just getting to know each other up here, Noron. It's been emotional but productive. Would you like to tell us about your overcoming?"

Noron's lip curled into a snarl. "Fucking overcoming? Fuck off. I'll tell you my overcoming. I killed a man who stuck his beak into my business." Blood dripped from the skillet. "What do we need a fucking musician for? What you doing here? Laknir says you shat yourself. We should fucking eat you, useless twat."

Slatre said nothing while Arjier regained his feet, clinging to the mainmast for support. Noron spat and withdrew to his lair.

Karelud gave a little "Oop," scampered down to the main deck and handed the spit-pot to Arjier. "Here you go," he said.

Arjier stared at the pot in confusion. Through broken lips he mumbled, "Thank you."

"Captain says to clean it." Karelud clapped the boy on the shoulder and thumped his own chest. "Strength, brohir."

The boy gazed upwards with the pot in both hands, as if hoping deliverance would drop into it from the sky. Karelud returned to the quarterdeck and took his seat. The soldiers resumed their make-believe battles.

Slatre grimaced, shook his head and returned his attention to the men. "Hunvir, I'm sure your overcoming is a tale of dignity and sublime adroitness. Let's hear it."

Hunvir smirked. "I diddled it. Dad was a cooper and wannabe intellectual, but he was thick as a bag of hair, not proper clever like Yav. He wanted to me write some religious essay to impress the gauldr. This lad, a simpering little shit, I caught him trying to have his way with his little sister, behind the temple of all places. 'You'll be doing my overcoming for me, lad. Make it smart.' He didn't argue. Couple of days later, he gives me this bundle of papers, with the title, get this, 'Sublimating Demythologisation of the Weaker Sex in Widdith Casuistry, and its Applications for Battlefield Strategy in the Final Conflict with Dregva.'"

Millitre frowned. "The fuck?"

"That's what I thought," He popped a piece of ship's biscuit in his mouth and spoke as he chewed, brushing crumbs from his chest. "It backfired though, see. This essay was the tits, best thing anyone'd ever seen. They all thought I was some prodigy. Registration was coming up and they were gonna put me forward for seidhr college at Silves, but I'd have to defend the essay to the reg officer. I didn't even know what it was about, never even read it. So fuck that.

"Now, real early one morning, I takes myself off to this local pond, where lads like to fish. I hid behind a bush and spied a few fishers coming along, so I waded into the pond, and lay there, face down, like I was drowned. The lads pulled me out, all panicky like. 'Someone get 'is mum!' I just lay there, looking all thwarted like. Oh, sorry Yav. Anyway, they carry me all the way back to the village, me dribbling with a daft look on my face.

"Over the next few days, I mooned about, like my mind was gone, getting spoon-fed by my folks, pissing myself, the lot. Registration came up and they showed me to the officer, displaying me all sad like. He looks me up and down and I stands there making noises at him." Hunvir hooted and squealed. Dalind peered at them from the quarterdeck, shielding his eyes from the sun.

"Gets worse. I was sat there at the table, smearing myself with porridge, and my fucking parents start talking about drowning me for real. 'I can't take it anymore! Look at him! We'll say he slipped away in the night.' All this stuff. Fuck! So, then, I starts making a miracle recovery, managing to blurt the occasional bit of sense and coming back to myself, bit by bit. My parents had mixed feelings on that, if I'm honest. Good times." Hunvir shook his head at the memory.

Slatre applauded, chuckling.

Ekkero's voice was cracked and thin, and his head swivelled around for support, in vain. "You should be ashamed, Hunvir. You've had no overcoming. Still a child, you are."

Hunvir's expression hardened, though his smile remained fixed. "You need to lighten up," he said. "Werdom, if I give you a boiled egg would you strangle this miserable bastard?" Karelud touched Werdom's forearm and shook his head a little. "Maybe you'll like this one better, Ekkero," said Hunvir. He turned to the bard. "If you don't mind, Slatre?"

Slatre gestured, *the floor is yours*.

Hunvir cleared his throat. "I was labouring for a geezer in Lepe, and a few of us used to unwind at the Moderation Inn. Dodgy place, very seedy. You know it, Ekkero? No? Ask your wife." Ekkero got to his feet, stomped to the main deck and disappeared below.

Canna spoke. "You push him too far, Hunvir."

"He'll wank it off. Shall I go on? Anyway, a group of us was playing cards one night, hunt the maid, and this guy was there, a real silly bastard. Sure of himself, you know. He's got this metal tankard he was real proud of, inscribed with his name and overcoming date, or some shit. But because of where he's got this tankard, I can see his cards. I'm robbing him blind, over and over, sitting there with this big pile of marks.

"By the end of the night, it's just me and him and he's desperate to claw something back. For a stake he offers a night with his daughter, to do whatever I want with, versus the whole lot I've won off him. Well known, she is, this daughter, a beauty. Prim with it, though. 'No, no,' I says, 'You're getting silly.' He throws a fit, and yells at me, 'One! Fucking! More!' He swipes this fucking tankard of his off the table. Shit. But I thought, why not, life's too short. So, we play this final game, fair and square, and I beat him anyway. The guy just hangs his head.

"Couple of nights later, he comes to my dump, with this daughter, looking fucking terrified. She's made up all pretty, but I can see she's got bruising to her cheek. 'You treat her right, or I swear,' he says. So, he goes off and his girl sits there on my bed, hands in her lap, all demure like. 'Get it over with then,' she says. Now, I'm a prick, but

I'm not a rapist prick, so I just got her to clean my place up a bit, cook me some eggs and whatnot. She kips the night, knackered, and toddles off in the morning. All good, no harm done.

"But then, that night, the dad barges into my place, a couple of his pals as backup and they give me a pasting. 'Take the piss out my daughter, would you? Taking the piss out of me?' he says. 'She just cooked me some eggs,' I says. Twat was okay with me raping his daughter, but not with her doing a bit of cooking and cleaning. Some people! They drag me down the docks, tie my hands up and feet and bundle me in a row boat. We row out half a mile and they're gonna push me overboard, this guy still muttering on about people taking the piss out of him.

"Now, these lads can't tie knots for shit. My hands are behind my back and, piece of piss, I slip the rope loose, but I'm keeping my hands behind me. I start begging, 'Come on, just untie my feet, yeah? Give us a chance, at least. I gave you one more game, didn't I?' And I swear, no shit, that while I'm talking to them dead in the face, I pulls my hand out, scratch my nose, and put it back again. They didn't notice shit. Dad of the year looks at me for a bit, unties my feet and then they chuck me overboard. I just swam back to shore and went about my business. No harm done. I avoided the Moderation from then on, though."

Slatre applauded. "Well children, what have we learnt today?"

#

Below deck, Ekkero's teeth clenched and he slapped at his naked torso. In swift, jerking movements he dropped to a squat, kicked his legs out behind him and then forward again, knees meeting his chest. Then he jumped, his crown striking the overhead, hard, and dropped back to a squat. Over and over, he moved through each stage, accelerating through them, breath deteriorating into hoarse panting. Glistening with sweat and blood, he collapsed to the deck, empty and purified.

"I am your faithful servant. I abide as you abide."

# 9. THE AUSTERI

*10th day of Poori, 893 AZ.*

Yavilad Slowater dangled at the outer hull with ocean spray stinging his eyes and wind numbing his fingers. A stiff leather harness cut into his groin and armpits, and was attached to ropes with metal clasps. By means of a wheeled hand winch on deck, the weary marionette could be manoeuvred fore and aft, higher or lower. Vagaries of the ship's heeling sent him swinging away from the hull and back towards it, at pace. He hissed as his knees smacked the hull, hawked and spat, and set about jimmying another barnacle from the wood with an iron trowel.

"Keep her steady, Dalind, for fuck's sake," he grumbled. Slimy life squirmed inside the shell he beheld, then he tossed it away.

Knuld's wizened head appeared over the gunwale. "Alright down there, Yav?"

"Yes, sir. Just one bolt showing a little greenness, so far, otherwise all well. These barnacles do not consent to their eviction without considerable persuasion though, sir. Stubborn tenants if I may say so. Lower when ready." Knuld disappeared and the winch creaked above.

Yav juddered downwards until his lower half dangled in the sea, his testicles now wet and freezing as well as strangled. They retreated for the warmth of his abdomen and he gasped. "God's puckered arse, that's cold." Fighting the instinct to shiver, he hacked at barnacles with gusto.

The captain's bearded face appeared and his voice was clear above the ocean's roar. "Yavilad, cast asunder every last interloper and stinking rag of seaweed. Inspect every bolt as if it were something you found on your cock."

Yavilad gave a thumbs up. "You mean ask my wife to take a look, captain?"

Skuld laughed, and withdrew.

Yavilad wondered how the innumerable choices he had made in life had led him to this position. In one sense, he thought, perhaps we are all hanging by our freezing balls, scraping sea creatures off a boat in the middle of nowhere at the behest of a narcissistic madman.

A shelled thing pinged off his forehead and plopped into the water. My problem, he considered, is that I'm reasonably competent at everything but excellent at nothing. Reasonably reliable, reasonably personable, reasonably intelligent, married to a reasonably attractive wife. I have neither Werdom's strength, Ulter's brain, Ekkero's faith or even Karelud's low cunning. A reasonably miserable existence, terminating in a reasonably meaningless death. Ah well, he thought, I suppose to some poor shits a reasonable life's an elusive fantasy.

On deck, Knuld locked the winch handle into position, cleared his throat and squinted at the captain. Skuld chewed his lip and stared at nothing. Ulter leant on the gunwale, filling a pipe.

"Thoughts, shipbuilder?" Skuld said to the distance.

Knuld scratched at his arse with one hand, his beard with the other and sniffed. "A little excess roll could be slowing us, nothing to alarm ourselves. Plus the barnacles and whatever shit might be dragging on the keel and rudder. Maiden voyage, new-type ship, y'know. Can only figure out so much before you set sail. Never know how it'll perform in ocean currents till you get there." A gnarled finger pointed to the galley and he cackled. "Mayhap the cook's starved his boy so much we've lost ballast. Stuff him down in the hold, maybe. Could be worth fitting bilge keels when we turn her over at Hrno. Runners for 'em are already there, simple job to attach. Can remove 'em while afloat if need be."

High above, the bard teetered along a spar, bottle in hand, swaying in a parody of drunkenness. "Excuse me, my lady," he yelled to the mast, "I seek the outhouse. Have you seen it?" Falling forwards, as if in a faint, his body curled into a somersault and landed tangled among the rigging. He burped and shook his head.

Skuld nodded. "Very well. She's a sexy wench of a ship, but I must squeeze every drop of milk from her udders." Ulter peered at him. "Set about your calculations, lads, put your heads together. Worth sending a diver under?"

Ulter shook his head at the captain. "Not worth risking a man for the sake of the little speed we've lost, I'd say, captain. We're still pushing on. We'll be at the Orns in a few days."

"Not even Werdom? We could just rig him up and have him tow us along. Level of intellect around here would increase markedly if that one drowned. Not sure he'd notice though."

Hearing his name, Werdom paused scrubbing at the deck, grinned and waved at the officers. It was the enthusiastic wave of a small child. They smiled and waved back.

Ulter whispered around his pipe stem, "Wave back or the bastard might eat you." Knuld spluttered a laugh.

#

In the lower deck, Canna and the Austeri hand, Qed ij Qed, sat cross legged before a pile of wooden barrel staves and iron hoops. Dust motes flickered in a shaft of radiance from the overhead grill, and the hull's creaks and groans offered sorrowful accompaniment to their exertion.

Qed held a pedagogical finger aloft and spoke in a thick accent. "Boring, yes. But important job, Philos. Do proper. Barrels no good? Food spoil." He mimed being sick. "Like this, see." He smoothed the curved staves with a sanding block using long, regular strokes, and brushed sawdust from his legs. Canna copied, his strokes short and uncertain. "No no. Glide, you see? Like glide hands over woman. Be nice, yes?"

Qed was shirtless, his upper body and arms taut and wiry. An angry pink scar bisected his trunk diagonally, obliterating his left nipple, but a scholarly, angular face contrasted with his ravaged torso. Hunvir and Millitre traded fraternal banter over an expanse of sail material, inspecting, treating and repairing. Life at sea, Canna reflected, largely involves rubbing things and shouting.

Chewing jamweed as his hands toiled, Qed told Canna something of his past, growing up in the warren backstreets of Karidth. Cosmopolitan, febrile and dusty, the city sweltered in the heart of the Langbar region. Ostensibly a centre of learning and philosophy, the economy of the place was as much founded on rumour, favours, grudges, debts and brutality as on silver and gold yekels. While the people scrabbled among themselves for the meagrest advantage, the city Fathers nurtured their envy and disdain for the rival city of Sardan, nexus of Austeri industry and technical innovation.

Young Qed was skinny and quick of thought and body. He stood lookout for the criminal gangs which ran illegal gambling dens and brothels, eventually heading a loose collective of twenty such urchins, while still a boy himself. While his booze-addled mother slumped and gibbered in their hovel, he devoted his evenings to learning. He pored over stolen candlelit texts, finger trailing along dense script, and imbibed the teachings of stony-faced patriarchs who glowered from the pages. He gorged on theological mechanics, parallel linguistics, and the great philosophical schools: Kahl's dogmatic brutality; the effete elitism of Zahir's cultivation theory; the Sardanic school of self-deception.

"Good theories, very clever," Qed said, and spat a gob of jamweed juice into a tin pot. "How organise life? Who to be in charge? Nice, nice. But missing thing? Simple goodness. Austeri so cruel, cruel." Qed stroked his chin theatrically and looked down his nose. "Rich Karidth teacher sit, gaze at flower, weeping, 'Ah, life so beautiful, gods favour us,' then raping slaves, making pregnant, drowning baby."

Qed's cultivated network of slave-spies chanced upon highly damaging information concerning the aging Father, Darahiz ed Molak. Despite the sexual hedonism of the ruling class, such information would be an affront to the city's most fundamental standards of human dignity, and ruinous to the Father himself. Gifting the grubby details to a rival Father, Qed gained a long-term patron, and steadily rose through the echelons of non-criminal society. Increasingly respected for his academic learning as much as his propensity for getting things done, he settled into a sedate role as tutor to the spoiled children of the privileged.

Piles of sawdust grew around them as Qed explained, "These children. Clever but blind, you see? No understanding of life, of suffering. I took clever old learnings. Put together with…" Groping for the words, he mimed bringing two objects together. "Human feelings. Basic, you see? Love, sympathy. Control anger, be steady, see as others see. Improve self. But I, what would captain say? Fell in shit. Fathers turned against me." He smiled.

A pregnant slave woman, despairing and aggrieved, killed her owner-rapist, leaving a fat-bellied corpse in a bath of blood with a new mouth smiling in its bloated throat. As a mere commodity, the woman had no right to advocacy or trial by her peers; a committee of Fathers decided her fate, quaffing sweetmeats and wine. As per custom, the seriousness of the crime required that not only would the guilty be executed, but the entire coterie of household slaves also; twenty-six individuals, including elderly amanuenses and child drink servers. While a normal outcome in principle, the unusual number of condemned brought the case into the realm of public debate.

Qed sensed an opportunity to nudge his society away from barbarism, and campaigned for clemency and amendments to the law. His instincts, for once, were misguided. Fearing threats to their comfort, the forces of tradition and bloodlust proved too powerful and well-connected. At staggering speed, Qed was ruined, his patronage withdrawn, his history of criminal enterprise dragged into the light. Fathers who had utilised Qed's nefarious services lamented his perfidiousness and with regret, called for him to be flogged. It was a death sentence in all but name. The night before his trial, he rallied favours owed and secrets kept dry for such an occasion, and secured passage aboard the ship of an Ibrian trade envoy by name of Skuld Heel.

Canna clutched his sanding stone motionless, halfway along a stave. "What happened to the slaves?"

Qed held his hands flat in front of him, horizontally, and brought them together in a single, slow clap. "Piercing. A very big board, er…platform. All slaves tied down on platform, lie flat." He lay back with his limbs spread. "Like this. No water. No food. Hot sun." Qed sat up and grimaced. "Also, big platform above, spikes on underside, thin, long. Is all like big machine, you see?" He narrowed his eyes at Canna. "A crank is turned, little bit each day. Click. click. click. Turned by victim family, Fathers, special guests. Day after day, top platform is lower, lower, spikes coming down. Statue of Neheb looking on, god of revenge. If lucky, victims is pierced here, here." He indicated his forehead and heart. "But maybe, is pierced here. Here. Here." He pointed to his groin, mouth, and thigh. "Take many, many days to die. Great pain. Children, old peoples. Flies, wasps come. Holes in bottom platform catch blood, collected, fed to animals, make fields grow."

#

Karelud watched Werdom wave at the officers. Ulter said something, and Skuld and the shipbuilder chuckled. Karelud crawled forwards and resumed scrubbing at the deck with the pumice stone. His hands were raw, and his knees screamed, despite the wads of sacking he had tied about them.

"It's no way to organise labour, Werdom, I tell you. Rotate the tasks a bit, it's not hard. Too much for that slothful wretch Dalind to figure out. How many times have we crawled around doing this shit? Ruin and decay, my knees are fucked. Second watch on piss-easy swabbing every day." He jerked a finger downwards. "Millitre's down there wanking off Hunvir."

Two of the drengrs, Tala East and Tala West, sat cleaning their blades in silence. They were identical twins, and their eyes lifted to Karelud with uncanny synchronicity. He turned away, flustered. Werdom scrubbed and hummed, muscles rippling in his broad back. Then he stopped, dropped the stone and sat, tears welling.

"Still sad about your nubbly, Werd?"

Werdom nodded. The nubbly was a small wooden toy Karelud had crafted for him, with projections which could be spun, depressed, or fiddled with in one way or another. It helped distract him from biting away his cuticles.

Karelud patted him on the thigh. "I know, Werdom, I miss my pamphlets too. Someone took them like they took your nubbly."

"A bad person, Kare?"

"Yes, a bad person."

"Do you think they're on the ship?"

"Yes, I think so, Werdom."

"If I find out who the bad person is, I'll smash their head off!" Werdom smiled and reminisced. "Remember the bad people who hurt you, Kare? I helped—"

Karelud hissed at him, "Quiet, for ruin's sake."

Werdom leaned into him and whispered. "Sorry Kare."

A snapping noise and a cry interrupted them. Knuld stared in mute shock at the broken wooden handle clutched in his hand while rope unspooled from the broken winch in a whining glissando.

Ulter dropped his pipe and ran to gunwale. Yavilad's head disappeared underwater. "Ah, shit, he's under, captain!"

Skuld grabbed at the rope, looped it around his wrist and heaved, foot against the gunwale. Against the drag of the water, he could only halt the unspooling and he turned gritted teeth at Werdom, who sat docile.

"Get here and haul, ruin take you."

Werdom stood slowly, but didn't move. Confusion crumpled his face.

Karelud jumped to his feet and shook the big man. "Help the captain, Werdom, for God's sake. Quickly."

Werdom trotted over, took the rope from the captain and hauled Yavilad's weight with ease, hand over hand. The other men stared at his arms. A hacking cough and spluttering from below, and the bedraggled hand was dumped on deck. He groaned and vomited a thin stream of bile and seawater, then held his shivering body. A gash in his forehead bled freely.

Skuld removed his jacket, spread it over Yavilad and levelled his gaze at Karelud. "The laknir, now." He turned to Knuld. "Did you not check this piece of shit winch?"

"I checked it myself, captain, only yesterday. Handle just broke off in my hand, I don't understand it. That winch could take five men."

Werdom picked at his fingers, then recoiled in surprise as the captain shoved him hard in the chest. Skuld grabbed his shirt collar with one hand, jabbed a finger between his eyes and hissed up at him.

"I say haul, you haul, shit for brains. You don't wait for your girlfriend's say so. If I say jump overboard you do so with no hesitation or concern for my reasons."

Werdom's nostrils flared and his upper lip twitched. A vein popped in his neck.

Skuld raised his eyebrows and took a step back. "Oh? Not happy with that? Would you like to take a swipe at me, you lump?" Tove materialised at the captain's side, hand hovering at the hilt of his sword. Knuld wrung his hands in the silence.

Yavilad stuttered through his shivering. "Th-thank you...c-captain...Werdom." Tove's hand relaxed.

Skuld glared at Werdom. "I've shit bigger. Leave my sight or be flogged."

#

Canna and Qed looked up as Skuld trotted down the steps to the lower deck, the hatch banging behind him. The captain grasped Hunvir's neck in one hand and shook him; too hard to be definitely friendly, not hard enough to be overtly aggressive.

"Hunvir, my favourite lazy spawn of a slut. Teaching the young pup here the dark arts of labour avoidance?" Skuld's bearing was intense, coiled and ready. Canna held his breath without realising he was doing so.

"Ah, yes sir." Hunvir grinned. "He's a natural, sir. I've little left to teach him."

"Good, good." He raised his fists to Millitre and sparred, ducking and weaving, throwing out playful jabs and hooks. The boy reciprocated, darting this way and that.

Skuld laughed and moved on to where Canna and Qed toiled over a partly-assembled barrel. He squatted beside them and stroked the wood, nodding his approval. "Good as new, gentlemen, good as new. Qed, you're a credit to your barbaric people. Canna, join me for a sup, would you." It was not a question.

#

Skuld glugged wine from a clay bottle into two cups and pushed one to Canna across the table. He ran his hands through his hair, scratched at his neck, seeming to quiver with words unsaid. A thick book lay open on the table, filled with reams of tabulated figures.

Canna asked, "Was there a problem on deck? We heard a commotion."

"Nothing to worry about, the hull winch failed and Yavilad got a little wet." He waved away Canna's unspoken question. "He's fine, he's fine." Then he sniffed and stilled, arching his fingers and smiling. "How're you doing, Canna?"

"I'm well, captain. Trying to make myself useful, learning a lot. Looking forward to the Orn islands."

"Ah yes. They're beautiful, you know. A little sand between our toes is what we need, I think. The islands are ours in name only and Irna's interior is unexplored. We should take a look."

"I'd like that."

"I bet." He drummed his fingers; a slow, expectant rhythm. "You've never left southern Ibr have you, Canna? Before this, I mean."

"No, captain. I'd never been further from Riverbend than Qeren. I thought the town exotic, because their streets are paved with a different stone from Silves. But my God, speaking to Qed earlier. His history, ruin."

"Told you of his downfall, then, the slave girl who undid him." Canna nodded. "What did you think? Of the Austeri, their way of doing things?"

Canna rubbed the back of his neck and grimaced. "I'm sure they're people just like us, deep down, but the cruelty of them beggars belief. How does that happen? That normal people consent to such things. I wonder to myself; would I be there cheering on an execution? I thought I knew. But I know Qed's a decent man. Brave."

"He is, he is. But the Austeri, you know, they're so far ahead of us. Engineering, philosophy, trade. Their women are prettier."

"All built on suffering, though, is it not?"

Skuld peered at Canna through slitted eyes. "If you happen to be the owner instead of the owned, life's not too bad in a sink or swim sort of way. Less intrusive than the Overdrengr's edicts in many ways."

"How do you mean?"

Skuld relaxed, pleased with the opportunity and ability to impart his wisdom. "It comes down to distance and speed, Canna. The Austeri dwell in sprawling cities dotted around a modestly sized region, and their animals, the mairs, allow fast movement between them. New laws, goods, slaves or troops can be moved around quickly. This means the rulers can allow the populace a level of personal freedom, because, when necessary, ideas or draconian measures can be delivered at speed. The ability to intercede at any time means you mostly don't have to. And that brings us to Ibr; small, isolated communities, spread around a vast area, with no means of travelling quickly between them. So how to govern? With fist and boot, yes."

He reached a hand towards Canna then retracted a fist, as if pulling his heart out. "But also, by reaching into the day to day lives of the people, by defining their very habits and customs, so that organising their world in a different way does not even occur to them. This is why registration exists, to demonstrate that the Overdrengr has absolute control over you, the power to take your very children from you, wherever you are. Why do you think even the humblest settlement in Ibr has its very own bridgewarden? He is the embodied will of the Bryggn." He drained his cup and poured more wine into it. "If you want to know upon what a civilisation is based, look to its severest punishments. You and Qed committed affronts against the means by which your rulers operate, so in that sense, the results were proportional."

Canna struggled to absorb this. "Isn't there a better way?" he said. The words sounded lame even as he spoke them.

Skuld snorted, and responded to a more nuanced question which Canna had not asked. "You know, if another captain suddenly appeared aboard this ship, one of us would have to go. One, and one alone, would come to dominate. Perhaps I'd allow him to call himself captain, give him a job counting weevils, or simply hurl him overboard, but we'd not operate on an equal footing for long. It would be inevitable, the only way to keep the ship moving forward. Ways of life, civilisations, are similar. Sooner or later, as the lives of Austeri and Widdith people overlap, one will dominate, the other, perish. I don't fancy our chances, as matters stand, not least because the seidhrs are backward zealots. Perhaps the Fathers, in their mercy, will tolerate us cowering in our temples of Svangur. Or not. Your grandchildren may worship strange gods."

Skuld chuckled, raised his palms and waggled his fingers. "Listen to us, trying to reorganise the world. I should be more concerned with matters aboard this boat." Sober once more, morose even, he stared at the table before him and his voice dropped a register. "You know, Canna, I've sailed with miscreants and thieves, murderers and rapers of women. I've broken up more brawls than I can remember, had men flogged and hanged. But always, I've hewn the men God grants me, moulded them into an efficient machine in which all parts function for the good of the whole. But here on the *Improbable*...I cannot place it, but there's something wrong among these men."

# 10. GROWING UP DIFFERENT

*1<sup>st</sup> day of Poori, 893 AZ.*

Javic Silver perched atop the thatched hut, and smiled down at the wizened form of Frei Yederic Jomar, one of the oldest citizens of Riverbend. Inevitably, she was rumoured to be a witch by credible youngsters. She was harmless, but age lent her the freedom to speak to men or women of any station, unfettered by conventional niceties or fear of opprobrium. Even in his earliest memories she had appeared a crone; frost-blue eyes twinkling in a face wrinkled beyond reason. Perhaps she had always looked so. Perhaps she was born a little old woman. She leered, picked her nose and pointed the finger at him, as if inviting appraisal of her excavation.

Through a sock puppet mouth, she said, "You're a good boy Silver, not like your dad. I thank you for your trouble, fixing my humble dwelling. Lazy one, your father, and getting fat. Never sullies his lady hands with the likes of us. My Yederic, he's preparing with God now, he made a beautiful iron shield for your dad. The oaf shafted him, if I may say so. Paid him not half what it were worth. I hope he dies before I do, so I see you in charge."

"Very nice of you to say so, Frei Jomar."

She cackled, and disappeared into the hut and he heard her muttering and pottering about below him, no doubt with that mangy vit coiling about her legs, pestering for treats. Stroking his chin, he inspected the ugly hole in the roof, then pulled away fistfuls of sodden, mouldering thatch. The stuff smelled warm and damp, not entirely unpleasant. With a wooden board he plugged the gap in the roof, and set about sealing it with sticky tar and handfuls of straw and wheat reed. In truth, he had no idea if the fix would hold and he cared even less. Clouds obscured Yfir and the Sun, but the air was close and sticky, so he removed his cotton shirt. He yawned and stretched, enjoying the loosening of his aching muscles.

Poesha Jalana and her cousin, he couldn't remember her name, passed beneath him, probably headed for market. The cousin turned and glanced up at him over her shoulder, biting her lip; a coy imitation of shyness. He flashed the smile at her for the sake of form, and she smirked.

By the time he entered the wardenhouse, the air had cooled, but he remained shirtless. The woman who thought she was his mother fluttered about him, pressing a hunk of home cooked cheese-bread and a flagon of weak beer into his hands. She had no inkling of how much he hated both. He bent to kiss her cheek and she cupped his face in her hands, pride and approval stripping years from her. Despite her elevated station as wardenwife of a prosperous community, her humble origins in the mountain village of Rovan were betrayed by her stoic self-reliance and unaffected warmth.

"You're a fine man now, my son. You make me proud. And to think what trouble you gave me as a boy, fighting and running wild. There's naught more humble than simple acts of kindness and folks appreciate that, whether you be Overdrengr or pauper. Even Frei Yederic Jomar. Dregva himself fears that one."

His mouth formed the shape of something that looked like a smile but wasn't.

After forcing down a couple of bites of bread and a mouthful of beer, he retreated to his room, stripped and cleaned himself with a bucket of water and a cloth rag. He studied himself in the ornate mirror which hung above his dressing table, and assumed a sorrowful look.

"There'd been a fire. They're both dead." He cleared his throat, looked sad but not as much. "They've gone. There was a fire." This time he tilted his head, lowered his voice, aiming for an impression of sober disquiet. "There was a fire. They are both dead." He dressed in clean, formal attire and left to join Javic Tor and Poesha Cairn in the heimver.

The bridgewarden's face brightened as Silver entered the room, as it always did. "Here he is! Sit, boy, sit." Javic clapped him on the shoulder and returned to his own seat. Poesha Cairn stood and offered a tiny bow, an unprecedented formal gesture of submission; a welcome development.

Javic sniffed and pushed odds and ends around the table to no particular purpose. "So, my boy, you've completed the delicate task I asked of you? You visited Bradden and his wife?"

"Yes, father." He paused, his face blank. "Both dead. Fire."

Javic winced at Poesha, leaned back, then ran his fingers through his hair. "When?"

"The remains were quite decomposed, a couple of weeks I'd say. Bradden was quite incapable, by all accounts. I imagine some foolishness of his caused the fire."

Poesha spoke. "Where's this leave us?"

"Poesha," said Silver, "Your concerns are well intentioned. That's your job and you do it well. But we're taking stories of monsters far too seriously. Bradden was an idiot, his words meant nothing."

"His wife believed it. She was shrewd, that's why she married the fool in the first place. Canna believed, and you'll not find a more sceptical man. Those who've suffered torpor aren't capable of flights of fancy, Silver. Something happened on that journey, I'm convinced of it."

Javic was silent, content to watch his trusted men bat the argument back and forth.

Silver shrugged. "They fought, got robbed. It happens."

Poesha shook his head. "Something happened. We need to take this seriously. There's no such thing as monsters. But there're animals we don't know about. Why couldn't there be another type of man, who to us would seem a monster? Slipskins exist. Who would believe in them if they hadn't seen one? Or what if it were a disease of some kind, that made this Fioror attack the others? We should call on Silves, the seidhr. Their library might have something." Poesha slapped his leg and scowled. "This fire. Shitty luck."

Silver's gaze rested on Poesha for a beat, then he turned to Javic and saw the same concern written there. This was not going well. He closed his eyes and exhaled. There was a fire at Bradden's farm but it had not killed the couple, because Javic Silver had already killed and partially eaten them. Then he set the place ablaze. Pleasant heat bloomed in his chest as he remembered the woman's screaming, the man's hysterical blubbering, piss spreading down his legs, as Silver unsheathed his wrist spikes, and stretched his jaw. He could still taste their brains and livers, the morsel of soft-boned humanity growing inside the woman.

Talk of monsters would not do. Poesha had to die. As did Canna, if he ever returned. As would his putative father, if he continued to pursue this line of enquiry. Silver scratched at his wrists, feeling the hard bony lengths under the skin there, trying to scratch around them. They itched maddeningly if they were not unsheathed regularly.

During his adolescence, the maturation of the wrist spikes predicated his dawning understanding of what he was, and what he was not. They began as tender, irritated swellings, and less than a half-year later he sat alone in the outhouse, weeping in pain as they forced their way through his skin, pink and glistening. He shuddered, remembering the prolonged agony of his upper jawbone dissolving, to be replaced by the strong, flexible tendons that now held the lower part of his face in position.

Had he always known he was inhuman? It felt true, but perhaps he was projecting his current knowledge onto his past. Other children simply absorbed and replicated the thousands of tiny gestures and reactions that constitute being human; the sceptical flick of the eyebrow, the quivering lip of distress, the eye flashing in rage. Like spiders spinning webs, they just knew. They just did it. It was not like that for him, but neither did passing for human require the tongue-protruding focus of learning letters and numbers. It was something in between. A natural replication, but lacking the heft of genuine human emotion. Feelings certainly directed his actions, as they did for humans, but his fears, desires and frustrations were of a different order to those around him.

Childhood transgressions, slaughtering hokrs and vits, pummelling other children, gave way to a well-mannered dispassion, as instinct told him that to reveal his true nature was to flirt with doom. In gratitude and relief, his human family saw this abatement as a sign of maturity, and in a sense, they were correct. He was not prone to introspection, but subduing his appetite for carnage allowed him space to wonder what he was. Unravelling himself was a process complicated by the maelstrom of the usual teenage dynamics among his peers. Their need to belong while appearing interesting and unique, and the wildfire transmission of ideas between them, did not leave him untouched. He tried on and discarded new identities; the rebellious loner, the aloof aesthete, the popular clown. Eventually, his developing body insisted he confront and accept himself.

Caustic expectoration was the last of his trinity of weapons to emerge, only maturing at the end of his second decade. Stomach cramps, raw constriction of his throat, and a sensation of a great fiery lump lodged in his torso kept him bedridden for days. But his first blinding, some drunkard in a Teoton back alley, was a gleeful rite of passage. The whimpering human pawed at its eyes, increasing the damage caused by the acrid stuff.

Javic Tor turned his glum face to Poesha and Silver in turn. "Poesha's correct. We can't ignore this."

# 11. HRNO

*A Naturalist's Diary. 16th day of Poori, 893 AZ.*

I write by firelight at the conclusion of a tiring and extraordinary day. We are camped in the interior of the island of Hrno, largest of the Orn islands. Laknir Hal, Hirdrengr Tove and Hunvir murmur quietly in the tent, though I'm surprised they did not choose to sleep under Yfir's light; the night is wonderfully mild and full of flying insects which flitter about the campfire. No doubt the light confuses their usual means of navigating by triangulation of ring and moon.

I visited Haugr Wood as a boy, one of my mother's bedsheets trailing behind me. With the sheet strung up and a small fire behind it, insects would gather, framed by the sheet like some piece of moving, natural artwork, to be gently coaxed into my tin for later study. I would love to catch and study some of the exotic insects here, but unfortunately, I have nothing with which to catch them; foolish of me.

However, the curious creature which squirms in my knapsack has made this island visit more than worth my while. It is too beautiful and spirited to be picked apart by a clumsy human; I think I shall release him...there. As I watch, it is investigating the tent pegs, watching me all the while. Mischievous fellow! Ah, it has slithered away into the darkness. God hone your tentacles, and do not scare Ekkero again!

Despite the day's exertions, our ardent believer has wandered off somewhere to perform his punishing exercises. I am sure he believes this brings him closer to God, or at least farther from Hunvir's teasing. The two men are possibly the most unalike individuals ever to have the misfortune of voyaging together. I feel a little sorry for Ekkero; the world's imperfections seem to weigh upon him, rectifiable only through sheer labour.

Nijal strums his tagelharp, a calming accompaniment to my scribbling. It is a beautiful piece, all flowing curves, composed of dark, north Eyran caster wood and strings of the finest heidrn-gut. Its timbre is deep and resonant, rendering our bard's instrument a weak counterfeit in comparison. Becoming more acquainted with him and Tove has been pleasant; the drengrs have thus far been quite self-contained on this journey. Nijal, it transpires, is possessed of a lovely dry wit and eloquence; he regaled us around the fire with amusing tales of patrolling the less than salubrious quarters of Silves; the escapades of the riffraff have provided him a lifetime of campfire anecdotes. Hunvir, the *Improbable's* master of misadventure, produced a foul-smelling liquor from somewhere about his person, and shared it companionably. Even the stern Hirdrengr Tove unknotted his brow a little; he spoke proudly of his son's progress in the drengr academy. He became taciturn when I asked after his spouse, however. I suspect they are not on good terms.

In truth, this supply stop could not have come sooner; man requires space about him, and the confines of the ship frayed our tempers, not least that of the captain. His misgivings as to the crew's togetherness prompted him to organise a series of onboard competitions, inspired by the great Austeri sporting festival, the Aleab. Qed tells me that Austeri sporting heroes command almost as much fame and adoration as their gods. For some fine specimens, it is a route out of slavery. Winners of the inaugural *Improbable* Games, however, were merely rewarded with extra provisions of booze.

Millitre triumphed in the rigging race, which entailed scaling each of the three masts in turn. His agility among the spars and rigging was genuinely astonishing, and almost matched by that of our bard, who ran him a close second.

Slatre appears progressively unwell, looking drawn and haggard and clearly suffering abdominal pains, so ordinarily he may well have won. Our resident giant, Werdom, also inspired awe, winning the barrel-haul with ease. Striding along like some hero of Austeri myth, he shuttled weighted barrels back and forth as easily as I would the captain's spit-pot. His innocent delight in his achievement was quite touching. For the team rope-pull, the captain declared Werdom be counted as two men, so the opposing team had a man over. Werdom's team still won. Needless to say, Hunvir conquered the speed-drinking competition (wisely scheduled as the final event). A flick of the wrist, and a full flagon of beer simply vanished, to the cheers of his colleagues. Despite his swagger and boasting, it is difficult to nurture animosity towards one who inspires hilarity, although Ekkero (chin-up champion) manages to do so.

The fencing event took place with wooden armaments only, and was more an exhibition laid on by the drengrs than a competition. Their parries and thrusts were as elegant as any choreographed dance, though with a menacing undertone of controlled violence. Hands and officers fell silent as they watched Tove move with the grace of a prancing mair (I have never seen a mair, but I am told they prance and are graceful). I'm glad he is on our side.

Unfortunately, the captain soured the event at the last. He entered every competition, giving a fine account of himself in each; if all-round excellence were rewarded, he would conquer, no question. But he became increasingly tetchy as he was bested in each bout, and Slatre unwisely goaded him with unkind witticisms, picking at the scab of Skuld's self-regard.

"Perhaps there's a ladies' competition you could enter, captain?" and so on. The captain exploded at him, petulantly accusing him of undermining the spirit of competition, and threatening him with reduced rations. Later, as Skuld and I supped in his cabin, he was quite despairing. Whether of his own behaviour, or of being mocked in the men's presence, I am not sure. I do wonder if the jamweed he chews prodigiously affects his temperament. I tried the stuff on one occasion some days ago, and while it gave a lingering sensation of wellbeing, it left my mouth feeling sullied and had a devastating impact on the following morning's ablutions, to say the least.

So, it was a substantial mood of liberation, in which the men came ashore on Stink Bay. Despite the name, it is a beautiful cove, with white sand, azure waters (is the word azure ever used to describe anything other than sky or sea?), and blissful shade under the overhanging cliffs. Seeing the *Improbable* careened was remarkable. Having secured every movable object aboard the ship, the men heaved with hawsers and wedged bracing planks into place, and the ship grudgingly consented to having its belly exposed. It was vaguely indecent. Knuld, our shipbuilder and engineer, directed the hands and I to remove every living thing from the hull and while I picked at barnacles ineffectually, I tried not to think about the tons of wood balanced above me.

After the careening, the men enjoyed splashing in the rockpools by the shore, including a particularly deep one like a natural swimming spot. Noron led Arjier and Yavilad to gather fruits and vegetables while Slatre requested of the captain permission to explore alone. Skuld refused, instructing him (a little spitefully, I think) that he would remain at his side at all times during this stop-off. Slatre usually stands removed from events before him, casting satirical judgement from a position of ironic distance, but the glare he directed to the back of the captain's head was venomous.

A stone's throw from the shoreline, we were delighted to encounter a herd of pretty little creatures, about the height of our knees, called mintjak. With soulful eyes, dainty little horns and dappled, short brown fur, they were most tame, having I suppose never become accustomed to the dangers of men. Tove and his drengrs slaughtered them at will, pleased at the opportunity to put their archery skills to use. Noron eventually requested they desist, as we would not have capacity to salt and dry such a quantity of meat. The trusting little animals simply milled around incuriously, as more of their number fell about them. They have a kind of tough beak, with which they clip at the vegetation, and which looks rather like rows of teeth fused together. We also found the wooden sculpture of Yfir, mouldering and infested with termites, left by a previous expedition to claim this place for the Bryggn.

While the men busied themselves, and feeling myself of little further use, I wandered alone up the coast. Detouring over the headland, I disturbed nesting seabirds, which squawked and leered at me with their striking red-ringed eyes, their colourful head-crests flaring in warning. I descended into another, much smaller cove, this one pebbled and wilder than our landing spot. The *Improbable* would struggle to fit into the cove lengthways and the enclosing cliffs produced strange echoes when I hurled rocks at them and called out nonsense words.

Milling about at the water's edge, I was struck by the orderly, graded progression of smaller, regular stones near the water, to larger, irregular ones farther away. Vitgut Lake near Riverbend shows a similar phenomenon, proof that nature can of itself produce order of a kind; matter being arranged into a clear pattern, automatically, as it were. Suppose though, that further steps to this process could be added; order built upon order, sorting upon sorting. Could marvels arise? A stone shaped in a perfect replica of a Noron hunting blade, or even something alive. Impossible, I suppose, without the input of an ingenious Creator. Funnily enough, I looked up, and saw a cloud shaped rather like a hilted knife.

When I returned to Stink Bay, I was much abashed to find that the captain (the sullen bard still at his side) had considered sending a search party after me. Thankfully, he took the matter and my apology in good humour, and suggested that Tove, as an experienced man of the world, should keep me under close supervision on our little expedition inland. So, the Hirdrengr and I, along with Ekkero, Hunvir, Nijal and Hal, set off along the course of a shallow stream, to find what we may find.

The Orn Islands are the exposed heights of a string of undersea mountains, some of which are apparently volcanoes. Somehow, it never occurred to me that there could be mountains under the sea, and that some of these would rise above sea-level and be called islands. In my mind, the concepts: sea, mountains, islands, had simply been separate things, having naught to do with each other. It sounds stupid, but somehow this realisation seemed to shift my understanding of the world slightly, like discovering for the first time that your father's name is not in fact "daddy."

Hrno itself is dominated by two peaceful volcanoes, one in the north and one in the south. In general, the elevation of the island varies enough to be exciting, but not enough to be daunting. My general impression is that while the place is very green, there is too much bare soil and sun-blasted rock visible for it to be called truly verdant. The island lies somewhere between austere and beautiful. The volcanic soil is most fertile and a wide variety of cactuses predominate, with sparsely spread palm trees and tough, low-lying shrubs. I imagine if the place could be tamed, it would be a fine place to produce wine, although the lack of rainfall may hinder that, now I think on it.

Hal tells me a highly versatile plant grows here, called barbaden. Its spiky, fleshy leaves contain a slimy grey substance which can be used to treat abrasions, sun burn, and other conditions of the skin, though the leaves themselves are toxic. It can also be processed for use as a digestive aid and the laknir has gathered some to treat Slatre's ailment.

Hal, God hone his blade, is very much my mentor in all things, and he shared his wisdom as a secluded valley, deep and narrow, enclosed us. The trees here were a little denser, the air mercifully cooler. Ekkero teased Hunvir for his lack of fitness as they walked ahead of us, suggesting loudly to Tove that they stop so the larger man might rest. Hunvir declined the offer in ungracious terms. Hal and I withdrew from their bickering, to poke at interesting plants. Brightly coloured lizards flitted from one hidey-hole to another, always just too quick for us to view properly.

We chatted some, and without being specific I mentioned my interest in the mechanics of torpor. This topic was also of interest to him, not least because he had witnessed sailors with the condition being tossed overboard more than once. This is, I was shocked to discover (or perhaps not), the usual way of dealing with the torpid at sea.

"This whole notion of torpor being a weakness of the soul," he said to me, "is received wisdom. Your betters say it's true, so it's true. I prefer to find things out for myself, pull them apart a bit, get my hands dirty, see how they work."

I was aware that the Noror view torpor very differently from the Widdith. What I had not known, was that the Austeri have no great feelings about torpor either way, treating it simply as an ailment to be overcome, like a sniffle. It strikes me now, that while some Austeri practices are surely abominable, they might have a similar view of our treatment of the torpid.

"Your body does things it needs to, to stay alive," Hal said. "It doesn't really care if that's pleasant for you or not. The pain of a broken foot hurts like a bastard, take it from me, but it forces you not to walk on the foot, to protect it." He then lured me into a thought experiment of sorts. "Let's imagine, Canna, that the *Improbable* sprang a leak, too extreme to fix up. Water's pouring in, the stores are ruined. What would we do?"

"Why, flee in the rowboats, I suppose," I replied.

"Let's say we only have one rowboat, they're called dinghies by the way, and it only has room for five men. Then what?" I considered this a moment, imagining all the men lined up before Skuld, his appraising eye weighing up the value of each.

"I suppose the captain would choose his most valuable men and take them on the boat, and leave the rest to drown. And I would say to you it was nice to have known you."

I offered Hal my arm as he skidded a little over some loose rocks, and he winced as he put a hand to his lower back. Despite his years, however, Hal's mind is as fleet and sharp as any I have known. Indeed, it felt as if he were pursuing my line of thought, like a predator cornering some dopey prey. I enjoyed the grilling nevertheless.

"Exactly. The most important functions of the crew would be preserved." He extended his fingers, and lowered one for each lucky survivor. "Ulter's Navigation, Skuld's leadership, my medical training I dare say, Knuld's engineering genius, Noron's cooking skill perhaps, despite the man's lunacy. Extraneous tasks simply would not be bothered with. Not sure we'd need a naturalist, I'm afraid. Or a gauldr, come to that. Unless for food."

He grinned at me slyly and wiggled his eyebrows, not realising that consumption of men was something of a touchy topic for me. "Now, the point is that I believe torpor's the body's way of coping with a similar dilemma. It's starving, or riven by disease, or freezing cold, and just can't function properly any longer, like our sinking boat. So, it casts off the stuff it doesn't need. Stiffies, heart-warming memories, dexterity, hearing to an extent. All it keeps are the basics. The heart beats just enough for blood to trudge around the body, the feet shuffle along a bit, the eyes just about make out light from dark.

Pain, extreme heat or cold, register vaguely as stuff to get away from. You see?"

I did see, and it made to me a great deal of sense. "I suppose somewhere in the torpid body," I ventured uncertainly, "there must remain a facility which can detect, somehow, when matters have improved and that the higher functions can be restored, as it were."

Hal approved this speculation and I felt absurdly proud of myself, like a little boy being praised by his father.

"Exactly. Though we know that if these higher functions are neglected for too long, they're gone for good. The ship is lying on the bottom of the sea, as it were. Some men end up gibbering idiots for life. And torpor itself cannot continue indefinitely; the man simply dies after a while."

Hal circuitously revealed to me that he treats bodies as systems, with various machines and processes that work together to keep the whole thing working. An unwell person has simply had something go a bit wrong with one or more of these machines or processes, and this view extends to disorders of the mind. Virtue simply does not come into it. His view is akin, though in a more rigorous way, to Skuld's vague avowal that the world is a great system with every little thing fulfilling its role. I am perhaps being unfair to the captain. His methods for reading and predicting the weather are, as I understand it, genuinely at the frontiers of our knowledge.

It was sometime later that Ekkero and an unfortunate lizard cordially introduced me to my new tentacled friend. Our party halted while I stepped away to relieve myself in the shade of a short, squat palm tree. Midstream, as it were, I heard someone approach me from behind. It was Ekkero. He had overheard my conversation with the laknir, and complained at great length that Hal's views on torpor were "blasphemous and unscientific." The gall of it! Why he thought this was the best time to confront me, while I micturated, I do not know.

I finished up, and turned to engage him, prepared to defend my mentor. He stood a short distance away in the shade of another palm tree, leaning against its heavy trunk. The tree's crown of inward-curving, pinnately leaves created complex shadows over his face, giving him a mysterious and slightly disturbing aspect. I noticed a little lizard on the trunk near the man's head, limbs splayed, staying very still. It was probably enjoying the shade, as I had been. I struggled to pay full attention to Ekkero as he rattled off his grievances, my eyes drawn to the sweet little creature that perched beside him. The trunk of this tree-type was not jacketed with bark like the trees of Ibr, but with knobbly, rhomboid growths interlaced with desiccated hair-like material.

To my amazement, a small area of the tree's surface shimmered. A projection shot out from the shimmer, snared the lizard and reeled it in. It was a terrestrial octopus, about the size of a child's head, which had hidden in plain sight on the stem of the tree, and ambushed the lizard with one of its tentacles. Its camouflage ability was absolutely perfect. I lunged forward (Ekkero stumbling back in surprise, thinking I was attacking him), and grabbed the creature from the tree stem.

An absurd spectacle of buffoonery followed, in which I attempted to wrestle the struggling creature into my bag. Its tentacles were mighty strong, and wrapped and slapped about my arms and head. Every time I thought I had subdued the thing, another tentacle appeared from nowhere. Frankly, the melee proceeded exactly as one would expect a fight with an octopus to proceed. Nijal and Tove drew their swords, initially thinking I was in danger, but the party quickly descended into mirth.

Eventually I forced the creature into a bag and drew the drawstring closed. I laid the bag down, tittered in relief and took a breather with hands on hips. But then I watched in fascination as a tentacle emerged from the tiny aperture, a gap smaller than a Bryggnmark. The entire creature oozed itself out, like thick icing being pumped from a confectioner's piping bag. As it moved, it assumed a perfect simulation of the dusty ground. Not only the colour, but the texture also. It stilled, hoping not to be seen, I suppose. I bent to examine it, my colleagues gathered around me, and it consented to me lifting its tentacles with a small stick.

One tentacle, I noted, featured a prominent hooked claw, which was still coated in some of the lizard's blood, and I was rather lucky to have not been lacerated by it. Clearly, the ambush predator is well suited to hunting the available prey on this island. Hal bent close, and noted that across the head of the creature, a multitude of tiny bubbles swelled into visibility, before sinking back. The laknir suggested that these little bubbles were thin membranes, for the use of exchanging air from the environment into itself. In other words, its method of breathing.

Of course, octopuses of the sea have their weight supported by the water. My little friend has no such luxury. Instead, whatever miraculous facility which allows him to replicate the texture of his background, also seems to be used for constricting and hardening his flesh, to create, as it were, an improvised musculature for the use of locomotion and grip.

It is a profoundly different way of organising a body, compared to that of our own and other higher animals. Perhaps I should have kept the creature to study further, but I do not regret giving him his freedom. Ah, we have a long slog back to the ship tomorrow. I must rest.

# 12. IRNA

*A Naturalist's Diary. 21st day of Poori, 893 AZ.*

Hrno is full of wonders, but its sibling, Irna, is to it what a butterfly is to a moth. Or perhaps a more apt comparison would be between an inside-out bird and a hokr. Fortunate am I to have witnessed such sights, but I am equally glad to be back here, scribbling in the safety of my tiny cabin, nursing only a bruised knee. In the last few days, the world has grown older, more complex and mysterious.

The *Improbable* remained anchored offshore for this visit, fresh food and water replenished, scars and bruises patched up. A lighter mood prevailed among the men and the officers; even Noron broke into a smile, though it could have been a pang of indigestion. His poor slave remains on reduced rations, simply, as far as I can tell, because Noron despises him.

Speaking of people Noron despises (everyone), Slatre the bard appears in better health. Skuld, perhaps remorseful for his treatment of him, consented to him bringing aboard one of the little Hrno mintjaks as a pet, and the bard set about teaching it tricks. Of course, this was beyond the intelligence of such a dopey little animal, but the bard had now a comic sidekick for his japes. Sadly, Slatre reported that the poor thing stumbled off his hammock in the night and broke its leg, so he ended its misery and disposed of it. Skuld allowed Slatre to come ashore for this second stop-off, to set off on some adventure of his own, with the proviso that if he failed to meet us back at the dinghy, he would live out his days on the island. I could think of worse fates, though I doubt Slatre's hunting ability matches his gifts for music and acrobatics.

Our exploration party landed on the north-east shore of the promontory, which gives the island the appearance of a curled teardrop, if Ulter's charts are accurate. Like a hammerball trainer,

Skuld shuffled his team for this run-out, to give other players some match-sharpness. The only leftovers from the previous trip were myself, Hal and Hirdrengr Tove. Joining us were Karelud (winner of Slatre's 'Most Likely to be Hanged for a Farcical Attempted Mutiny' award); our exotic easterner, Qed; the twin drengrs, Tala East and Tala West; our First Hand, Dalind; and last and certainly most, Werdom. Come to think of it, Werdom must make a mighty hammerball player; I would not want to face him in the fray.

A spine of mountains runs along the coast of the island from the north-east to south-west, the rest of the island being relatively flat. Aside, that is, from the central plateau, upon which our exploration concluded. The air is more humid than that of Hrno, the vegetation denser, with forests and grassland the prevailing environs. Vying for dominance with the ubiquitous palms is an impressive, broadleaf species of tree, like a tropical type of oak, from which hang great strands of moss. We dragged the dinghy ashore and left it in the shade of such a tree, then set off along the course of a broad river.

We debated utilising the dinghy for at least part of the journey, but Tove and Dalind decided it would be foolish to risk the vessel on what is not, after all, our core mission. The humidity was such that, very quickly, we sweated as we marched, and our clothes clung to our forms. My breath had to be actively pulled into my lungs, while salty sweat stung my eyes. Wherever possible, we exploited the shade of the forest lining the river, and partook of a delightfully refreshing, pale violet fruit that grew in profusion. I examined a clutch of pale berries growing from a low-lying red-leafed bush, but Hal slapped them from my hand, thinking I intended to eat them. He suspected them to be most poisonous, as they resembled closely the bileberry which grows in the warmer climes of eastern Ibr.

Hal indulged me with authoritative observations and speculations upon the life we encountered. While very welcome, his wisdom prompted me to wonder, not for the first time, whether my presence on this journey to Eyra is truly necessary. After all, he makes copious records on the potential value of the animals and plants we encounter. Whereas I would say: we found a new type of fruit. It was round and blue and very delicious, Hal would include considerations of its potential nutritional and medical benefits, how it might be transported and cultivated in Ibr, and so on. The final insult to my fragile self-worth is that Hal is also a capable artist, and produced a beautiful, dynamic sketch of the Hrno hunting octopus. I am an imposter, I fear.

Finding a spiky yellow-petaled flower which piqued his interest, Hal fell silent as he pulled out a slate to scratch out some notes. Werdom fell back and chatted to me, not even breathing hard as he hauled more than his fair burden of the supplies, including the heavy cloth tent. He has such a gentle voice, that I asked him to speak up, to overcome the drones, chirps, rasps and trills that came from the unseen things of the forest. I do not mean this unkindly, but it was like speaking to a little boy. With childish spontaneity, he reeled off a list of things he likes: ship's biscuits, wooden toys, making shadow shapes on sunny days and so forth.

In his meandering, tangential way, Werdom revealed to me a fractured account of his history. He grew up somewhere in the north of Ibr, possibly with the Noror, but eventually found himself wandering south, alone, for reasons unclear. I doubt he ever completed an overcoming, which seems appropriate as he certainly has not left childhood distractions behind. Karelud first encountered him in Nifl Forest, wandering lost and hungry, and terrified he would be set upon by moaners, although those animals would likely be more scared of Werdom. He idolises Karelud; the smaller man is his saviour. To the latter's credit, he has borne on his shoulders the burden of guiding the big man through life.

After some hours, as the Sun's lower edge met the distant mountains, the river narrowed and forest gave way to grassland and rolling hills. Evening mercifully spared us the full glare of the Sun but the humidity remained oppressive, and the air shimmered. The mists upon the looming plateau looked wonderfully cool. Dotted about were thatches of a low, spiny, plant in which grew clutches of huge, hard fruits. These were yellow, hairy, and almost the size of my head, so I have dubbed them headfruits.

We stopped to take on refreshment and rest our legs, and a few of us stripped and hurled ourselves into the river, to splash around in the cool, unclouded water. Dalind and Karelud abstained, however, and I was surprised to learn, firstly, that they can't swim, and secondly, that most professional sailors cannot. Fatalistically, they reason that falling overboard at sea dooms them to a quick death, regardless of whether they can swim or not. Dalind likened teaching a sailor to swim to asking an icicle to work as a fireplace poker.

After a quick dip, Qed, the one among us most used to extremes of heat, sat on the bank with his ankles in the water, happily chewing jamweed and reading from a tiny volume of Austeri poetry. There is apparently a rich tradition among his people of epic poetry and drama, set upon the great ring that encircles our world. For them, Yfir is the home of the gods, from where they observe with disdainful interest the struggles of men.

Clambering from the water, I planted my semi-naked form next to the twins, feeling like a dumpy loaf of uncooked bread next to their chiselled frames, under the scrutiny of their piercing blue eyes. Tala East is the more gregarious of the two, though I gained the impression that he talks on behalf of both of them; if they are together, any interlocuter should treat them as a single entity.

They were registered for drengr training two years early, their youthful potential as honed weapons of warfare being so obvious. They tell me East is a specialist of the bow, whereas West is the superior swordsman, though I took this to mean that Tala East/West is formidable with both weapons. Incidentally, they gained their vital names because for their overcoming, they raced each other to the door of the famous Ballekka Pastry Emporium, one starting from the west, one from the east, though I forget whether each is named for the direction, or starting position of their race. They have the air of the uncanny about them. Occasionally, West smirks before East has finished some witticism, or they turn their heads in perfect unison, or East replies when West has been asked a question. I must ask Moshim about the orthodox Widdith view of twinhood. Do they share a soul? Perhaps Hal's medical insight would be more useful.

We continued on our way, wading through knee-high grasses of the plain. Hal and I grinned at each other knowingly, as Dalind's shoulders drooped ahead of us. Karelud was berating him about working conditions, proportional danger payments and so forth. So the first hand was more relieved than most when a loud cracking noise distracted us. It issued from one of the thickets where the headfruits grew. As I turned to the sound, I caught a scampering movement from the corner of my eye. A headfruit lay in pieces, pale green flesh exposed. I tried a little, and it was refreshing; sweet but with a muddy undertone. Staring around, I noticed another of the fruits was swollen and misshapen. I shielded my eyes from the glare, and it slowly dawned upon my confused senses that a land-octopus was perched there, squatting motionless like a hokr upon an enormous egg. Its skin was coloured and textured most miraculously, breaking up the outline of its form against the vegetation beneath.

With a flutter of my hand, I urged my companions to remain very still, and wondered what to do next. We waited, as the eyes of the creature regarded me levelly. Apparently deciding we posed no threat, it continued on its business; it contracted, quivering, and a sharp crack sounded as the fruit beneath was busted open. Tala East was by my side then with an arrow drawn, the muscles of his arm taught. He murmured from the side of his mouth, "You wish to study this?" I nodded that I did, and he loosed his arrow, spearing the creature's head, leaving it crumpled and oozing. I exhaled through gritted teeth, resisting the urge to swear at the man; I had not realised he sought permission to slaughter the poor thing. But for all my delicate sensibilities, I took the opportunity to investigate. The middle tentacle on each of the creature's sides were particularly short and thick. Each bore a narrow strip of rough, finely crenelated material along its length. Clearly, it uses these specialised tools to grasp the headfruits and squeeze them until they yield their contents, much like a nutcracker.

For all the world, it seems as if these creatures, and their Hrno cousins, had considered the tools Svangur gave them, and thought to themselves, *these are fine tentacles, very useful for swimming and catching fish, but I shall crawl out onto the land to see if I can find another use for them.* Gently squeezing the animal's head, Hal demonstrated that it shared the ostensible breathing bubbles of the similar animal on Hrno.

A further surprise; the creatures are noisy and social. Cheerful toots and whistles greeted our ears farther upriver, as we headed towards the island's central plateau. Dark, horizontal pupils in bulbous heads peeked above the grass, before quickly dipping out of sight. These sentinels stood on tiptoe, as it were, tentacles stretched to their fullest extent. Their gill parts, which for the normal undersea variant of the octopus are of course used for breathing, as with fish, flared from their heads, producing noises as complex as birdsong, setting off panicked scampering among their fellows.

We intruded into a large population of them, but they quickly became accustomed to us. Younglings cavorted, adults bore stones, twigs and lumps of fruit into burrows, where nurseries were located, perhaps. Some engaged in brutal fights, which escalated into mass brawls, but then stopped as quickly as they had begun, the combatants seemingly at peace with the whole episode. It was almost as if their tentacles fought of their own accord, while their minds wondered about what to have for dinner.

Though wildly different in appearance, these social animals pursue a similar life to that of the sweet little ground-perrits that excavate the fields of eastern Ibr. Two very different animals, living similar lifestyles. In some ways, the fruit-octopus shares more in common with the ground-perrit than it does with the hunting octopus of Hrno, even though it is almost identical to the latter. This raises, at least to my mind, the problem of how to name and classify animals. I have provisionally given these new creatures the unwieldy names of fruit-eating social octopus and tree-living hunting octopus. But these are quite arbitrary labels based on the briefest observation, and I have no doubt that the names of some well-known creatures are based on similarly shaky foundations. We look around us and say, "These two animals fly and have feathers, they are both birds. This and this are scaly and they swim, they are fish." But what if we ask, "What is an octopus? Why, it is a tentacled thing that lives in the sea." Well, I have a found a thing that looks like an octopus but it hides in trees and eats lizards. What does the word "octopus" mean now?

I am not sure I have illustrated my point too well, but nevertheless, there should be a more fundamental system for the grouping and naming of animals, based on some aspect of their essential essence or place in the world, rather than superficialities of their resemblances, or circumstances of their discovery. Animals new to the knowledge of man could be studied and slotted in, as it were, into the correct position in a great ledger of life.

We camped that night on a patch of rough ground at a bend of the river. A massive tortured tree yearned and groped for us from the opposing bank. Its main body resembled a multitude of narrow trunks squeezed like a bundle of thick sticks, as if some furious giant had squeezed and twisted a clump of normal trees together. The water here was shallow and turbulent, foaming and burbling over the rocks, and its noise soothed us.

Around the campfire, the twins murmured quietly, Qed withdrew into his book of verses and Hal undertook a solemn accounting of his medical supplies. The rest merely contemplated the fire, chewing ship's biscuits and fruit, comfortable in each other's company but each adrift on the sea of his own thoughts.

Later, we huddled together in the tent, sheltered from the surprisingly bitter night air. Karelud lay beside me, eyes fixed on the ceiling of our temporary home, while our companions slept. I admit I had not warmed to the man, because of his continual griping over conditions and pay, and I sought his admission that the wonders of these islands were greater reward than any amount of coin. He was disdainful, and hissed to me something of his early life, suffering grotesque mistreatments in the gauldrhaven where he was raised, at the hands of deviant tyrants who called themselves servants of His Intention. There are surely few tragedies worse than of a child's mind closed to the beauty of nature, by the abuse of those charged with nurturing him. I had no answer for him. Against the fabric of the tent, inquisitive, amorphous silhouettes writhed and probed in Yfir's pale glow.

#

We set off next morning in good spirits, the day cool and bright, the mysteries of the plateau our goal. Despite being a senior officer on the party, Dalind struggles to command the respect of the hands. Though likeable enough, he undermines himself, I fear, through his desire to please both his seniors and underlings. The former see him as grovelling, the latter as weak. By now he had abandoned any pretence of authority over the party, deferring in all things to Tove. So, it was the hirdrengr who dictated our next move. We would ascend the imposing plateau if a viable route presented itself, otherwise we would return to shore.

Hal and I were desperate to see what marvels awaited discovery on the island's upper storey. The other men were sanguine, inured to the principle of acting only at the behest of others. We marched for a few hours, following the river through grassland and small areas of woodland, where flowers of infinite variety grew in profusion, occasionally meeting little groups of the fruit-eating octopuses going about their mysterious business.

As the incline became more onerous, plant and animal life became sparser, although we saw here and there long-haired, heidrn-like animals, which tore at tough weeds sprouting from bare rock. Eventually, we clambered as much as walked and even Werdom began to pant. Our surroundings, as we neared the plateau, gave the impression of a huge, dissolved mountain, lumps of itself lying around hither and thither. Pale, rocky ground predominated, the stone marked by complex patterns of grooves and ridges, some wide enough to for a man to fall down. In the light of the fierce Sun, the pale rock was blindingly white, leaving afterimages dancing before my eyes. The plateau seemed to suddenly materialise a short distance before us as we left behind a smattering of hardy trees. It was perhaps thirty man-lengths high, and pockmarked with crags and caves.

There appeared no safe route up to the heights, but we followed the curvature of the river through an archway of rock, into a vast natural hall. It was illuminated by means of a grand hole in its ceiling, high above us. Our heads craned in wonder, and the dusty bones of animals that must have fallen from above lay about our feet. The river disappeared into the cliffs via a semi-circular cave, and Hal suggested the river descended from the plateau by means of a sinkhole and underground waterfall.

After some deliberation, and unbecoming pleading on my part, Tove acquiesced to entering the river cave, and continuing our exploration. Inside, the air was mercifully cool and fresh, the water shallow and fast-moving. We followed the narrow, muddy bank in single file, and the drengrs lit torches as we left daylight behind us. For perhaps half a mile we followed the underground river, which became deep and slow-moving. The bank was overwhelmed at one point, and we waded through the water and the darkness, each of us clutching the man before him. Dalind screamed as something brushed his legs under the water and Qed whispered supplications to his gods. We heard what sounded like the slow beating of large wings, and no doubt the men's imaginations conjured terrible flying beasts, watching with ravening curiosity from the shadows of their domain. By flickering torchlight, we negotiated forests of gnarled, glistening stalagmites, some conjoined to stalactites above to form imposing columns of rock.

We came to an underground lake, the size of which we could not ascertain; the men launched stones as far as they could over the water and every time were answered by a watery plop. Its surface was a sheet of darkened glass. Something out there, in the murk, gave a low, gurgling croak and Karelud swore. A narrow shelf around the circumference of the lake led to a natural rocky staircase, down which water cascaded into the lake. The "steps" were not steep, but the staircase was arduously long and perilously slippery. We scaled it with extreme caution (but growing excitement on my part), switching to all fours in places, so our arms became as soaked as our legs. More than once, the drengrs struggled to relight their dampened torches.

After our ascent, we came to a much smaller pool, fed by a waterfall from the unseen heights. Ducking under a low opening in the rock, we emerged in a dry, natural corridor, which we followed steadily upwards around meandering twists and turns. By now, I thought, we must be nearing the height of the plateau, and I was consumed by excitement. Whispering at first, the sound of rushing water swelled to a roar as we came to a long, straight section of corridor. At the far end was an opening to the world outside, so bright it was almost indecent. Halfway along the tunnel, the waterfall (presumably the one we encountered earlier) plunged down from high above, disappearing through a gap in the floor, around two manlengths long.

Tove approached the cavity and cautiously peered down, spray sheening his concerned face. He was about to proffer his considered decision, when, with a gleeful yell, Werdom took a short run and leapt the gap in a horizontal dive. He stood and turned to face us with a daft smile, though we could barely make out his features, silhouetted as he was by the light from the opening behind him. Karelud berated him like the angry but relieved parent of an impulsive child.

With trepidation, at least on my part, we jumped over to Werdom one by one, and I thought my heart would beat its way from my chest as I watched Hal, clever but aging Hal, steel himself to leap. In the event, it was me I should have worried about. Hal sprang over the gap with the grace of a man half his age, whereas I misjudged the thing completely, leaping far too early and landing with one knee striking the rock, the other leg dangling over oblivion. The men hauled me to safety and a demented giggle escaped my lips. The opening looked out over the side of the cliff, with a delightful view of the eastern side of the island; the river twinkled prettily and down on the plain I made out little groups of octopus pottering about. I even fancied I could see the *Improbable's* masts in the distance.

The drop was precipitous with no means of descent. As I peered down, Karelud slapped me on the back, exclaiming "Careful, Philos, don't fall now!" and he and Werdom burst into laughter. I shot him a glance and was about to rebuke him in no uncertain terms, when Hal clutched my arm and directed my attention to a stunning sight on the corridor wall.

Depictions of humans, animals and more were rendered in faded, red strokes. I thought them crude initially, but they possessed an artful simplicity. Humans were lined up in neat rows, carrying weapons of some kind. Horned, quadrupedal beasts fled from them. A flourish of smoke twisted above a roaring campfire. Then, a depiction of the world itself, accompanied by the Moon and a multitude of stars, but no Yfir; a profoundly unsettling omission. Strange feelings stirred; loneliness, grief, joy and kinship. Hal hurriedly set about reproducing the pictures on a slate.

Farther back along the corridor, a hollow shaft extended upwards and through it we could see the sky. It was a little wider than Werdom and about thirty feet long, eminently climbable, I suggested. Tove was inclined to bring our adventuring to a close, but Hal and I, stretching his goodwill to its limit, persuaded him to allow us to investigate further. Werdom took the lead, three of us combining to boost him upwards into the shaft. One by one we followed, until Karelud, the lightest of us, was hauled up by Tala East's powerful forearm. Bracing against the wall of the shaft, we slowly ascended in an ungainly column of haphazard human bodies, grunting and swearing. "Get your damn foot out of my face! Don't fart, Werdom, you'll choke us all." And so on.

Our escape shaft lightened as I toiled skywards, and I discovered the bodies of countless tiny creatures encased in the rock. Exquisite, swirling shells of remarkable variety, branching, leaf-like fronds and radially symmetrical things like edible treats. I had, of course, no opportunity to study these at length as Qed grumbled below me, but am confident they were creatures of the sea, though many bore no resemblance to any creature I am aware of. How did they get here?

Received wisdom tells us that Svangur cast unto the rock the creatures of his creation which displeased him. My confidence in this explanation has evaporated; it just seems too…small, too much akin to routine human petulance, somehow. This place must have been under the sea, but how could that be? Did catastrophe turn the world upside down or did the change happen gradually? Yet still, the most disquieting aspect of this episode was the rendering of our world with no great ring around it. Imagine, humans gazing at the sky and seeing only (only!) the Moon and a crowded curtain of stars. And what a profusion of stars there must have been, without Yfir's surpassing glare. Truths that heretofore underpinned my life are crumbling beneath me, leaving me to fall into the darkness of I know not what.

Our shaft opened into a rocky depression on the plateau, and we brushed ourselves down, checking all body parts were present and correct. The river was just a stream up here, and it disappeared into another such concavity. Scrambling to the rim of the sinkhole, we assessed our surroundings; the plateau was crowned by rolling, grassy hills, small patches of woodland and more rocky areas, with further gateways to the cave system below. Perhaps a mile away was a further cliff, an upper storey of the plateau, as it were. We stopped to eat and I discussed with Hal my thoughts on the sea creatures in the wall. I confess that I struggled to express the profundity of how my understanding of the world was shifting.

"Look around you, Canna," he said to me. "This place is carved by water. You can see the paths it's made for itself through the earth. It works slowly but inexorably, you see. Imagine how long it takes to scour the ground, drip drip drip, into such artful design." He took a swig from his bottle, wiped his mouth and stared into the distance. "The world's older than gauldrs would have us believe. And it changes beneath our feet. They tell us that without God's vitality and perseverance, Dregva's influence pulls all things towards decay and ruin. Balls, I say. The shaping of the world's an active thing, a creation that never stops and can't be separated from life. I'm convinced. Good and evil, vitality and ruin. These are human concerns. Why should the world care for such things?"

My musing on Hal's words was interrupted when Qed cried in alarm. A snake writhed on the ground near him, rearing its head aloft, as if in distress. A pretty little bird fluttered down to investigate, perhaps expecting an easy meal. An octopus burst from the ground, snatching the bird from the air and pulling it to pieces. The "snake" was a tentacle, coloured to emulate a snake, down to the smallest detail, even with two distinct "eyes."

A third type of land octopus then, I believe, though I had no chance to study it closely. A name for this one? Oh, I don't know. How about the trapdoor octopus? Three types of octopus, sharing many common features, but each with a specialised type of tentacle, or two, suited to its particular way of life. Orthodox knowledge tells us that Svangur created all living things (aside from bees, moulds and other simple, destructive life) and gave them the tools they need to prosper. But let us look at this with fresh eyes.

A family by name of Sveren lived in Riverbend when I was a boy; a mother, father, and three fine boys, the youngest around my age. The eldest, Sveren Mailow, became a carpenter, and by his teenage years his hands were callused and strong. The middle boy, Sveren Eitr, became a runner for the Bridgewarden of Arada, dashing over the hills to deliver messages to other villages. When I met him after many years of absence, he was wiry and slim, no trace of fat upon his frame, and I'm sure his heart was as robust as a Kyr's. The youngest, Sveren Jigeer, became of all things, a serving man to a fine lady of Teoton. His face was soft and feminine, welcoming and unthreatening. His hands were plump and delicate.

Life took these three boys from common stock, and shaped them, moulded their bodies, quite literally, into the forms most suited for their lives. What if the world also took a single tribe of octopus, separated them somehow, and moulded them into new, distinct forms, each adapted, as it were, to a new way of living? What if all living things were created this way from some simple Originator? Such a process would surely take almost an infinity of time, but considering Hal's words concerning the changeability and age of the world (drip, drip, drip), perhaps this is possible.

This raises further questions. Training helped the Sveren boys adapt to their vocations, and they chose (sort of) to pursue their careers. Animals surely do not "know" to change, so how could it happen? Perhaps their habits and bodies change through repetitive action. Sveren Mailow used his hands to smooth and shape wood, repeating the same movements over and over again, and his hands adapted to their function. Maybe something analogous occurred with the octopus; some of them pursued headfruits as a source of food, and their tentacles adapted over the generations, becoming more and more proficient at the task of breaking them. But this raises the question of how behaviours or physical features gained during life can be passed to an offspring. Will Sveren Mailow's first born son be born with hard little carpenter's hands?

My questions and speculative answers are driving me from God, I fear, so let us see if we can harmoniously resolve two opposing views. On the one hand, a world exquisitely designed by an ingenious creator. On the other, a world in which the variety of life arises through the vagaries of natural processes. Perhaps Svangur, rather than designing every living thing, merely created the rules, and dropped the handkerchief for the race to begin, as it were. Natural philosophy and religion could then happily exist as non-overlapping magisteria. There, that feels better. But no, I am merely apologising for the explanatory weakness of received wisdom; filling yawning gaps in knowledge with human stories, to explain forces that may care nothing for human desires. (It is striking that one when stops to examine stories of transcendent beings shaping the world to their will, they appear driven by the most conventional of human concerns). No. I must follow the facts, wherever they take me.

Our foray upon the plateau was curtailed in a most terrifying manner. We walked a little way along the stream with our clothes, damp from our underground traversal, drying in the noon Sun. A forest of tall, straight trees with lush canopies lay around a few hundred man-lengths to our left. From it came three lumbering, four-legged beasts, one clearly an infant. They were three times the height of a man at the shoulder and sported a covering of beautiful, iridescent feathers, with two narrow, backward-facing crests atop a blunt head. Despite their size, they seemed lithe and they honked and blared to each other in a remarkable cacophony. The biggest turned to us, performed a comic doubletake and tooted in alarm, prompting us to duck behind a jumble of rocks and observe from a position of relative safety.

"Shall we hunt?" Tala West asked with a grin, somewhat absurdly I thought. Then what, drag one back to the boat? I frowned at the twins and saw their jaws literally drop open in unison. The most terrifying animal I have ever seen burst from the forest. Tall as Werdom at the shoulder, it had sleek, dappled fur with a ridge of spiny black projections along its back. Those shoulders were bulky and powerful, and sat much higher than its haunches, making it appear like two different animals bolted together. It ran, I would say, twice as fast as the most able man, upon split hooves. Its head was the most frightening aspect; a long snout with small, forward-facing eyes, an eruption of dagger-like teeth, and bony protrusions sticking out from the sides of its muzzle.

The biggest of the feathered prey, the one which had glared at us, confronted the predator, lowering its head and flaring feathers in challenge. Its family cowered behind it, stamping and squawking, in vain, for the battle did not last long. The predator charged, seeming intent on dashing itself upon the giant's knees. But the prey reared, and the predator gracefully dodged to the side, then lunged forward to its victim's rear. Before the larger animal could turn, its tormentor clamped its jaws upon a hind leg, severing some vital tendon, and it was doomed. It bellowed and sank to its belly and the predator got to work upon its throat.

After a brief period of contemplation, Tove offered his considered view as to our next tactical manoeuvre, as follows: "F—ing run!" Despite my pretence of intellectual bravery, I concurred, and we squeezed down the sinkhole shaft quicker than we had ascended.

Sun kissed ocean as we reached the shore the following evening. We found the bard by the dinghy, splayed on the grass in a state of great lethargy. For a moment I feared he had entered torpor, but he responded to us intelligently enough, though his words were slurred. Hal examined him briefly and suggested he suffered a little in the intensity of the Sun, or had ingested some fermented fruit. A few stars had laboured into visibility by the time we roused him enough to stumble into the boat.

While the tireless Werdom, Dalind and Karelud rowed, Slatre lolled in the prow, staring at nothing but seeming in no distress. I felt for him; my muscles ached and my mind was overloaded, but Irna had kept its greatest spectacle in reserve. A hazy radiance appeared back on the shore. Coloured lights danced and swirled in the air while I stared open-mouthed. I looked beseechingly at Tove, who rolled his eyes in answer to my unspoken question.

We rowed back, and there on the sand was a great herd of octopus, hundreds of them, thousands perhaps, of which species I could not be sure. They had arrayed themselves in a vast circle, and coordinated patterns of light rippled through the horde. I scrambled up a tree for a better view, while the men remained by the dinghy. Alternating spirals of green and yellow; pulses of red appearing and disappearing in an accelerating, complex rhythm; circles of whiteness moving from the centre to the edge, like ripples from a stone dropped in water; branching, delicate fingers of pale blue, like forked lightning. And the creatures' bodies swayed, rose, fell and gyrated, moving to unheard music. My parochial, human mind had assumed that animal intelligence is merely a scaled down, simplistic version of our own. Now I know better. Of what consequence are the stories men tell themselves, to creatures of such alien intelligence? They were not put here for us.

# 13. GOD, HONE THEIR BLADES

*12<sup>th</sup> – 13<sup>th</sup> days of Gowan, 893 AZ.*

Werdom had always been a good sleeper, so he only awoke as the lower deck erupted in shouts and screams. He tipped from his hammock and crashed to the deck. Smoke teared his eyes and constricted his throat, but the air was a little clearer in his prone position. Everyone was shouting and running around. There's a fire, he thought, but no panic accompanied this realisation, no emotion, in fact, other than a vague satisfaction that he had used sensory clues to correctly deduce a significant change in the world. A rarity for him, to be cherished.

He reached a long arm up to his hammock, felt around and retrieved the new nubbly Karelud had made for him. It was even better than the old one, bigger with more bits on it to play with. He held it to his head, to hear above the racket the pleasing little boing it made, as he fingered its spring. Smiling, eyes streaming, he lay on the deck on his front, enthralled by the nubbly. My friends will sort out the fire, he thought, as flames licked around him. They always know what to do.

Skuld was there then, half naked and covering his nose and mouth with a cloth, shouting and hitting people, telling them what to do. He didn't like Skuld much. The captain used clever words sometimes to make him feel bad and he had hit him that time. Usually, if people hit him, Werdom hit them back and that was the end of it, but Kare had helped him understand that sometimes it was better not to hit them back, because…he couldn't remember why. Werdom gasped as something struck his ribs.

Skuld crouched above him, hauled him to his feet, and slapped him hard in the face. "Get to the pumps!" Skuld grabbed someone else in the impenetrable grey. "Furl the sails, boy, go now!" Someone dragged someone else along the deck. The man being dragged was moaning and breathing weirdly but then stopped.

Werdom put his nubbly back in his hammock and descended through the hatch into the hold. Yavilad was there, heaving one end of the big pump handle up and down, and he seemed to be crying. Werdom frowned. He liked Yav, he was funny and clever but didn't use his cleverness to be mean to people. Seeing Yav sad made him sad, too.

"For ruin's sake, Werdom, pump, man. I can't build the pressure on my own, I'm not strong enough."

Werdom grabbed the other end and together they heaved the pump handles up, down, up, down. Werdom smiled, enjoying the rhythm of it, the water's resistance as it was pulled from the sea and forced through narrow pipes. Loud hissing sounded above as mist from the fire-quelling system turned into steam. Werdom understood that his actions were helping his friends, and he felt a swell of pride.

Tove dropped into the hold, heaving in shaking breaths between coughs. Shoving Werdom aside and grabbing the pump handle, he said, "Werdom, go up and see if anyone needs help."

He turned to Yavilad. "Fire's under control. It's started pissing down up top, ship's safe, I think. Just keep the mist steady, stop a reflash." A weary shake of the head. "Qed's gone, Nijal couldn't wake up him up. The fucking jamweed. Nijal's in a bad way, he pulled me out."

Werdom returned to the lower deck, where the remains of barrels and boxes lay strewn about, charred and steaming. Gosh, he thought, all our stuff's broken. Someone whimpered and above the susurration of the mist leaving the pipe outlets, rain drummed on the blackened overhead. Skuld roared somewhere. In a sudden panic, Werdom dashed to the remains of his hammock, now just a string of charred material, and searched for his nubbly. He couldn't find it, and let go a high-pitched sob, his vision obscured by tears of sorrow.

Werdom emerged onto the main deck and blinked in surprise at the lashing rain, driving almost sideways in the night. Wiping a salty mix of tears, spray and rain from his face, he shook his head and looked around. The blurry shape of a man moved in haste on the quarterdeck. As Werdom ascended the steps he saw another man lying down. It was Hunvir, the funny fat man. He wasn't moving and there was something wrong with his abdomen; it was all bloody and there were little tubes and things hanging out of him.

"You alright, Hunvir?" Werdom asked, kneeling down. There was also something wrong with the man's eyes. They were open, staring, and the whites were bright red. "The rain's falling right in your eyes," Werdom tittered.

Werdom looked up and saw Slatre, tying a rope around himself, the other end of which was attached to the gunwale. "What are you doing?"

Slatre approached and placed bloody hands on Werdom's face, staring at him intently. "Ekkero's jumped in the sea, Werdom. He hurt Hunvir and then threw himself overboard because he didn't want the captain to punish him. I tried to stop him hurting Hunvir but I couldn't. I'm going to jump in the sea now, to try to rescue Ekkero. I'll need you to pull me out, okay? How will you pull me out, Werdom?"

The big man stared for a moment. "Pull on the rope."

"That's right. Good lad." With that, Slatre leapt over the gunwale and disappeared into the darkness.

#

In the drizzle of the morning, the sails remained furled and men huddled on the main deck, waiting for their captain, averting their eyes from two plain, wooden coffins that stood by the starboard gunwale. Hair was slicked back, shirts were tucked into britches, shoes polished and gleaming. Ulter stood sentinel by the ship's bell, next to the captain's cabin. Millitre's boyish face was crumpled in tears. Hacking, rending coughs punctuated the silence while a rainbow ornamented the horizon, a colourful counterpoint to Yfir's austere majesty.

An area of the deck, under which the fire had burned most intensely, was reinforced with boarding; an ugly, gleaming scar upon weathered skin. Moshim faced the men, in the plain, brown robe which signified the humility of his calling. His face was implacable, and he held the Book of Zarat in hands folded before him. Werdom frowned and stared around.

He nudged Karelud and when he spoke his voice was a coarse intruder into the reverential silence. "What's happening, Kare?"

Karelud winced and whispered his answer, while Moshim cast them a cryptic smile. "We're saying godo'lade to our friends, Werd. Qed and Hunvir are dead. We're just waiting for the captain."

"What about Ekkero? He's dead too, isn't he? Why hasn't he got a box?"

"Fuck him, Werd. That fucking lunatic killed Hunvir and threw himself over. He started a fire to cover for himself and now half our food's gone. We're fucked. Dregva take him."

Werdom considered this, and picked at his fingernails.

Skuld emerged from his cabin in full naval dress, his beard trimmed and his pristine, white coat crowded with medals. A couple of the men's eyes widened in surprise that the captain's breast bore the White Leaf of Reckoning, the rarest of naval awards, issued by the Overdrengr only for the most meritorious acts of service. He posted himself by the gauldr, who gave him a slight nod. He is a trinity of men, Canna thought. The father: indulgent, authoritative, harnesser of men. The weakling: addicted to approval and jamweed, envious, rent by doubt. And this new incarnation before us, the spirit: a manifestation of the comfort of Widdith theology, and the Bryggn's power.

Skuld raised a palm. The ship groaned and whimpered. "Men. We say godo'lade this day to our friends, Hunvir Leffen and Qed ij Qed. Gauldr Moshim's words will carry them to Svangur's side with our love and gratitude. But I give thanks to all of you, on behalf of Overdrengr Fan Parley himself, and on behalf of myself as your captain. You saved this ship, saved the man who stands beside you. Knuld Calldr, in my years I've never heard of any fire at sea that left a man alive. Your genius lent this vessel something of your own vitality and perseverance, and I thank you for it. Werdom." The big man started, and hopped from foot to foot.

Skuld spoke slowly, and locked eyes with the giant. "You saved us. You braved the flames and your work at the pumps with Hand

Yavilad Slowater, subdued the fire. I thank you both, and ask the privilege of your friendship." Karelud and Canna clapped Werdom on the back.

"Drengr Nijal Unsack recuperates in the lower deck, his wounds attended to by Hal. With no thought of his own safety, Nijal pulled Hirdrengr Tove from the flames. Alas, he could not save poor Qed. Finally, I wish to thank our bard, Slatre Run. He leapt into the freezing sea in a bid to retrieve Hunvir's murderer, whose name will not be heard upon this ship while blood flows in my veins, that the bastard might face the Overdrengr's justice." Murmured agreement from the men. Slatre, appearing in rude health despite his ordeal, watched on.

"Much of our stores are gone and rations will reduce. The *Improbable* is bruised and battered. And the rains which blessed us last night were but a prelude to the fury of a coming storm. Though the wound bleeds, a malignancy has been excised from our flesh, and we will be stronger for it. You've shown me what men you are, and we will abide. Quartermaster, distribute to each man an extra ration of beer tonight, if you please." Skuld touched Moshim's arm and nodded to him.

Moshim raised an arm to the horizon and smiled. "A rainbow greets us this morning, men, as it marked Zarat's journey over the Bridge. Only for souls of the greatest vitality, does Svangur provide this sign of His gratitude. With joy, He takes the arms of our brothers, Qed and Hunvir, guiding them over the Bridge to fight by His side. Qed's mistaken beliefs in this world are of no consequence, a mere accident of geography. In fact, the captain tells me that Qed fled Langbar because his principles transcended the barbarity of his people. Svangur will welcome him to His side as we welcomed him to ours. Qed's wisdom, clarity of thought and generosity of spirit were assets to us, as they will be to Him, and we proudly call him brother.

"Hunvir's spirit was so vital, his sense of fun so irrepressible, that men's laws struggled to constrain him. He brought laughter and a joyous recklessness to this ship, and Svangur smiles upon those who bring light to the dark places of world. Our brother Millitre, I know, values the kindness Hunvir showed him." A sob escaped Millitre, and he wiped at his eyes.

"Zarat lay bleeding and bruised in the jail of the warlord, Satheen, and word came to him of the death of the guard, Chamal, who had shown him kindness."

Moshim opened the Book of Zarat, and read. "Fear not the darkness, for Yfir guides you, and God hones your blade. My murmured song circles into flight, to sound clarion by your side."

The men responded in clear voice. "As He abides, we abide."

Dalind, Millitre, Canna and Skuld stepped forward and hoisted a coffin to their shoulders. Ulter pealed the bell, and Moshim continued. "Qed, Hunvir, listen while you tarry in this life, for you will be in the next before our peal has ended. In joy, we will meet again." The coffin was released, and with another peal of the bell, the other followed.

Hal emerged from the lower deck while the crowd dispersed, and beckoned to Canna and the captain. "A moment of your time, gentlemen. And you, Moshim, if you would." They gathered in the captain's cabin, and Skuld loosened the top gold buttons on his formal tunic.

Hal opened his mouth to speak but the captain interrupted him. "How is Nijal, laknir?"

Hal kissed his teeth and rubbed at his neck. "In a bad way. His throat and lungs have taken great damage from the heat and smoke. He can take no food, can barely drink and his breath comes with difficulty. I've applied salve to the burns to his arms, which are extensive. He risks dehydration because of the fluid lost, and if the injuries become befouled, he's done for. On top of that, he's lost an eye and that side of his face is a mess. He suffers greatly. If he abides the next few days, he'll have a chance at life."

Canna felt prickles over his skin and his heart race, as if his body were reacting to the mere description of such bodily assaults.

Skuld grimaced and drummed his fingers on the table. "Let me know if there's anything I can do."

"Captain, gauldr," said Canna. "They were fine words you gave. I'm sure the men, all of us in fact, appreciate it. They were good men. Poor Millitre was close to Hunvir. He looked broken."

The captain stood, retrieved a bottle and four cups, poured and handed them around. "Good wine this. Austeri, very expensive. A gift from Qed, for my affording him safe passage from his tormentors. Did you know that caused a diplomatic incident? Fan himself got wind of it, sent a diplomatic team to smooth things over. Cost him, personally. Qed was a mere hand to us, seemed happy enough with the life, but he was a man of consequence in Langbar."

Skuld raised his eyes to the overhead and breathed out through his nose. Then he smiled lopsidedly and snorted. "Hunvir was a lazy bastard. But funny with it, got away with a lot. Good man to have aboard any vessel." The captain's face darkened. "To have been murdered by a sneaking, zealous little shit."

"That's what I wanted to speak to you about, captain," said Hal. He faced Moshim and Canna in turn, and his voice was little more than a whisper. "And the two of you. I briefly examined Hunvir's body this morning. The wounds to his abdomen were extensive, a mess, basically. But his liver and heart were gone. Torn from his body, it seemed. And I found teeth marks within and around the wound. Many of them. One of his lower ribs was snapped, with gouges at the rending point, as if it were bitten clean through, which before yesterday I would say was not within the capability of a man."

Hal allowed the words to penetrate while outrage and disbelief battled for dominance of Skuld's face. With liminal awareness, Canna's mind shifted from sympathy to detached curiosity. He sat straighter and brushed a stray hair from his forehead. Moshim's chin sank to his chest, so the others could see little more than his troubled brow.

"Moshim, the murderer came to you for advice, did he not?" Skuld said. "Was he capable of this?" Moshim raised his eyes and Canna saw an overwhelming sadness there.

"I would say not. He was troubled, yes, and zealous. Lonely, I think, and conflicted. He took umbrage to Hunvir's frivolity and Hunvir goaded him. But I don't think he had such evil in him. He pushed his body to its limit through exercise and labour, which offered him some release from his distress."

"And yet the facts remain," said Skuld, fixing Moshim with a cold stare.

Hal broke the silence. "There's more I'm afraid, gentlemen. Hunvir's eyes were damaged by some caustic substance. His corneas, the outermost layer, you know, were burned. He was rendered blind before he died."

Skuld covered his face with hands, then slapped them down on the table and said, "I thank you for bringing this information to me, laknir, but I'm not sure what I'm to do with it. We must apply ourselves to our own survival. A storm's coming, and I will turn into it. Ships, like men, are stronger when they face their enemies, instead of running from them." His eyes blazed. "Speed. Agility. Defiance."

#

"Relax lad, you're stiff as a plank. Here." The captain pushed a pouch of tobacco over the table to Yavilad. "For you. Have a sniff, it's good stuff. From Langbar."

"Thank you, captain," Yavilad said, and his head shook in a brief spasm.

"Touch of the twitches? You're not the only one. Don't worry, it'll be days before you start fitting and crapping yourself." The captain chuckled, then sat straighter, his face pained. "Ruin, sorry. This is no time for levity. How many times have you sailed under me, Yav?"

"Nine times, sir."

"You should be first hand by now, but your devotion to your daughter's a credit to you. She's well?"

"Yes, sir." Yav relaxed and his smile was a mix of pride and something else. "Finally walking, last time I saw her. Talks, after a fashion."

"She has your perseverance, I'm sure. You're a good man and a fine hand. You take orders without complaint and when I ask something of you, it gets done. I trust you, Yav, and that's why I ask a favour of you."

"Of course."

Skuld laced his fingers on the table and leaned forward. His voice lowered. "These thefts, under my nose, on my ship. Yesterday, a rung halfway up the shroud-ladder broke under Millitre's feet. Only the boy's quickness saved him. And your dunk in the sea; Knuld's thorough to the point of madness. When he says he checked that winch, I believe him. Someone's screwing with us, Yav. This morning I was happy to believe it was Hunvir's murderer, but it's been gnawing away at me. It doesn't fit, doesn't smell right; he was a lunatic but he didn't have the cunning. I want you to keep your eyes open, root them out if you can. Hands will always be on their guard in the presence of officers, it's the way it is. But the men trust you, and the miscreant won't see you as a threat, especially now as he'll think the heat's off him. Report to me daily. Discreetly. Anything you notice, no matter how irrelevant it seems, I want to know."

"I agree with you, sir, having known the murderer. And I'd love to help catch whoever's messing us about," Yav said. It was true, but he gave a pained expression.

"What is it, Yav?"

"If I may say so, captain, I've never trusted the bard. Something's off about him."

"Really? Why d'you say so?"

Yavilad ordered his thoughts. "Nothing specific. But for every man on this ship, I can say something of his character. Moshim's solemn, Karelud's vexatious, Canna's timid."

"He's not. Canna's got something about him. It's not obvious, but it's there, believe me."

"Okay, I may be wrong about them but that's not my point. What I mean is, there's something of the man there for me to interpret, rightly or wrongly. My Jari, now, she's a funny little thing, very sweet. If she feels something, she'll act on it. There's no barrier between what she feels and what she does, there's no performance, no negotiation between the feeling and the action. Hang-faced kids are like that. With Slatre, all I see is performance. I don't know what lies underneath."

Skuld fixed him with a stare and chewed his lip. "I've not known him long, you know." A pause, and Skuld wagged a finger. "You're a smart man, Yav. I'll consider your words. Go now. Eyes open, eh?"

# 14. CLEAVE FLESH FROM BONE

*15$^{th}$ – 18$^{th}$ days of Gowan, 893 AZ.*

Storm transmuted ocean into bludgeoning mountains of white-tipped water, and men cowered within and swarmed atop the *Improbable*. Ulter and Dalind staggered on the quarterdeck, clinging to the helm and each other, tripping on ropes which secured their bodies to the mizzen. Hail and spears of rain traced arcing attacks, stinging their skin, jabbing their very eyeballs. The ship groaned and shrieked, bucking and heeling like a wounded beast refusing to die.

Millitre scampered fore and aft, relaying messages from the forecastle, where the captain roared orders into the faces of men and refusal into the face of the wind. Though bedraggled and gawky, Millitre moved with the grace and invincibility of adolescence. He pirouetted, crouched and side-stepped, resisting the yaw of the ship and the storm's craving to hurl him overboard.

Scrambling to the quarterdeck, he grinned, clutched Dalind's head close to his mouth and yelled above the wind. "Big boy coming! Rudder amidships. Brace!"

Dalind fell on his arse as the ship reared, bowsprit pointing skyward as if the *Improbable* were disillusioned with sailing and yearned to fly. For a heartbeat all was silent, and Skuld was framed against the sky by a flash of lightning, frozen with an arm aloft, mouth wide in a silent bellow of defiance. Sound and terror returned as the *Improbable* crashed through a wall of water, thunder roared and the main boom snapped with an explosive crack of defeated wood. It flopped beneath the storm sail like a broken arm. Dalind puked and the puke was vapourised in the wind. He tottered to his feet. Millitre lay unconscious on the main deck and his body slid around on the frictionless wood at the mercy of the ship's throes.

Arjier and the bard appeared in the doorway of the galley. Slatre shoved and yelled at the boy and pointed at Millitre. Arjier lurched across the deck, fell face forwards, rose and shook his head. Millitre's limp form tumbled and bounced towards portside as the ship heeled with a mournful howl. Arjier dived towards him like a hammerball forward and both boys disappeared as foaming water swept over them from starboard. Dalind clutched his head in his hands and moaned, but then punched the air and roared in triumph at the sight of Arjier hauling Millitre to his feet. He half slid down the steps to the main deck and rushed to help, leaving Ulter grappling the ship's wheel. Together, they carried Millitre between them to the sanctuary of the galley.

Below deck, Gauldr Moshim Vitchum struggled to hold his gorge and write legibly. One forearm secured parchment to his table, the other held a stylus, while his inkpot was braced between his knees.

# 

*Gerwen,*

*Happy birthday, my sweet one. You would be twenty now. Not long after you turned ten, farmer Faye came to the gauldrhouse, to complain that you had been sneaking into his barn of a night, somersaulting from the rafters into the hay below, feeding unhealthy treats to his livestock. A slave to order, that one, more concerned by the discord you brought to his property than for your safety. But as I promised him, I castigated you and kept you under curfew for a five-day. You clenched your little fists and called me boring, and your mother averted her face to hide her laughter.*

*If you could see your father now, girl. An adventurer, bravely facing the worst punishment the high seas can muster. Well, not quite. In truth, I have taken shelter from the storm while more able seamen steer the ship through danger as best they can. I do my duty by staying out of their way.*

*You would like our captain, I think. A risk taker, like you, fearless and determined. Clever, too. By means that I do not fully understand, he foresaw the storm that ravages above, and took actions that may have saved all our lives. He would make an excellent uncle; wonderful in small doses, but perhaps a little trying for longer periods. You would adore Canna, our naturalist. He is humble, unconfident and self-deprecating. Easily embarrassed, which you would tease him for. Untrained in the ways of science, he nevertheless knows much of the beasts of earth and sea, and enjoys sharing his knowledge with those with an appetite for wonder, like you. His lack of rigour is countered by a freshness of perspective and an ability to see through distractions and strip questions to their fundamentals.*

*Canna's questioning of the world intrigues and vexes me in equal measure. Life arose from less complex forms, he reckons, from simple things that strived for greatness, and all things are related, somehow. These ideas insult God, but I do not feel the insult. And if God did not create this world, what of the next one? I delivered you into the world and from it, your mother with you, and we will not meet again. Zarat teaches that the souls of the torpid are unworthy to fight by Svangur's side in the final battle with Dregva. The Book, the dusty old Book, claims your spirit is consigned to nothingness, while Dregva cleaves your flesh from your bones.*

*I remember your tears when dear Frynki left us, the vit you adored since before you could walk. Perhaps that tenderness of heart, always there under the scrapes and bruises of a full childhood, left you ill-equipped to fight for your God. I cannot accept this, will not, ruin take me. The gauldr bows his head in solemn humility, the father rends his clothes in grief and wails his refusal. Does God not love the tender of heart? The lonely and vulnerable?*

*Yavilad, a good man, told me of the birth of his daughter. She was born hang-faced and sickly, and he did not warm to her. Night after night he willed in silence for Dregva to take her, yet she persevered and as the months passed, he realised she had taken residence in his heart. In her infancy an illness almost finished her, distressing poor Yav almost to madness, as if the world were asking him, "Is this not what you wished?" Now he simply adores her, and the promise of seeing her again helps him endure the privations of the seafaring life. If Yavilad can recentre his world around such an unfortunate*

*creature, cannot God? Where is His humility? Perhaps there is something to Canna's anti-theology after all; life has a start and an end, and in between we must simply make the best of things. There is something bracing yet terrifying in that absence, and I cringe from it, but perhaps love can flourish there.*
*Your father, always,*
*Moshim.*

#

Grey calm settled over the ocean, hungover and embarrassed from days of revelry. A band of blue sky peeked from greyness at the horizon. Yfir's base disappeared into murk, as if broken by the storm. Battered but dignified, the *Improbable* wobbled onward while her men ministered to her with tender gratitude. The storm sail was released and inspected for damage. Main and foresails were heaved from lockers, readied for rerigging. Spars and booms were tested, splinted or replaced. A few fish had expired on deck and were turned into a rich broth, which revived the men's bodies and spirits.

Skuld's officers sat in the wardroom, staring at him in silence. He spluttered a laugh, seeming on the verge of rage or hysteria. "Dear God, we're still here. We abide, do we not? Blessed, I am, with such a ship, and such men. Ulter, Dalind, my kings of the sea…" He composed himself. "I'll come to you in a moment, Knuld. Laknir, how's the boy?"

"Fine, sir. He took a blow to head and was knocked insensible, but there seems no major damage aside from a great egg on his forehead, which is a good sign. Better than the damage turning inward. I recommend light duties for a few days, if that's feasible."

"Agreed. Arjier saved him, did he not? Fair play to the lad, I didn't know he had it in him. I'll compose a citation." Noron scowled, and turned his flask around and around. Skuld grinned at him. "You must've instilled some backbone in him after all, Noron. Knuld, the ship?"

"She's taken a pounding, captain, between fire and storm, but the sails and rigging are functional. The lower deck pillars and many strakes were badly compromised and I've prioritised these for the safety of the men, but I lack wood. But most seriously, the rudder only obeys the helm with reluctance. I dangled Yav down there and he says the sternpost and apron have taken a beating. We're limping, or rather, we're forced to limp by our dearth of manoeuvrability. She needs careening again."

Ulter caught the captain's eye and Skuld nodded to him. "I need clearer skies for a more accurate report, captain, but I estimate we're two hundred and fifty miles off course to the west. All is uncharted now, so we've a choice. We can tack due east for the coast of Eyra and seek landfall for resupply, but this'll delay our mission. Or continue south-east into the unknown. But in our state, the stores and the damage, we'd need to make like Austeri and ask a favour of God, to deliver us an island. If we saw no land before Eyra, we'd be in a bad way indeed."

"I ask no favours of God," Skuld said, glancing at Moshim. "Noron, the stores?"

"Fucked," Noron growled. "That murderous prick fucked us. Don't know what shit you fed him, gauldr, but it didn't work. Two thirds rations or we all starve, and that's if we tack for the coast. Half rations if we maintain course. At least the boy's lost weight, fat prick."

Skuld turned to Dalind. "How's morale among the men?"

Dalind, addled, opened his mouth and closed it. "A mixed bag, if I'm honest. It's understood that rations will be curtailed, but while they receive their booze and baccy they'll abide. Peril's brought them together I think, and they feel cleansed of Ekkero." The captain's jaw twitched. "Oh, sorry captain. But the bard's words concern me. He says he's come upon men grumbling in twos or threes, breaking off of a sudden when he approaches, because they know he has my ear."

"Seen this yourself?"

"No, sir."

"Report any signs of insurrection to me immediately. Managing the men will become more difficult in the coming days. We maintain our course."

# 15. STEALING MEAT

*28th day of Gowan, 893 AZ.*

Yfir narrowed and extended across the sky as the *Improbable* crept south. Clothes hung loose from dwindling frames, and heat cracked the men's lips, quickened their hearts and unmoored their thinking. Hunger left some twitching and numb, hugging themselves to assuage waves of cramps. Malnourishment exacerbated an inherited difficulty in absorbing certain nutrients, an heirloom from a tiny population of their distant forbears, forgotten people who cowered in pockets of survival and prayed for the Sun's return.

Yavilad sprawled on the forecastle steps, filling a pipe, shaking life into his tingling fingers. He lit the pipe with a candle and puffed, feeling his misfiring nerves settle as smoke filled his lungs. A crash of metal startled him and he jerked, dropping the candle and his pipe, the contents spilling around his feet.

Noron exploded from the galley, brandishing a rolling pin, his face insane. "Where the fuck is that snivelling fuck?" he roared.

Yavilad gazed sadly at his empty pipe and sighed. He pushed himself to his feet and retreated to the lower deck. His eyes slowly adjusted to the dimness, and he trod softly between barrels of beer, crates of weevil-infested flour and victuals, stacks of firewood, coils of spare rigging and swabbing brushes arranged neatly in a wooden frame. Noron's muffled bellowing continued. On shelves were bundles of candles, stacks of parchment, pots and pans. He prodded a toe at a stack of folded hammocks and the men's chests of humble belongings.

Rasping air, forced into scorched lungs sounded from behind a hastily erected screen of sail material, where Nijal clung to life.

Yavilad grabbed a lantern and poked his head around the screen. Hal glanced at him in mild surprise, a spoon of some milky substance in his hand.

"I'm sorry laknir, could you spare a flame?"

Hal nodded and obliged, proffering a lit candle to Yavilad's lantern.

"How is he?" Yav whispered.

"Responsive. He speaks in whispers and gestures, so I believe his mind is unharmed. He clutches to life with a tenacity that does him credit. If he dies it will not be for want of perseverance."

Yavilad nodded and retreated, and descended to the hold, handling the lantern carefully as he negotiated the ladder. Slatre stood down there, motionless in the darkness with no lantern or candle. Yavilad approached and raised the light to head height. Slatre squinted and shielded his eyes from the dazzle, and Yavilad caught a flash of red light reflected there.

"Get that out of my face, would you Yav," the bard whispered. He looked awful. His lips were dry and cracked, angry sores suppurating under his nostrils. His eyes were hollows, sweat beaded his brow and his cheeks were sunken. It looked as if his hair had receded a little. Yavilad kept the lamp where it was.

"You look like shit, Slatre. You need to see Hal?" The bard smiled and Yavilad recoiled at the sight of dark, receding gums. "What're you doing down here, anyway?" There was silence then, and Yavilad felt the hairs rise on his arms as Slatre's smile remained frozen in position, with unnatural prolongation. A fist clenched and unclenched.

They turned towards a thump and scrape from somewhere nearby. The sail locker. Yavilad approached the waist-high doors, glancing back at Slatre, and noticed the latch was disengaged. He crouched and swung the doors open. Arjier, the cook's boy, sat amidst a halo of crumbs, clutching a fistful of hardtack biscuit and dried meat. His eyes widened and he burst into tears.

"Please don't tell, Yav. The bastard's been starving me. Come on, Yav, please."

"Out, boy. Now."

Slatre grabbed Yavilad's elbow from behind. His voice was hoarse, menacing and unhealthy. "Yavilad. He's just a boy. You've seen how the cook treats him. They'll flog him for this. Tove's monitoring us, for signs of disobedience. Did you know that?"

Yavilad looked at the bony hand which clutched his elbow with surprising strength, then raised his eyes. "Why are you down here, Slatre?"

The bard's mouth tightened and after a moment, he released his grip.

#

Dalind and Yavilad dragged Arjier and tied him to the mainmast by hand and foot. The boy bled from the mouth and wept. At the captain's insistence, every man was on deck to witness the flogging, save Nijal and Hal, who was instructed to prepare another sickbed. Sympathy was as atrophied as the lining of stomachs, and the mood of some was of undisguised eagerness, the break in routine bringing its own elation. In tones of haughty pedagogy, half-remembered anecdotes of public retribution were traded and exaggerated. Surreptitious bets were laid as to whether Arjier would survive his ordeal, or for how long. Noron leered. Tove was impassive. Werdom looked on the verge of tears.

Karelud nudged the big man and whispered. "Don't cry Werdom, for fuck's sake. He's a thief, he deserves what's coming."

Canna slowly exhaled through dry lips. He imagined vomit scouring his parched throat, and his nausea intensified at the sight of the bard's wretchedness. Skuld appeared from below deck, strode through the crowd and turned to face them, sparing no glance for the restrained boy.

His voice was strong and clear but lacked its usual theatrical intonation. "Men. Forgive me for detaining you from your work, and settle down. This is not a mummer show. You are not toothless peasants giggling at a lynching. You are here because good men must bear witness to justice."

The crowd quietened and chins dropped.

"Hand Yavilad," Skuld said. The man stepped from the crowd to stand before the captain. "Do you swear by the Intention of Svangur, that the testimony you now give is truthful, to the best of your knowledge?"

"I swear it."

"Describe the events that took place in the hold, earlier this day."

"I was down there looking for a spatch-handle as you had commanded, captain. Slatre was down there. I asked why but before he could answer we heard a noise from the sail locker. I opened it up and Arjier was in there, eating food from the stores. Jerky, ship's biscuit and the like."

Skuld turned to Arjier for the first time. "Anything to say, boy?" Arjier blubbed nonsense and the captain sighed.

"I find this man guilty of theft. The punishment for this crime is twenty-five lashes of Mother's Disappointment. However, in light of the boy's age and his proven bravery, he will receive ten lashes of Vettr's Tongue. There will be no further repercussions. He has committed a crime and pays with skin and blood. I alone bear the responsibility of dispensing justice. We have the saltwater ready?" Knuld lifted a full wooden bucket aloft and nodded.

"Very good. First Hand Dalind."

Dalind shuffled forward carrying a small wooden case. His lips were bloodless. He withdrew a leather whip, with two loose knots tied at the end.

Skuld lifted the back of Arjier's shirt, pulling it up over his head in a tight roll. "Bite down on it, boy." Arjier whimpered and did so.

Dalind cracked his knuckles, shook out the whip and released a single, explosive breath. He unleashed the ship's justice, and the boy's screams concatenated into a single, fluctuating wail as red streaks decorated his skinny back. Werdom covered his eyes and wept. When Knuld doused him in saltwater to prevent befoulment, the boy passed out. Ulter and Canna untied him and lowered him to the deck, face down.

Slatre emitted a weird, high pitched keening and heads turned. The bard dropped to the deck, shivering, hands curled into claws, and his jaw locked into a grimace. Foam flecked his lips, his eyes rolled and his limbs jerked. His back arched and piss spread around him.

Hal prepared another dose of elixir, bending over a table and mixing small amounts of alcohol, honey and lavender oil.

He prattled as he worked. "I feel for the boy and will treat him as best I can. We all do our duty, do we not?" A low whisper was the only response. "We're all hungry now but Noron starved and beat him from the start, took an instant dislike to him. His system's suffered much punishment already. Skuld'll go as easy as he can on the lad; he's not a cruel man, whatever else you may say of him, but he should keep his cook on a shorter leash. At least Arjier'll have us for company, eh? Eh Nijal?"

The laknir turned to his patient and his smile disappeared. Nijal's remaining eye stared, unseeing, at the overhead. Hal bent to him, put an ear to his mouth, pressed knuckles to his sternum. Nijal's hands were cold and his mouth opened very slowly. Hal took his pulse; for every six heartbeats of Hal's, Nijal's beat once. Not dead, nor fully alive.

A flurry of stomping feet and Karelud's head appeared around the sail-curtain. "Laknir, come quick, please. The bard's having a fit or something up top." Karelud's eyes flicked to Nijal and he frowned. Hal pushed him back out of the sickbay.

"Show me."

#

Tala East wrestled with the bard's jerking arms, as if straightening them would end the seizing, while men crowded round. Skuld and Yavilad stood together, expressionless.

Hal pushed through the crowd. "Drengr, release his arms for ruin's sake, that's not helping. Dalind, put something soft under his head, let him ride it out."

Canna removed his shirt and threw it to Dalind, who knelt over the bard, gently lifting the twitching head. Slatre thrashed and growled. His eyes rolled down and darted about, awareness returning with something else. Dalind blinked as the eyes met his with an animal intensity. Slatre bared his teeth and his mouth juddered open, and kept opening until his chin met his breastbone and the mouth was an inhuman gape. Dalind recoiled and the men backed away.

For a beat, Dalind and the bard were isolated in a private bubble of space and silence. A quick wet noise, and a glistening, bony spike erupted from Slatre's left wrist. A flick of movement, and the spike punched into Dalind's neck, blood spraying. Before Dalind's face could register shock, Slatre leaned forward and his yawning mouth tore a massive chunk from his throat. He swallowed, eyelids fluttering, and shoved Dalind's corpse aside.

Werdom bellowed and charged. "Stop hurting my friend!"

Before Slatre could rise, Werdom grabbed his neck and hurled him through the air, crashing him into door of the galley, wood crunching. Slatre retched, shook himself and lurched to his feet, to face Werdom. In a fighting stance, both spikes extended now, he panted and swayed in readiness. He snarled and opened his bloody mouth to its full, awful extent. Tove and the twins were at Werdom's side, swords drawn, but Werdom ignored them and dashed forward. The bard retreated a step and spat a gob of pale fluid, aiming for the eyes. Werdom dodged and Slatre hissed, driving a spike towards his belly. Werdom darted left, and in a single, fluid movement caught the wrist in one hand, and swept Slatre's feet from under him. He pinned him to the deck, face down, braced a knee on his forearm and yanked upwards, snapping the arm. Slatre howled, and the howl intensified when Werdom stood and destroyed an ankle with a stomp.

As he went about his work, Werdom's violence was almost transcendent in its controlled efficacy, and the men's fear turned to awe. The captain stood frozen. Werdom knelt again and yanked Slatre's head up by the hair, arching the spine to its limit, then drove his face into the deck with brutal rapidity. Teeth skittered.

Ulter called out in a quivering voice. "Enough, Werdom. Tove, twins, tie it to the mainmast, quickly now."

They dragged the insensible bard across the deck and secured him to the mainmast in a kneeling position, arms yanked backward. Bone protruded from the snapped forearm. Arjier woke from his stupor, pushed himself to all fours and stared around with wide eyes, wailing as pain washed over him.

Skuld's paralysis broke and he called, "Karelud, Knuld, see to Dalind's body. Gauldr, Millitre, help Arjier. Yav, you're acting first hand. Canna, laknir, with me."

Yavilad stared at the thin strip of ruined flesh connecting Dalind's head to his body. "What the fuck...what the fuck..."

#

"What the fuck is that thing? Laknir? Canna?" Skuld spoke in an urgent whisper. He ran his fingers through his hair, leaving it a disorderly jumble, and swigged from a bottle. He hissed as liquid burned down his throat and passed the bottle across to Hal.

"I know of no such creature, outside of tales to scare children," Hal said. He took a swig and passed the bottle along the captain's table to Canna. The naturalist was staring into his lap, a muscle in his jaw flexing. Hal nudged him. "Canna?"

Canna looked up and spoke in a monotone. "Bradden Scar, the Riverbend man who was renounced. His wife told me his party was attacked by a thing such as this."

Hal stared. "You spoke to a renounced man?"

Canna ignored the question and passion entered his voice. "We need to know what it is, where it came from. How did it come to be on the ship, captain?"

Skuld wiped his mouth and grimaced. "Me and some of the men were at the Three Bridges Inn. You know of it, full of transients and rogues. I'm known there. Slatre was juggling, playing his harp and whatnot. He caught my eye and came over, with drinks for me and the men. Made us laugh he did. Told us some nasty character in a high position was out to get him, some rivalry over a woman. Said he'd join the crew for half pay, see a bit of the world, let things settle down. Ruin take me, my guard was down. Played me like his fucking harp." Skuld reached for the bottle and took another swig, coughed a little and shook his head. "Poor Dalind, ruin."

"I put him at the creature's mercy. It should have been me," Hal said.

"Nonsense. See to Arjier, Hal. Canna, interrogate that thing tied to the mast. If you want it tortured, ask Tove, he's experienced. I want to know everything about it before I destroy it."

"Captain, there's something else," Hal said. "Nijal is torpid. Just now, as Karelud came to fetch me."

"Throw him overboard then, for fuck's sake."

"Captain, please. He's recoverable, I think. He's been unable to heal properly because his throat's too painful to take food. Torpor may relax his pipes so I can feed him high vitality foods. Ruin, much of our certainties of the world lie in tatters, do they not? This is no time to indulge naval superstition."

The captain glowered, then nodded. "Crisis is innovation's father, eh? Very well. Go. We reconvene in the wardroom when you are done, Canna. The officers and Moshim, too."

Canna left the captain's cabin and fought to control his shaking.

# 16. THE PASSION OF THE UNNAMED

*28<sup>th</sup> day of Gowan, 893 AZ.*

Slatre sagged before the mast, head lolling.

"Slatre."

No response. Canna nodded to Karelud, who stood aside with bucket and swabbing brush. Karelud lifted the bucket, crept towards Slatre and threw the water over him, then retreated in haste. The bard's head snapped up and he winced in pain, breath rapid and shallow. Watering eyes fixed on Canna. He spat blood, grimaced, and writhed around to find a tolerable position. His slack mouth drooled, but his skin had lost its unhealthy sheen. My God, Canna thought, feeding on Dalind has restored him.

Canna approached, leaving a wary distance between himself and the bard. His heartbeat pounded in his ears. Karelud stood regarding them, still clutching his bucket.

"What are you?" Canna was disgusted at the fear in his own voice.

Slatre grinned at him and lisped through shattered teeth. "What's that, Canna? Come closer, so I can hear you." He licked his broken lips and winced. His accent had changed.

"I think not. What are you? A demon?"

Slatre dry heaved and spat. "I'm a man like you," he wheezed. "Except not."

"Save your riddles. Tell me what you are."

"A wretched beast of the Earth, as are we all. I look human but I'm something else. Will I be in your diary, Canna? Sit here with me, and I'll tell you all about myself. I'll tell you what you are, also."

"What's your real name? Not Slatre, I presume."

"My kind don't need names, any more than you need a dorsal fin. Some called me Abal. Your friend, Bradden, knew me as Fioror."

Canna took an involuntary step backwards, and blood rushed to his face.

The unnamed grinned. "There's no keeping secrets from me, my hearing's too sharp. My name…my name…what's a name for? It's a handshake for humans to mediate their interaction. If you'd been born into loneliness Canna, had never seen another human, would you bother giving yourself a name?"

Without really thinking on the question, Canna said, "Yes, I think so."

The unnamed sniffed. "You'd like to think so. You're a little master, steering your body around like the Austeri with their tame mairs. Is that right? No. The mair does what it wants, Canna. You go where it pleases. It lets you think you're in control." There was no sense of ill will in the bard's voice. "You're not even a discrete individual. You're a node, in a network of other nodes, and you don't exist without it. The network can't be denied, because you're not a lone animal. It's in your very bones. Even a hermit defines himself by the network, his separation from it. I am a lone animal, Canna."

"You killed Hunvir, correct?"

"Yes. I ate his liver and heart then threw Ekkero in the sea. The fire was a distraction, obviously."

"Why?"

"I was hungry. Your food doesn't agree with me. Give me a break now, would you, Canna? I can take a lot of pain but I'm in agony here."

Canna gazed up for a moment at Yfir, straddling the sky. The waxing moon was faintly visible within the arch. "Not yet. So, your kind, what, pretend to be human, blending in, and then you eat people?"

Slatre stared at him a moment. "It's more complicated than that. Or simpler. 'Blending in' is more accurate than 'pretending.' I don't pretend anything. I am what I am. I'm born with drives, fears, survival techniques, like you. Your species survives in networks, cooperating and battling each other. Mine survives by blending in with yours, exploiting your instincts and living off your meat and goodwill. I don't just eat humans, by the way. Any fresh meat's good."

"Do you have no conscience? Pity?"

"No. Pity, love, shame; they're lubricants that help the network run smooth. I'm not part of the network, remember? But my body rewards me for actions that help me survive, as does yours. My sensations are as real as yours, I imagine."

"But different."

The unnamed nodded. "A good meal gives you pleasure. Because its goodness is some innate property, like the wetness of water? No, it only tastes good because your body knows it's good for it. You get a pat on the back, a sensation of goodness, for doing something to help it. Some lower animals get a similar pat on the back when they eat shit, maybe. Ever eaten shit?"

Canna snorted. "And what gives you pleasure?"

"The thought of you untying me from this fucking mast." Slatre leered. "Remember playing Garor with the men? Hunvir took the piss out your inexperience but helped you learn the game. You smiled at him and felt good, because the men were accepting you. Your body knows, somehow, that solidarity's good for you, helps you stay alive. I felt good as well, for different reasons. When men laugh with me, shake my hand, applaud, I feel good, because my body knows I'm blending in, that the humans don't know my true nature. This is key to my existence. Anything I do which distracts humans from what I am, feels good. I play on the connections within the network as I pluck the strings of my harp. Disruption and chaos in the network distract it from turning on me, while I exploit it. If I feel the network's becoming aware of me, this fake node, I feel fear. Analogous to your fear of rejection, maybe. I've no plan. It is what it is. Watching things die gives me pleasure, too. Ease up now, Canna, I'm tired."

Canna glanced at Karelud, who sat cross-legged, watching. "You've distracted us from what you are? How?"

"Lots of things. Little thefts, sabotage. Stoking antipathy between men who already dislike each other, undermining the officers. I stood up for Arjier, made him rescue Millitre in the storm. This was because he was a figure of ridicule; though he suffered, he united the others in their disdain, and relief that they themselves were not despised."

Canna was silent then, replaying scenes in his mind, analysing them in a new light. "How do you do blend in?" he said "How do you know how to respond to people when you have no pity, no normal emotions?"

The unnamed sucked his remaining teeth; one of them visibly wobbled. "Good question. Do you speak Austeri, Canna?"

"What? No."

"Nor me." Wracking coughs and a dry heave. Blood and saliva dripped to the deck. "Imagine, Canna, you're stuck in a room, alone. Someone slips notes to you under the door, and expects you to write back. But the notes are in Austeri. If you were fluent in Austeri you'd just write a note back, but you can't. All you see on the parchment are little squiggles that mean nothing to you. Now, in the room with you's a thick book. It's got tables and tables of instructions which tell you how to write a response to the notes. All you do is compare the Austeri symbols in the notes with those in the book, follow the instructions carefully, and you can write a note back. You've no idea what any of these notes are saying, yet you take part in a whole conversation. I've a book like that, Canna. In my mind. But it tells me how to pass for human. This is happening now, as we speak. You see?"

"Yes, I think so." Canna felt something fall away from him. It was the barrier, or maybe a bridge, that exists in every human interaction: the sense of observing and evaluating oneself through the eyes of the other. That was not applicable here and he felt a sensation of lightness. This thing would not, could not, judge him, at least in human terms.

"How do you reproduce?"

"Really, Canna?"

"Tell me."

Slatre exhaled. "Alright, I'll do my best. It's a cycle, so my starting point's arbitrary. I'm an adult male, going about my business, blending in, eating your hokrs and heidrn when you're not looking. I pick up a powerful scent in the air; we've good noses, you know. It stirs new feelings. A female. I know without knowing and I'm horny and terrified. The females are very different, Canna. Formidable. She's been venturing from wherever she's holed up, leaving gifts of scent." Karelud looked disgusted.

"I know she wants a gift. Food. The harder to acquire, the greater the risk to me, the better. If she's unimpressed, I'm in the shit, to say the least. But this is a happy story. I track her down, dragging along some poor innocent, and the female's happy with it. She lets me mate but my role isn't finished. When the baby's born, I'll smuggle our bundle of joy into the network. Switch it with a human baby or leave it at the door of a gauldrhaven.

"The kid grows into an awareness of itself. The maturation of our wrist spikes hurts like a bastard, let me tell you, and if you think toothache's bad, try the feeling of your jawbone dissolving. You have your overcoming, we have ours. We males just carry on into adulthood, blending in, feeding when we can. The females, though, transform." His eyes were glassy, and he spoke to the sky. "They leave humans behind and become something…better. They fend for themselves. Whether they retain language or self-awareness, I don't know."

Canna closed his eyes a moment and remembered the tree-octopus materialising from nowhere and snaring the tiny lizard. "You fled Ibr, didn't you?"

"How did you know?"

"Just a guess."

Slatre grunted. "I became aware of another male in my territory."

"Territory?"

The unnamed nodded, then flexed his neck and hissed in pain. "Ah, fuck…I'm not sure Werdom's human either, to be honest. What were you asking?"

"You mentioned territory."

"Ah yes. We don't play nicely together, my sort. Remember the network. My life's a game of numbers and probability. Two fake nodes in the same network would raise suspicion, trigger a response. A young male in my territory had reached maturity, and I had a close call with his female. A young male in a very advantageous position. I was hemmed-in on all sides, so I left on a whim, to find a new territory of my own. It was a risk. I don't even know whether our kind exist in these far-flung corners of the world."

"Who's this other male?"

"The son of the Riverbend bridgewarden."

Canna's mouth fell open. "Javic Silver?"

"That's him."

"You lie, surely. I know the man, myself."

The unnamed managed a slight shrug, despite his restraints. "Clearly not. Why would I lie?"

"I don't know," Canna admitted. "Why are you telling me any of this at all?"

"I'm trying to survive, by giving you what you want: information. And it's easier to be honest than lie, right now. Skuld would have Tove torture me if I refused to talk and I don't enjoy pain any more than you do. If I was speaking to Hal, I'd appeal to his duty and generosity. If it was Skuld, I'd convince him of my usefulness and subservience. But I'm speaking to you, to your curiosity. I tried intimidation, at first. I smelled your fear, but your curiosity won out, so I played on that, stoked it by begging you to lay off."

Canna forced his expression to remain blank.

"There's more to learn, Canna, a lot more," Slatre said. "I'll show you how my wrist spikes work. I won't attack, I'm knackered anyway, my ankle and arm's bust. I'm crippled. And I think you understand I bear no malice, for any of you."

Canna shuddered as a stab of fear returned. "You know I can't."

Slatr's smile was warm, yet imbecilic and predatory. "I have to try, Canna. By talking to you openly, I've made it more likely that you'll help me survive. Whether you realise this or not, makes no difference. Fake medicine helps a man recover, and here's the important point: fake medicine works even if the man knows it's fake. Ask Hal. That's why I'm being honest with you. Persuade the captain for me. Leave me at the next landfall and you'll never see me again."

"It's not my decision," Canna said, flatly. "The octopuses on the islands, I believe they came from common stock and adapted to their current forms. Do you think humans, and you…unnamed, come from common stock?"

"Interesting idea. Maybe. And what of our slipskin brothers? Persuade the captain and we'll find out together. You can study my body."

"I'll be doing that, regardless."

Canna held the unnamed's eye for a moment, then turned and walked away.

# 

In the wardroom, Canna gave a halting account of his conversation with the unnamed. The captain invited comments and Noron spoke up.

"Just kill it, for fuck's sake. Who cares?"

Hal had a faraway look about him. "Dear God."

"What is it, Hal?" Skuld asked.

"I just remembered. I was sent to Hakela when I was young. The wardenwife had awful monthly pains, you see. One of the serving girls came to me one night, desperate. Her sister's baby was not feeding, and weakening. I went to see them and the little thing was fading fast, I doubted it'd see another morning. I visited next day, and the baby was bonny as the Bridge, feeding happily at his mother's breast. The parents were overjoyed, as you can imagine. It took me a moment, but it was a different baby. I thought they must've taken another family's child, but there were no reports of such, and it's a small place, you know. I put some pointed questions to the parents but saw no sign of guilt and they were disinclined to probe the origin of their fortune."

Yavilad caught the captain's eye in the silence.

"Yav?"

"If what the thing says is true, Riverbend has a big problem. The villagers are at risk."

Skuld nodded. "I understand that, but there's not much we can do about it now." Then he slapped the table and hurled a cup at the bulkhead. He shouted, "Ruin take the wretch! It was on my ship, doing this under my nose. Picking away at us, at me, all this time." He composed himself and continued. "Moshim, hold a service for Dalind. And for Ekkero, may his soul forgive us." Nods around the table.

"I recommend the unnamed is kept secure upon the ship, captain," Moshim said, "that he may face interrogation and justice on our return to Ibr."

"Justice? For that? It's not a 'he' Moshim, it's an 'it.' Where's this creature fit into your neat understanding of the world? Of the vital and the unworthy? What's your Book got to say? Bugger all. We should throw it overboard."

"The captain's right, gauldr," Canna said. "Justice is a human concept. It means nothing to the creature. And it's too dangerous to keep aboard. We've seen how it manipulates men. Captain," Canna tiptoed carefully between his words, "your anger's understandable, but it's not the same as being taken for a fool by another man. That's not how it works, I think. It may be hard to accept, but it's not evil, more like a dangerous animal. It just needs putting down. No need for ceremony." Canna looked over at Hal. "But Hal and I would appreciate the chance to study its body, to learn more."

Skuld nodded, calmer, and spoke to Tove. "Fetch your bow."

A short time later, on deck, the unnamed raised its head, eyes widening. Tove stood a few feet away, an arrow cocked.

"Captain, wait! You don't understand. There's another like me aboard, I can help you."

Skuld nodded and Tove loosed. The unnamed fell silent.

# 17. KINSHIP

*A Naturalist's Diary. 2$^{nd}$ day of Einmandr, 893 AZ.*

All my life I have been told God would hone my blade upon my death, readying me for His final battle. But the blade of my reason is sharp enough. My Dangerous Idea takes shape, and while it offers no comforting promise of a glorious ever after, it demands a reckoning with the kinship of all of life, the ubiquity of suffering, the struggle. A man who accepts this demand must make his own choice as to the purpose of his life. He must take responsibility for his actions, for the actions are his alone. Such a man is, I think, harder to control than a man who regards himself a mere tool of superior beings. Slipskins were a mistake of God, supposedly, but I believe God is a mistake of man.

My Idea is incomplete, but there are four principles which underpin it. The first is that individual living things of the same type vary from each other. Some have longer or shorter legs, different markings and so on. Secondly, features can be passed on from parents to offspring. The third principle is that animals and plants have features which make them more likely to survive and pass on those features to their young. These offspring are then more likely to survive and pass those traits on to young of their own. Creatures that do not share these advantageous features are punished by death, and do not pass on their features (or pass them to fewer young). So, among a population of organisms, certain successful features become more common. The final principle says that over time, this process of selection leads to animals changing into quite different forms, adapting as it were, into forms of increasing complexity and excellence. If a group of organisms is somehow cut off from their brethren, the selection process can get to work on the separate populations, leading, in a kind of branching process, to new distinct forms.

So, death, not God, drives creation; a blasphemous conclusion. Survival (or immortality?) is not dependent on the worthiness of your soul, but the excellence of your tools. The Idea is deceptively simple but wields explanatory power. There are gaps, however, which trouble me and I may never rectify. For instance, the changes to animal forms, which lead to the variation of life we see around us, must be incremental and take vast swathes of time. Is the world so old, then? If life is a great, branching tree, this implies a single Originator at the tree's base. I struggle to comprehend how the sheer variety of life could begin from such a humble beginning. Perhaps this is merely a failing on my part, my imagination too small to handle such profundities. And from whence came this Originator? And how do animals pass on their traits? Until these mysteries are solved, my Idea remains an unproven curiosity, a mere exercise in reason. Volley after volley of facts must be hurled at it, to test its foundations.

I have no name for my Idea, as yet, and shall have to think of one. And so, I crudely segue to the unnamed. I struggle to conceive of their origin. One can imagine a population of octopuses becoming separated, by for example, crawling onto two separate islands, then diverging into different forms by the process described above. Similarly, if men found themselves trapped in caves, the engine of death and success could shape him to his new environment, hence the slipskins. But whence the unnamed, living among us all this time? Perhaps in some forgotten village, some of the men were shunned, a kind of social separation, so death was free to work upon them in their isolation, changing them into a new kind of pitiless creature with man's appearance but none of his capacity for goodness and cooperation.

Hal drew a comparison between the unnamed's notion of human networks, and the way parasites infect the "network" of a host's body. The parasite feeds on the host, but it is not in its interests to overwhelm the animal on which it depends, or to instigate a powerful counter-response. And it is against the unnamed's interests to overwhelm us. Now I think on it, my Idea implies that parasites and hosts would forever be locked into a battle for supremacy. Parasites that are better at exploiting their hosts will pass on their traits to many young, and proliferate. Hosts which can resist parasites will have an advantage over those which cannot, and will also pass their beneficial traits to their young. Host and parasite drive change in each other.

So many things fall into place. Creatures frozen in rock, for instance. Not the failed experiments of a starving god, but creatures in their own right which ultimately failed death's challenge and were extinguished. Perhaps down there, in the rock, earlier forms of ourselves lie in rest. What were they like, our kin?

Families are the basic unit by which our people group themselves, a sub-network as the unnamed might put it, and this points to a logical means of grouping and naming animals; by their relation on the great tree of life (an original phrase of mine, I believe, which I hope becomes commonplace). We and the unnamed surely sit on proximate twigs, sharing a joint ancestor in the relatively recent past. The implications of this are profound but I cannot think on it now; my head hurts already. I must remember my principle of graded simplification so as not to drive myself mad. But, God's ribs, the Idea is like a pair of powerful new eyes that see into the past and future, and I cannot help but turn them hither and yon.

I must guard against the seductiveness of neat little explanations that seem to slot nicely into the theory. Follow the facts, always. Hal told me something of the great famine which I had not known, which provides a cautionary tale against certainty of any kind.

During the famine, Overdrengr Fan Clour was powerfully influenced by his adviser, Seidhr Trofim Ysen. Trofim believed seeds could gain vitality and perseverance through exposure to cold and other forms of assault: drying out, heating, exposure to acids and so on. He believed the seed would pass on what it had "learned," to its descendants, and that crops would therefore become stronger and stronger over time, if treated correctly. Fan latched onto these ideas, attracted perhaps by the prospect of a simple solution to a grave problem. He decreed that all farming across Ibr must follow Trofim's principles. The famine was exacerbated, and thousands suffered starvation and torpor. Infamously, the Overdrengr was by this time manic and haunted by paranoia, and instigated Red Harpal.

Hal and I performed an examination of the unnamed's dead body. Or rather, Hal performed the examination, his dextrous hands slicing and peeling, while I looked on and listened attentively to his observations. The creature provides a lesson in how the selective engine of death shapes an animal, such that one part can be co-opted for some other use. The adaptive process seems rather akin, in fact, to floating on a piece of wood and gradually building an entire ship all around you, all the while making sure you never sink. At some point you might decide that an oar could serve as a mast and you whip off your trousers for a sail. Your boat moves faster but now your legs are cold. It is all trade-offs.

The unnamed's frightening wrist spikes are made of bone and are analogous to the small "boat bone" found in the human wrist. It is tucked between the forearm bones and is sheathed by means of three special tendons. It emerges through a small muscular slit in the wrist, which is virtually invisible. Hal demonstrated, unnervingly, how the spikes could be unsheathed by manipulating the tendons, just so. The creature must have powerful healing mechanisms to resist infection, for the viscera of its prey must surely enter its body via these weapons. And I am sure its tolerance of pain far exceeds that of a man.

The jaw lacks the firm mandibular joint of humans, and is instead secured by flexible tendons which allow the mouth to open very widely. Thick, densely packed muscle provides powerful biting force, complemented by the teeth. While appearing normal at first glance, the incisors' edges are exceedingly sharp (a couple were left intact by Werdom's fury), allowing for slicing through flesh. The rear molars are larger than those in humans, the rearmost ones fused together, so the creature could perhaps have crunched bone. A small, bulb-like structure sits within the nasal cavity, just below the brain, similar to structures found in many animals with advanced scenting abilities. The pupils of the eyes are unusually large, and there sits an extra, reflective layer in the back of the eye, bearing comparison with some nocturnal creatures. It is intriguing to imagine the rich sensory world in which the unnamed must have moved, although Hal suggests that like many animals, the unnamed's nocturnal vision may be traded off by a poor capacity to distinguish between colours.

Aside from the wrist spikes, the most striking difference between the unnamed and humans is in the digestive system. Typically of a carnivore, the tract is relatively simple and short. The stomach is large, flexible and muscular, geared towards infrequent gorging of large meals. I recall the unnamed's almost torpid presentation when we met him on Irna; he must have recently digested some poor victim, and was reduced to lethargy while his body broke down great quantities of meat. His mintjak was no pet.

The stomach features a sort of annex, filled with a foul-smelling brew, and the food pipe is particularly muscular with a protective lining on its inner surface. This suggests the creature's weaponised spit, used to blind its enemies, is actually an adapted form of projectile regurgitation. Perhaps the fluid from this annex mixes quickly with the stomach acid, to create a potent mixture which is vomited at will.

Before Tove ended it, the unnamed left us a sour, parting gift of suspicion, by claiming another of its sort was aboard. The captain believed this a desperate attempt by the unnamed to forestall its doom, and I concurred, but he could take no chances. At the point of Tove's sword, each man was subjected in turn to having his jaw and forearms palpated by Hal (with his customary sort of quiet bravery), to detect any sign of unnamed anatomy. Skuld and Tove were subjected to this test first, and I carried it out upon Hal. All clear. The idea of kindly old Hal being a predatory monster seems laughable, but I would have said as much of the bard. I wonder how long they live.

Without the benefit of an intrusive, post-death examination, the only outward clue to the unnamed's true nature is the unusual muscularity of his jaw. Oh ruin...Javic Silver shares this facial characteristic. And is given to regular walks, often leaving for days at a time. Hunting. Like "our" unnamed, Silver is popular, personable and handsome. The people of Riverbend adore him for his sympathy for the poor, his mercy, his humble willingness to help those less fortunate than him. It was he who persuaded his father to let me live and to have me join this expedition, and I have no doubt that Javic is completely in thrall to the creature he believes to be his beloved son. Why let me live? Let us pretend for a moment, in an ironic reversal, that we are the unnamed, weighing the value of different courses of action.

Canna brought a warning, from Bradden, that monsters may live among us. I [the unnamed], must ensure such stories go no further, lest the network turn its attention to this potential threat. I could persuade Javic to kill Canna, box him. But no, Canna is well liked, well known. If Canna is destroyed by Javic, this reflects on me, lowers my standing in the eyes of the people as a wise, merciful leader-in-waiting. If he is boxed, people will ask why. What did Canna do or say that was so damaging? What did he discover that was so dangerous to the bridgewarden? I cannot allow wild rumours to spread through the network. I could simply kill Canna myself, make him disappear or stage an accident, but this brings its own risks and leads to the same problems. No, I shall have him join this journey to Eyra, get him out of the way. There is a good chance this weakling, who has never been to sea, will never return. There is an added opportunity here to demonstrate to Poesha that it is I, not he, who wields power through the puppet bridgewarden. Good, it is settled. Canna is dealt with, for now, and I will steer Poesha and Javic away from silly stories of monsters. But Bradden and his wife must die.

Enough. Seeing the world through such eyes leaves me queasy, and I will only torture myself trying to anticipate its course of action. My friends are in danger. I am in danger, but powerless. We know, at least, that it is possible to examine a living unnamed and reveal him for what he is. Perhaps Skuld and Hal will help me persuade Javic that Silver is not what he appears. Humanity must be told of this threat; the hunters must be hunted. But oh ruin, the cure could be worse than the disease. Too easily can I imagine warring families accusing the other of harbouring unnamed, gauldrhaven children massacred...

Throughout the unnamed's body we saw trade-offs between the competing aims of killing efficiently, and blending in with human hosts. Such trade-offs, Hal says, are found throughout nature. Bird bones are light and contain air sacs, allowing flight but limiting the size to which they can grow while retaining that ability. Women's hips are wider than a man's, to allow for giving birth, but this reduces the support provided by the soft tissues of the knees.

What of the female unnamed? If they do indeed hide away from humans as they reach maturity, then their body is free, as it were, to devote itself to killing without the need of retaining human appearance. "Formidable" was the word the unnamed used, though it still must start from a point of human appearance in its childhood. And it is a sad indictment of us that the females' propensity to flee their hosts is camouflaged by the sheer number of human children who disappear from their families, never to be seen again. Young girls vanish all the time. Aside from the family, nobody really cares.

I imagine there are many less obvious trade-offs in living things, in anatomy and behaviour, which could only be sufficiently appreciated through the application of mathematics. Relationships between growth-rate, body size, number of offspring, foraging behaviour and aversion to risk; life steering a course through unseen calculations, moulding itself to their limitations. Dare I say, there is something god-like in this great calculus of life and it will take minds quicker than mine to dissect these secrets of the world. Ulter perhaps, if he ever tired of the seafaring life, could bend his will to such a task. Many disciplines must be brought to bear for the Idea to fully mature: mathematics, geognosy, alchemy, natural philosophy, engineering. I leave the Idea now, tucking it away in my mind like a child unwillingly storing his favourite toy before bedtime.

Happy news: Nijal is recovered. In his torpid state, he was able to swallow high vitality foods with the aid of Hal massaging his throat, and within two days he was aware and talking. During his torpor (which was known only to myself, Hal, the captain and Moshim), his wounds healed at an accelerated rate. It was as if, modifying Hal's ship analogy, the crew of Nijal's body abandoned navigation and rigging to focus on scrubbing all mould from the deck and fixing the hull. Hal subjected him to a suite of tests to determine the functioning of his mind; counting backwards from one hundred in leaps of seven, walking in a narrow line, identifying pictures and so on. A little grudgingly, Skuld acknowledged that Hal was justified in his refusal to renounce Nijal. Gauldr Moshim, meanwhile, is quiet and graver than usual. He is a good man, but the recuperation of Nijal and the unveiling of the unnamed stand as challenges to his very purpose. I hope he will be alright.

# 18. CONTROL GROUP

*3rd day of Poori, 893 AZ.*

Javic Silver shivered naked in the freezing stream, washing blood and scraps of fur from his face, hands and wrist spikes. He splashed from the water and flopped on the grassy hillside, wrapped a cloak about himself and idly picked flesh from his teeth. Warmness spread through his bones and meat weighed heavy in his stomach. He yawned, feeling his eyelids droop. Riverbend torchlight wavered and pinpricks of stars dissolved into fuzzy splodges. His thoughts tripped over themselves.

He awoke with a start, looked around in panic. The Moon had risen, a circle of radiance behind Yfir's eastern leg. He had dreamed of hunting; a human child, a female, fled through the trees of Haugr Wood, weeping and stumbling, and he smelled her terror. It collapsed at the Moon Pool clearing, whimpering and then laughing and swelling into a terrible beast, all horns and teeth. From an altar of sinew and bone it looked down on him, imperious. He dropped to his knees before the beast, terrified and erect, and carved runes into his thighs with his wrist spikes.

He yawned, dressed himself and trudged up to Beggar's Leap, the huge shelf of rock jutting from the brow of the Beggar's Hills. Somewhere down there, in the Horn Valley, lay what had been Bradden's farm, now a charred tomb. Vettr's Horns, twin mountain peaks named for the twisted creature sent by Dregva to hunt the errant Svangur, framed the evening star. Qeren's faint radiance in the east would be undetectable to humans from here.

This would not do. Poesha had asked him to send a runner to Silves, to search the library of the seidhr for information pertaining to monsters who look like men. The unnamed pondered on the chilly rock. *By asking me to complete this task, rather than instruct the* runner himself, Poesha hopes to re-establish his superiority over me in the social order, and Javic's favour. A fortunate decision for me, but I can only delay so long. Regardless of his strategy, my ascendency to bridgewarden is inevitable and he will answer to me, if I allow him to live. Perhaps he lays the groundwork for when I hold official power, demonstrating to me that whoever holds the title, he holds the levers of control.

The unnamed's forearms itched and he flossed his wrist spikes in and out a few times. Poesha is not motivated by power for its own sake. He cares nothing for material rewards and titles. He finds pleasure in seeing decisions translated into actions of consequence. Canna's report of monsters piques his interest, because he understands there are potential consequences for his ability to exert power, and for the safety of the few people who matter to him. He cannot be dissuaded from this path, so he must die. Javic can be distracted easily enough. Some other crisis could be generated to occupy him.

Something moved in the valley below, a stain of shadow. He blinked and squinted into the gloom. Definitely human. It approached the foothills, heading towards the old mine entrance. Lying flat on the rock shelf and peering down almost vertically, the unnamed took a long breath in through his nose. There was no scent; the wind was wrong. He sniffed again. No, there was just a hint of something, maddeningly familiar. Metal struck flint, and a torch flared. A human male. The torch bobbed up the hillside, lingered a few moments, then disappeared. The unnamed dropped thirty feet from the shelf, crouched into a roll as he landed and sprang to his feet. He skipped down the steep hillside in silence, dodging rocks and plants, revelling in his agility.

Tumbled rocks were strewn about the exhausted mine entrance, and cart tracks leading to it were faintly detectable. The entrance was partially obscured by spineberry bushes and was sealed by planks of wood nailed to its wooden frame. Javic had spun tales of monsters haunting the old mine, preying on unsuspecting, errant children. Probably a wise ploy, these tales, to keep children from danger, though it was not impossible that a female once dwelled here and really did eat the odd wayward child.

The unnamed considered the entrance and took a deep breath into his lungs. That hint of a scent was stronger now, and unmistakable. Poesha. Fancy soaps could never mask his underlying essence. In proximity, the unnamed had noted a trace of decay, wrongness, in Poesha's breath, on his skin. Some disease of the blood, perhaps. Ending him now, early in life, might spare him years of later suffering, the unnamed reasoned, though the conclusion carried no emotional weight.

The planks covering the entrance were nailed securely to the surrounding frame, yet Poesha had surely gotten in somehow. The planks were old and weathered but the surrounding frame and the nail heads appeared quite new. A faint arc traced the dirt. Spitting into his hands for grip, he grasped the frame and heaved. The whole frame, planks and all, lifted and swung outwards easily. The unnamed smiled in the darkness.

Ducking beneath overhanging bush, he entered the mine and pulled the door closed. Even with his excellent vision, the blackness was overwhelming, and he crept forward. A few paces, and his foot met a thin resistance. He froze, stepped back, breath held, heart racing. He took a moment, exhaled, then bent to one knee. A tripwire stretched across the tunnel, connected to spindly wooden supports, which secured a jumble of large rocks above in a web of netting. A crude but effective trap. With care, the unnamed stepped over the wire and moved on.

Farther into the darkness, his vision was rendered useless, and he moved with the ponderous gait of the torpid, feet scraping, feeling their way before him. Poesha's scent waned in silence, and blackness seemed to dissolve the barrier between him and itself. He was unmoored, insubstantial. Then a new, foetid stink announced itself. Death; not the aroma of a fresh kill, but the stench of disease and putrefaction. He followed it for a time, wrinkling his nose, then stopped. Something about the airflow had changed. He licked his fingertips, spread them before him and allowed his thoughts to empty.

A fork in the tunnel. The unnamed sniffed and followed the right-hand passage, descending into the earth towards the smell of death.

From somewhere came the faintest illumination, allowing him to make out a deeper darkness spread across the way; a chasm spanned by a bridge of rope and wood. Testing each step, the unnamed crossed the groaning bridge, pausing in surprise as something skittered over his foot. A glimmer of orange beckoned in the distance.

The light grew, and he shielded his eyes as he rounded a corner; the route was lined by blazing torches fixed to the wall. More turns, then a descent down a twisting ramp, and the unnamed came to a small room. Wooden struts held at bay a bulging ceiling of earth, which he eyed warily. A broken cart decayed on its side among a heap of rocks, and tools and buckets lay scattered about. Water dripped. Several tunnels led from the room but only one was marked by torchlight and the stench. Stones tumbled somewhere in a black side tunnel, but the unnamed ignored it, focussed on his quarry.

The tunnel terminated at a wrought iron gate, which sagged from a single hinge and marked the entrance to a large natural cave. Death flooded his nostrils. He backed up, grimacing, and squatted to reconnoitre from a shadowed, natural alcove. The cave was lit by torches, revealing a flight of wooden steps leading up to a walkway, which ran around the left side of the cave. Atop that was a row of cabins; tool sheds, sleeping quarters or some such, he supposed. Near the centre of the cave, a pile of five or six human bodies lay stinking, a macabre artistic centrepiece. Though the smell assured its deadness, the pile jerked and shifted. A trick of the light, perhaps. No, an arm in the pile flopped in a grim, lazy wave, and there were noises. The unnamed frowned, shoved the iron gate aside with a howl of protesting metal and entered the cave.

Krets swarmed among the bodies; sleek forms scurrying over, under and through the dead. Sharp beaks nipped at fingers, earlobes and thighs, clever little arms wrestled for choice tidbits. A corpse of indeterminate sex bulged and rippled as animals snuffled in its torso.

"Silver? What are you doing here?" Poesha stared from the walkway above.

"Watha, Poesha," the unnamed replied with a smirk. "I followed you, wondered what you were up to."

Poesha sighed. "You could have just called after me. Shit, you were lucky not to be flattened by the rocks. How d'you find your way through, anyway?" He flapped a hand. "Never mind, come on up. I want to show you something."

The unnamed ascended the steps and joined Poesha by one of the cabins.

"You ever been in here, Silver?"

"No, never."

"Me, Jalana and Canna used to play in here as kids. I got lost once; I was terrified. My dad told me a teenage girl got lost and never came out." He pointed down to the corpses and grinned. "Sorry about the mess by the way. Hold this a moment."

Poesha handed his torch over, pulled a key from his pocket and unlocked the cabin door. Skinny humans stood unblinking in the torchlight, mouths hanging, pupils huge. Some were naked, some not. Many had cuts and bruises, one had a smashed nose and a missing ear. The room stank of shit. They huddled together in the centre of the room in a dense knot, then turned, and shuffled towards the light and warmth, clacking teeth as they collided. The unnamed stepped back. One of the torpid struck the doorframe, fell backwards and lay still.

A pile of rags in the corner rose and blundered its way to the door.

The boy was unhealthy and filthy, but cognisant. He sobbed and clutched at the unnamed. "Oh God, please! He's kept me here for days, I haven't eaten. Please, my father has money, help me, please!"

Poesha stepped forward and drove a fist into the boy's midriff. "Shut up, you." The boy crumpled, and Poesha heaved him to the rear of the cabin where he lay clutching himself and moaning. Poesha herded the torpid back with kicks and shoves. He moved to pull the fallen one to its feet, but then shrugged and left it where it was.

After locking the door, Poesha turned to the unnamed with an expression of wry amusement. "You're probably wondering what's going on."

"I could take a guess."

"Please."

"Turning people into cheap animal feed?" The unnamed licked his lips.

Poesha frowned and sniggered. "Nope, but I like the way your mind works. No, listen. Why are the Widdith so far behind the Austeri in engineering, technology, standards of life?" The unnamed shrugged. "I'll tell you. Cheap labour. Free labour, in fact."

"Slavery."

"That's right. Austeri have the time to dream up ways to improve their lot, write their poems, whatever, because slaves do all the shit work. Widdernity forbids that because we're all of us potential warriors for Svangur, right? Overdrengr to pauper. Apart from?"

"The torpid."

"That's right. Torpid souls aren't worthy for the afterlife, so there's no proscription against enslaving them. But they're useless if they're under too long, if they revive at all. Dribbling and shitting themselves." He jerked a thumb at the cabin door. "But what if we could control the torpor? Use it. Keep them in that state for just long enough; not too short, not too long. And then revive them, so they're not too far damaged that they're useless, but damaged enough to take orders, carry out simple tasks, without question. 'Carry this pile of wood over there. Chop this tree down.' Whatever. Pliant, you see?"

"I don't understand, Poesha. What about Skuld's plan? Where'd you get these people, anyway?"

"It's the Overdrengr's plan, not Skuld's. How d'you know about that? You're a sly one. Anyway, the chances of his success are slim, it's just a leap in the dark. As for this lot, I got them from Three Bridges mostly, fuck ups from all over. I've got a thing with the landlord there."

The unnamed offered no reaction and watched Poesha gnawing his lip.

"Listen Silver, I've got a lot of work to do before the process is reliable. The results are all over the place 'cause I've struggled with how to set up a proper test. Canna would know what to do. Not that he'd be up for it; we used to argue all the time about what to do with the torpid, Red Harpal and that. God, I'm rambling. Listen, don't mention this to your father, alright?" Poesha turned from the unnamed and stared down at the pile of bodies. "He's not ready yet, and I want to present him with a complete solution."

The unnamed unsheathed a spike and poised the tip close to the base of Poesha's skull, but was struck by sudden curiosity. He sheathed the spike and wondered, what would Poesha's face look like if he realised he was trapped alone in a cave with a monster? It would be interesting to witness his amazement that someone so close to him was not human, that the thing from Bradden's story was real. Perhaps the fear reaction would be mixed with satisfied validation; Poesha was right to pursue the story, after all.

Poesha turned back to him and the unnamed laughed. "Poesha, it's brilliant, but can you imagine dad's face?" he said, still laughing. Poesha laughed back, nervously at first but then louder, with a gusto fuelled by relief.

The thing that called itself Javic Silver laughed and with each laugh, the mouth opened a little wider. Wider and wider still, until Poesha stopped laughing and pressed himself against the cabin door in horror, sank to his knees and whimpered.

The unnamed stopped laughing, bent to Poesha and extended a wrist spike very slowly in front of his face. "What are you thinking, right now?" Was there a trace of validation there, lurking under the terror? No. Something else though. Guilt, that was it. Strange.

"You're...you're...one of..."

The unnamed nodded and drove the spike through Poesha's eye. Then, for some reason he did not understand, he squeezed Poesha's body on the knee. He found the key and pocketed it, then sat cross-legged on the walkway. The torpid here would make an excellent source of food; captive, ready to be fed upon without the need to hunt. But they would need feeding to stay alive, until required for slaughter. Poesha's corpse would sustain them, and the lively one could be kept in good condition as a gift, potentially, for a female. He had accidentally become a farmer. The unnamed smiled to himself, a rare occurrence among his kind, an atavism, in fact, from his distant, social forebears.

Behind the iron gate, Poesha Jalana cowered in the small alcove where the unnamed had stood, and pressed a hand over her mouth to stifle a moan of grief and terror.

# 19. GERWEN

*18th day of Einmandr, 893 AZ.*

By the time Arjier died, even Hal could barely stomach being near him in the makeshift sickbay, such was the stink from the boy's putrefied wounds. Red streaks inflicted by Vettr's Tongue merged into an undifferentiated mass of hot, angry flesh, blisters and leaking pustules. Fever took him and the boy's mind fell apart.

A mercy in the end, Skuld thought, crouching on the beach and letting sand run through his fingers. Screams had given way to incoherent mumbling as the boy's system succumbed, already weakened by malnourishment, the heat, and unhealed injuries at Noron's hands. Hungry men kept to themselves their relief that Arjier's wailing had given out, and that the end was surely near. In a final bid to save him, Hal attempted to debride the injuries, cutting away ruined flesh, which served only to prolong the boy's agonies. He died blind and shivering, each juddering breath weaker than the last, and Hal did not correct his belief that the hand holding his was his father's.

Noron's sneering reaction to Arjier's death brought the captain's guilt and frustration boiling out. "Fucking sap. Couldn't even take a flogging. And you went easy on him."

Skuld grabbed a fistful of Noron's hair, punched him hard in the throat, followed up with jabs to the jaw and ribs. Noron collapsed to the deck, moaning.

"You ruined him, you sadistic fool," Skuld hissed. "You know his who his father is? Are you going to his door to explain what happened to his boy? No, that would be me. I took him on as a favour to toughen him up, not fucking kill him. God's ribs, you're a piece of work, Noron."

Arjier's father, one of Lepe's wealthiest wine merchants, would never learn the truth, however. He would step on the Bridge believing his son died bravely rescuing a shipmate during a storm. It would not be the first merciful fabrication of Skuld's career.

Skuld snorted in amusement as the twin drengrs play-fought on the beach, hurling at each other the smooth orange fruits that grew in abundance among the tree line. The island had brought salvation, and the half-starved, twitching men were giddy with ebullience. But unless this place held a secret store of jamweed hereabouts, Skuld would feel the cold tendrils of his old trouble wrapping around his mind even before the home leg of their journey had begun. Ever since it became apparent that his crew was infiltrated by some obscure deviancy, the mystery of it had gnawed at him, and he chewed the sticky brown leaves at twice his normal rate. The thing fooled him into harbouring it aboard his ship, played him for an arsehole, bringing death in its wake. And now, rationing the weed as best he could, despair haunted the edge of his awareness, whispering mantras of self-disgust and madness.

Skuld's eyes widened, then he smiled. Qed's belongings. There's bound to be a stash of jamweed among it. The possessions of men who perish at sea should be returned to the family, of course, but Qed had no family, no connections in Ibr at all, in fact, and was completely estranged from Austeri society. It wouldn't be missed. He could offer the rest of the stuff around to the officers, subsume his own desperate theft within an act of pragmatic generosity. Skuld stood a little straighter.

The *Improbable* was careened, it's belly rude and exposed in the bay. Knuld and Yavilad perched on ladders, patching and hammering at the rudder. They bantered around their tobacco pipes, while Karelud stood beneath them, staring at nothing.

"Chisel, Karelud," Yavilad called. "Karelud, wake up, man. Hand me that chisel there."

Ulter had taken a dinghy on a circumnavigation of the island, surveying it with Werdom as his oarsman, while Moshim assembled a bridge icon on the beach to claim the place for the Bryggn and the Widdith people. Canna scraped and hacked at shelled things which clung mindlessly to the hull, and stared in wonder at raking claw marks on the wood.

As on Hrno, the Drengr were blessed with an abundance of docile prey, in this case a grey, leathery skinned, waist-high creature. It had flapping, expressive ears, small tusks and an elongated, muscular proboscis which dangled to the ground and ended in a hand-like radiation of foraging tentacles. These snufflers, as Canna dubbed them, were good to eat and their tusks could be of value. Noron constructed an impromptu spit on the beach and handed out slices of glistening roast meat to an impatient huddle of hungry sailors.

He roared cheerfully, "Back you greedy bastards, back. There's plenty to go around. One at a time, ruin take you."

#

The crippled ship had hobbled towards the waistline of the Earth. Yfir tapered and stretched, a thin line across the sky demarcating the familiar north and the unknown south. The captain ignored pleas to tack eastwards for land and salvation. Something broken and nihilistic in him was seduced by the course of greatest deprivation and glory, the endlessness of the ocean. And on third rations, teeth loosened from darkened gums, atrophied muscles spasmed and jerked, and minds reeled between lethargy and mania.

On the third day of the month of Einmandr, Ulter Wan and Tala West paused their selfhoods and descended into torpor, and on the following day Karelud joined them. Skuld, shaken now from his mania by the loss of his navigator and dwindling cadre of men, pored over neglected charts, dredging up half-forgotten lessons in the use of the astrolabe and the bridge-compass. He cursed his over-reliance on Ulter, and reluctantly tacked the *Improbable* eastward.

Renouncement of the torpid was a thing for another time and place, he declared to his crew, but the remaining men were beyond caring either way. On this, the gauldr kept his own counsel, but Werdom could not. The heuristics by which he navigated life were simple levers; if this event happens, that action must follow, and his mind was unable to shift into a new gear of understanding. He pestered officers and colleagues, questioning in childish perplexity why the torpid men were not simply cast overboard. Tala East snapped and attacked him, suffering a smashed nose and bruised ribs for his trouble. It took four men to restrain Werdom, and Yavilad's pleading to dissuade the captain from flogging both belligerents.

With honey, fish oils and patience, Hal ministered to the three stricken, shuffling men, keeping them tied to an upright in the lower deck for their safety. He prioritised the rejuvenation of the navigator, bending to the uncaring pragmatism of his captain's will and resisting his egalitarian medical instincts. And as the dark line of Eyra's western coast manifested, Ulter and Tala West returned to themselves, while Karelud languished in the space between life and death, a space bred into him by ancestors who clung to survival in the frigid super-winters of Yfir's shadow.

The *Improbable* approached the Eyran coast, and the featureless strip of dark land resolved into topography; green-crowned hills and a welcoming smear of yellow sand. Lean men salivated and cheered with gap-toothed delight at the prospect of fresh meat and vegetation. They knelt in thanks to Svangur, despite His disdain for interference, and contusions bloomed on their knees. Then, their eyes were drawn to a phantasmic emergence from the water. Pale yellow, bubble-like pustules rose to the surface, to bob with the swells. Each was larger than the wardroom table, and they were densely packed in a wide, sinister barrier around the coast. Some claimed to see dark, streamlined bodies moving beneath the surface of the poxed ocean, acting with intelligence and purpose. Wind was spilled from the sail until the sheets were luffing, and the *Improbable* crept towards the coast.

As the hull touched the pustules, the globular things burst, releasing a green gas, which hung over the water in a miasma. The men's eyes stung, their throats closed in protest and their skin burned and blistered. They scampered up masts or cowered in the hold while the captain and his first hand steered the ship back into unblemished waters. By the time the air cleared, Skuld and Yavilad were at the brink of suffocation, half blind, their skin angry and peeling. They clung to each other at the stern, pulling clean air through scoured throats. Later that day, Karelud woke from his torpor.

#

Moshim sat on the sand, facing the sea, eating plump red berries. Skuld dropped down next to him, pinched a berry and popped it into his mouth.

"Gauldr. So, we welcome this place into the warm bosom of the Overdrengr." The captain twisted and pointed to the Bridge icon, a man-high thing constructed of woven vines, stone blocks and decorated with leaves and flowers. "A fine icon, but we need a name for the island, before we declare it to the men."

Moshim faced him and smiled lopsidedly. "Skuld island, perhaps captain?"

Skuld chuckled and shook his head. "It has a sinister ring to it, even to me. I suggest Ekkero Island. I cursed his name, ruin take me, and he was innocent. A decent man."

"There are many dead from which to choose. Qed, Hunvir, Arjier, Dalind. They all had their qualities." He said nothing for a time, then, "I thought I failed him. Ekkero. That my counsel exacerbated his murderous intent. But I failed you all. A gauldr, unable to see that one among us was a thing without a soul."

"It fooled us all, Moshim. And I let it aboard the ship. I insulted you before the officers, when we were wondering what to do with it."

Moshim stared at the sand between his legs, then lifted the locket which hung from his neck. "You were right. There's locks of my wife and girl's hair in here. I ended them during Red Harpal. Held them under the Moon Pool. To spare their suffering or to validate the Overdrengr's edict, I don't know anymore. My wife was torpid for weeks. She would just stand by the hearth, staring. She was done for. My girl though, Gerwen, she was only under three days." Sourness twisted his mouth. "She could have come back. I could have brought her back."

"You would have been renounced."

"She would have been alive. You said Canna illuminates God's creation, and I bring it meaning. That seems a long time ago now." Skuld had no answer for him. The dinghy had appeared around the headland, Werdom's frame dwarfing that of the navigator.

"Here's our man. The island is obviously of modest proportion. I'll speak with him and then we'll convene the men for the naming."

A short time later, Skuld stood framed by the icon with the men gathered before him.

"I, Skuld Heel, declare this place a domain of the Bryggn, in the name of Overdrengr Fan Parley. Whomsoever dwells in this place will be faithful, and will bear true allegiance, devoting their perseverance, vitality and humility to the Intention of Svangur, in accordance with Bryggn law. I name this place Gerwen Island."

Quizzical looks greeted the name. Moshim's chin dropped to his chest and he closed his eyes. Skuld smiled at Moshim then continued, his posture relaxing. "Tonight, we make merry upon the beach. Hier Noron, in his devious magnanimity, is working on transforming our fruity bounty into a potent, mind-altering brew. You deserve it, you poor bastards." Men laughed. "We're explorers and tomorrow we shall. Hier Ulter has surveyed the island, and believes there are signs of architecture to the south. Tomorrow, myself, Canna, Hal, Tove, Talas East and West, Ulter, and Karelud will follow the coast and investigate on foot. The remaining officers will oversee repairs and restocking of the ship.

"I also wish to make it known that Hier Yavilad Slowater is promoted to the rank of first hand, substantive, and I will be citing him for the Golden Leaf, for his outstanding bravery and service, steering the ship from danger on more than one occasion. Werdom will be cited for subduing the enemy who infiltrated our ranks. The wretch never stood a chance." The captain grinned, enjoying himself. "Hirdrengr Tove will cite Nijal for military honours; he pulled men from the raging inferno at enormous cost to himself. Make space upon your chests for medals, men. But for all you, upon our return I will recommend a twenty percent dividend for distinguished service in the face of exceptional adversity. If His Vitality disagrees, it will come from my own pocket, I assure you." The men gave a ragged cheer. "But hear this, men. We've subverted the will of the Overdrengr, by reviving our men who descended into torpor. You will never speak of this. Think what you will of the fate of their souls, that's for your conscience. They've proven themselves in this world, and they are our brothers. Thank you, gentlemen. Until the dawn greets us, your time is your own."

Moshim caught the captain's eye and they nodded to each other.

# 20. SCOPAESTHESIA

*19th day of Einmandr, 893 AZ.*

"No Werdom, you're not getting twenty extra marks, you're getting more than that. You're getting twenty percent more than normal."

"What's percent again, Kare?"

Karelud pursed his lips and looked skyward. Pain throbbed in his side, and had been there since he emerged from torpor, varying between a dull, pulsing ache and a sharp stabbing sensation. Gorging on food the previous night had not helped.

Waking from sleep brings with it an awareness of time having passed, albeit unwitnessed, but his memory of nine days in torpor was not like that. His consciousness had dimmed like the last traces of daylight, but something of himself had lingered, like a protraction of the liminal state between sleeping and wakefulness. He remembered an impression of longing, craving almost, and of dreadful sorrow.

The two of them lagged behind their fellow explorers, trudging along the coast of Gerwen Island. Skuld held forth, recounting tales of travels in the frozen north and exotic east. Canna and Hal stared up to the weird, long-snouted bat things that nested in the cliff. They moved over smooth, vertical rock as if by magic and one sprung from there, soaring over the waves. It compressed itself into an aerodynamic lozenge, and hurtled into the ocean. Flapping water from wing membranes, it heaved itself back into the sky, clutching a wriggling fish in its maw.

"Percent means for every hundred," Kareud said. "So, for every hundred marks you earn, you'll be getting an extra twenty." Werdom looked at Karelud, innocent and uncomprehending. "Alright, think of it a different way. Let's say we want to know how much taller you are than me, okay?"

"I'm much taller than you, Kare. And your soul's buggered."

"Yeah, thanks Werdom. So you're, what, one and a half feet taller than me, right? Understand?"

Werdom brightened. "Yeah, I know what feet are."

"But what if a demon came, and made us both grow forty times as big as we are now? How much taller than me would you be then?"

"One and a half feet!" Werdom squealed. "Is that right, Kare? Kare?"

Karelud had stopped walking and was staring into the distance, with an expression of mild puzzlement. His mouth hung open and waves lapped at his ankles. He blinked, then trudged onwards.

"You alright Kare?"

"Yeah, yeah. What were we talking about?"

"Can't remember."

Werdom jiggled the massive pack on his back, pawed at the straps. "This pack's all lumpy, right pain in the bum it is." He lowered mournful eyes. "I feel a bit bad, Kare. I said the captain should throw you overboard when you was torpor, but I'm glad he didn't. Sorry your soul's dead."

"God's ribs."

Karelud glanced back over his shoulder. Not for the first time in recent days, he felt an acute sensation of being watched.

The sky was overcast and a cool breeze ruffled the waters and buoyed the men's spirits. Tala East tossed little rocks to his brother, who swung at them with his sword, hitting a fair proportion with a cheerful ding of stone on metal. One skimmed by Tove's ear.

"Children, please," the hirdrengr said, without ire.

In the near distance, three huge, triangular skerries pointed from the sea, like giant's teeth. Waves crashed at their bases, foamy tendrils grasping up the craggy sides before slithering in retreat. Hal pointed to them, explaining something to Canna, in a pose of teacherly authority.

Ulter stopped, pulled a bridge-compass from his pack, and raised a hand. "One moment, if you please, captain." He set the intricate device on a small tripod and crouched beside it, twisting dials, adjusting axes, peering at the sky and sucking his teeth. He plopped to his rear on the stony ground and began scratching figures on a slate. Werdom stood aloof, pulled from his pocket Nubbly the Third, and fiddled in happiness. One of the twins plucked Skuld's hip flask from his waistband, and danced away with a whoop. The twins tossed it between each other, fainted and dodged, taunting the captain. Skuld flailed after them, cursing and laughing.

Karelud sat himself beside Ulter and wrung his hands. The navigator's brow was furrowed in concentration, chalk squeaking on slate.

"Sir...Hier Ulter."

Ulter face remained on his work. "What is it, Karelud?"

"I just wondered, erm, how you'd been feeling since...you know."

Ulter turned to Karelud, pocketed the chalk and stuffed the slate back in his bag. "Fine actually. Apart from the whole, my soul is condemned to everlasting oblivion thing, you know? Not disappointed, if I'm truthful. I'm tired enough as it is. You been alright? You were under for a while, eh?"

"Yeah, fine. Just a bit of gut ache. I'll talk to Hal maybe, or..." The words dwindled and Karelud turned away, biting his lip.

*Sorry I left you, Skiff.*

Karelud's head whipped back round to the navigator. "What?"

Ulter peered at Karelud. "I said nothing, lad. Come on, we should get going. The ruins aren't far." They got to their feet and Karelud drifted back to Werdom's side.

Skiff. Only one person ever called him that. A young boy, underweight with a shock of dark hair, patchy backfur and haunted eyes. A young boy who ended himself many years ago, lost in despair and self-loathing, fleeing the tyrannical horror of the gauldrhaven. Karelud released a shaking breath and rubbed at his face with both hands.

Sand and pebble gave way to a chaos of rockpools and boulder fields. Skuld and Tove picked a way through, with care, pointing out the worst of the hazards to the men following. The twins leapt from rock to rock, outdoing each other's graceful bravura. Canna and Hal's progress was interminable, such was their fascination at the array of life in the pools and niches: striped, giant starfish; iridescent spiny urchins; seaweeds of red, brown, yellow and green; crabs with carapace markings resembling the face of an angry warrior; things that waited patiently in shells, darting out a mess of tentacles to snare tiny fish.

"If your theory postulates a common ancestry for all life, Canna," Hal said, grunting as he clambered up a rock, "places like this would be good candidates for its origin. The tide provides a regular cycle of sunshine and wetness, away from the fluctuations of the open ocean. Nutrients would build up in great concentration in these little pools, I should think. A good place for creatures to adapt and morph."

Canna stared at him. "Morph?"

"That's the word Zahir used, the Austeri philosopher, for animals changing into new forms. He believed all life was in constant flux. He was vexed by the remains of sea creatures he found in the mountains of Montalino, and postulated that the Earth itself was subject to gradual upheaval. Mountains rising from the sea, landmasses crashing into each other and moving apart. Like you, Canna, he saw parallels between different forms, human hands with bat wings and such." Hal stopped to perch cross-legged on a rock, looking down at Canna. "Creatures changing into new forms isn't a new idea, Canna, ask Yav, he's read far and wide. He'd tell you there are no new ideas under Yfir." He grinned at the complex expression on Canna's face. "Ah don't be sore now. Your genius is to have hit on the mechanism by which changes occur. The how as well as the what of it. But you need to lay it all out, with clarity and evidence, and be prepared to defend it if you wish to secure your place in history. If the Overdrengr doesn't have you skinned and burnt at the stake first."

Canna slipped, soaking an ankle in a shallow pool. He cursed, shook his leg then squeezed his body between two large, slimy boulders. He stood there, wedged, as he answered Hal.

"So, the theory could be named morphism by selection. That covers the what and the how."

"What type of selection though?"

Canna considered. "Natural selection, I suppose."

Rounding the headland, they came to a sandy bay, maybe half a mile long. At the far end, an enormous rocky arch extended into the sea. Hundreds of feet up, a torso and head were carved into the arch's apex. Stern disapproval upon the titan's face could still be made out, despite the weathering. Muscular arms extended down each column of the arch, as if the figure cradled a ragged image of sky and ocean before its midriff. On the cliffs, jagged, ruined structures stood out against the pale grey sky.

"God's ribs, look at that grumpy bastard," Skuld said, shielding his eyes and squinting at the carved figure.

Tala East or West said, "It's like he wants you to sail through his belly. Wait." His brother finished the sentence. "Is that a path?"

To the left of the archway, a vague line wound its way through greenery from the beach to the clifftop. Quickening their stride, they headed for the path while the cloud cover dissipated a little and the air warmed. Shafts of sunlight beamed through breaks in the cloud, creating yellow ovoids of glowing ocean. The archway grew until it towered over them. Waves tickled the giant's fingers.

"How do you even go about creating a thing like this? They must have been advanced," Canna said. "I wonder what happened to them?"

Skuld grunted. "Their shit smelled as bad as ours, trust me. People are people wherever you go, Canna, and societies go one of two ways. They get buggered, or do the buggering. Down to luck, mostly. You're blessed with docile, useful animals that you can ride around and eat, nutritional crops that grow easily, or you get wiped out by a volcano, or a plague. Another, stronger people come and absorb you into their way of life, whatever. Saying that, a people's religion and laws can hold them back or drive them forward, it's not all down to chance."

The men clustered around Skuld as they marched now, and he raised his voice for his audience. "Widdith law holds us back in some ways. You wouldn't believe the palaver I went through with the seidhr council. I presented my methods of weather prediction to them, refined and proven through extensive experience and insightful analysis, even if I say so. I wanted it ratified for all exploratory voyages, and for farming, all sorts, but those torpid old buggers knobbled me. Dust puffed out their arses when they farted, I'm sure.

They bogged me down in theologics, debates about whether storms were the doing of Svangur or manifestations of Dregvaic decay. Nonsense, it was."

They reached the base of what was, evidently, a constructed path, encroached upon by rockfall and dense shrubbery. Shallow steps were rounded by the years, and among the plant life were glimpses of a rusted metal rail. The drengrs unsheathed broad cleavers to hack at the greenery, and the party climbed incrementally.

Skuld continued his monologue. "In every obscure corner of the world, in the future and in the past, people are people. Back in '89, you know, with that mild winter we had, the ice retreated a little and we surveyed Dunvein, the northern archipelago, as much as we could anyway. Yavilad was with me, and Noron of course, on the *Resplendent*. Tribes of fat little people live up there, bundled up in their furs. Tremendous fisherman, you know. They eat blubber from their sea-kyrs. Disgusting stuff but extraordinarily high in vitality. Burn it for lamps, use it for soap, the lot. Everything they see has its own god, with its own name. God of the clouds, god of snow, god of the fluff in your belly button, and a ritual for every occasion. 'I farted without shitting myself, uncle, let us sacrifice grandfather to the god of sphincters!'"

Skuld huffed as the path cleared and steepened. "Anyway, we were at Jylla, the nearest thing they've got to a town, and some cheeky sausage pinched my dinghy. So, we took one of their lads hostage, leverage to get the boat back, you see. We called him Clickclick, because that's what his name sounded like to us. You have to make the sound in the back of your throat, though. Not easy. Clever old Yav traded a bag of jamweed for some information, and we tracked down the boat. It was knackered. Noron, with his usual diplomatic clarity, wanted to butcher the whole town.

"But I thought to myself, I'll take this Clickclick back to Silves, smarten him up. See if he can't learn our ways, then send him back to civilise his people. Well, he was the centre of attention in Silves, let me tell you, women cooing over him, invites to the most exclusive events, and whatnot. The seidhr took him under their wing and he was a fast learner, picked up Ibrian easy as you like. He got poorly, just a sniffle, but it flattened him and he died, poor bugger."

"Sounds a little like slavery, captain." Canna had not meant the words to sound so harsh and accusatory.

The captain chewed and spat, staring straight ahead. "You know, Canna, I asked an Austeri slave once what he'd do if he was free. He told me he was happy as he was. His owner treated him like a prize possession."

"Was the slave master there when you asked the question?" Hal said.

Skuld's face darkened briefly, then he relaxed and smiled indulgently. "Canna, laknir. If you continue to besmirch my spotless character, I shall withdraw from you the privilege of hearing my rousing tales of adventure."

Grunting and sweating, the men reached the top of the path, emerging among the shadows of stone towers and broken walls. To the south, a ridge of land spread beneath them. To one side, the ocean cliffs, to the other, a steep drop into a green valley, where a lake twinkled in the sunshine. A ruined settlement sprawled over the ridge, the size of a large village. Nestled among curling trees and undergrowth were clusters of square and circular buildings, some with roofs intact. Toppled pillars lay strewn about, and there were open areas, like market squares. Paved thoroughfares crisscrossed the place, slabs bulging as if frozen in the moment of explosion, a majority skewed and broken. Everywhere, nature overwhelmed design, pulling it back into the Earth. An elevated area at the far end of the ridge overlooked the settlement. A wide circle of dark, narrow obelisks stood there, and from the men's vantage point it was difficult to judge their height.

After resting and refreshing themselves, they descended into the settlement, silence deepening as the ruins enclosed them. Tall, thick trees and low stone buildings lined their way along a narrow street. Trunks erupted through shattered buildings, and some grew atop them, with roots as thick as men's bodies drooping, like frozen liquid, over mossy gambrels and black entranceways.

In the hush, Karelud's sensation of being observed was almost a physical pressure on his skin, and he fought the urge to glance back every few steps. His attention was drawn to an alcove, which housed a row of slender female figures, rendered in greening, corroded bronze. Each was blindfolded and held an indecipherable object reverently before her. He shivered as he passed.

"Canna, captain, look at this," Hal called, his voice brazen in the silence. "Look familiar?" A large frieze dominated a wall, remarkably well preserved. A bare-chested warrior, in a sweeping headdress, brandished a curved sword. A naked enemy crouched before him, either cowering or preparing to strike upwards with the spikes which protruded from its wrists. Behind it was another figure, the sight of which caused Canna's mouth to run dry and a hollowness to bloom in his stomach. The thing was larger than the swordsman, nightmarish and hallucinatory, quadrupedal but bursting to its hind legs to attack. Those legs were digitigrade, animalistic, with bulging haunches that spoke of explosive power. The wrist spikes were twice the length of its companion's and its fingers ended in curving claws. A bald head bore a cluster of sharp teeth.

"G'ribs," Canna breathed. "A female, right?" Hal nodded. Sunshine broke through the clouds then, and the blackness of the stone entryways deepened. The men hurried on.

None suggested entering any of the buildings as they moved through the deserted place, and they breathed easier in the more open areas. Reaching the far end of the settlement, they hacked their way up a short slope through a tangle of thickets, clambered over a fallen column and reached the circle of dark obelisks. Each was perhaps five times the height of a man, triangular in cross section and pointed. They curled inwards slightly at their peaks, creating an impression of confinement. Within the circle, jumbled paving sloped downwards, to a dark, rectangular entranceway to some realm beneath the settlement. Another path led away, down into the bucolic valley.

Skuld peered into the subterranean blackness, hands on hips. He shook his head and kissed his teeth. "Nope. I don't mind admitting, men, this place makes my sac crawl." The captain led the men down the hillside on a wide roadway, paving just visible here and there beneath the grass, to finally disappear completely amid a profusion of shrubbery and purple and yellow flowers.

At the rear of the column of men, signals misfired in a small, damaged area of Karelud's brain. He mumbled as he trailed his companions.

*You see, Skiff? Everything's decay. It's the way of things, and in the space left by the defeat of order, freedom lies. You won't have to fight for God. He doesn't want us. He hates us, as the gauldrs hated us.*

"I got them for you, Mino," Karelud muttered.

At the base of the valley, the remains of stone archways and tumbled columns demarcated a neat, oval depression in the earth. An arena. Qed had spoken to Canna of such places, where Austeri Fathers grew intoxicated on expensive wine and cheap blood, spilled from slaves and wild animals. The remains of stone bleachers and holding pens were here and there on the slope, separated from a flat central area by a head-high wall. The barrier was punctuated by a tunnel leading away under the bleachers. The men scrabbled down into the arena, where insects buzzed among the flowers and grasses, which grew from fertile soil. They wandered aimlessly, imagining.

"An ocean of blood's been spilled in this place, I'd wager," Tove said.

Skuld nodded. "Good spot to camp. Put the tent up if you would, Karemund, Werdom." The big man shook the huge pack from himself and dumped it to the ground, then stood, stretching his arms high above his head and flexing his shoulders. Karelud stood a little way away, near the tunnel. He whispered, eyes closed, hands dancing. Hal watched him, and frowned.

A thundering of paws, and a herd of snufflers burst into the arena from the tunnel. Karelud stood unresponsive as the herd flowed around him, dashing in all directions, hooting in panic, colliding with the wall and each other, before veering away. Then Karelud screamed, clutched his ears, and fell to his knees.

Four huge predators loped into the arena; quadrupedal, seven feet tall at the shoulder. Smooth, streamlined bodies arrayed themselves around the space, conical heads sweeping back and forth as men scrambled over the wall and fled up the bleachers. The predators were black with pale, mottled bellies, white patches standing out on their flanks and heads. Long tails divided into flat, horizontal flukes, and three of the animals had extravagant, triangular crests upon their backs, like colourful dorsal fins. The other was smaller, with a plain, black crest. Karelud sat frozen, staring at the creatures in terror. One paused, turned its head to him, and jerked its mouth quickly, upwards. Karelud screamed again, clutched his head. Then the beast returned to its group, to focus on the snufflers. Karelud staggered to his feet and stumbled away through the tunnel.

The smallest beast commanded the others, with glances and jerks of its head. Two beasts flanked the prey from each side, while the leader steered the other directly towards the herd. They kept low to the ground, moving slow, and their muzzles juddered in silent vocalisation. The prey flinched and stumbled. One broke from the pack and a predator whipped around, mouth quivering. The snuffler froze, collapsed to its knees then lay still.

On the heights of the bleachers, the men regrouped to watch the spectacle below.

Canna grabbed Hal's arm and whispered. "They're herding them with sound, using it as a weapon."

Millitre winced, hands pressed to his ears. Gritting his teeth, he stared at the other men in pain and confusion. "Fuck, can't you hear it?"

Tove hissed to the twins, "Fetch Karelud" and the drengrs sprinted away.

The predators converged on the trapped prey, leapt forward and tore into them. Honks and squeals echoed around the arena, rising in a crescendo before dying away, then the only sound was of ripping and crunching. Canna forgot his fear, crept down the slope for a better view. Red and slick with blood and gore, the predators rested. The small leader sat neatly on its haunches, impassive, front legs straight with its tail curled around itself. Its companions splayed on the ground, limbs spread, licking blood from massive paws and nuzzling each other. As Canna watched, the more colourful members of the pack rose again, stretched, then adopted hunched positions. They shook, and from some invisible opening between head and crest, hordes of shelled, red insects emerged, each the size of a thumbnail. They swarmed down from their giant hosts in a living river, flooding over the corpses of the snufflers. The twins and Karelud were making their way around the upper rim of the bleachers, casting wary glances to the arena below.

Slapping his pack, Werdom turned to Skuld. "I managed to grab the tent, sir, but I think I've shat myself a little."

Skuld spluttered a wild-eyed laugh and punched his shoulder. "You're a good lad, Werdom. God hone your blade."

Below, rays of the lowering sun glinted off shifting waves of chitin, and the air cooled rapidly. Yfir, ribbon-like, glowed with a crimson radiance.

# 21. EYRA

*A Naturalist's Diary. 4$^{th}$ – 5$^{th}$ days of Harpal, 893 AZ.*

And so, we arrive at Eyra, and Yfir is no longer the austere bridge, frozen in the southern sky of my childhood, but a thin line, seen in cross-section. Some apposite analogy could capture how it, and I, have changed over the course of this voyage. But I have no appetite for such niceties anymore; too much has happened. Our mission feels of lesser import now than the wellbeing of my sailing companions, who, for all their faults, I regard as brothers.

We tacked along the narrowing estuary for some miles, Yavilad zigzagging us upriver in a masterful harnessing of wind and momentum. Ulter dropped his lead-line frequently to sound the depths, and yelled his findings to the captain and first hand. Conditions eventually failed us, and now we are towed by Werdom, Karelud and Millitre, rowing one of the dinghies. We dropped anchor briefly, to prepare the little rowboat, and for Moshim to assemble one of his icons on a rather beautiful riverbank, supposedly claiming all of Eyra for the Bryggn. I admire the gauldr's artistry; from naught but rocks and vegetation he constructs quite lovely representations, which speak powerfully of who we are as a people, of what we hold dear. They move me deeply, yet I am floored by the hubris of it. Laying claim to this vast, unknown place seems like an ant biting a man's arm and declaring his entire body the Kingdom of the Ants (so much for my disdain for analogies).

We swelter between borders of dense jungle which close around us along the narrowing river, and the air is so humid that sweating no longer serves to cool one's body. Insects here are the size of Ibrian bats (I exaggerate only a little); four winged things with huge compound eyes and mandibles drone with lazy interest around the ship, materialising from the mists. As I watched, dripping and panting at the bowsprit, something large moved beneath the surface of the water, perhaps a third the length of the *Improbable*. It gave the dinghy a warning thump, knocking its stern alarmingly sideways and prompting Werdom (fearless, feckless Werdom) to hack and poke at the thing with an oar. It retreated with a flick of a chunky, scaly tail.

This brings to mind the claw marks etched on the *Improbable's* hull, and the shapes which moved among the bubble-traps that lined the Eyran coast. I interrogated Millitre, whom I have come to respect as a highly intelligent, observant and proactive fellow, despite his illiteracy and modest origins. From his sanctuary atop the mainmast, he spied shapes through the noxious gas, moving among the bubble-traps. They sported arms and humanoid heads, according to his testimony, and their bodies culminated in a long tail. They propelled themselves with the up-down spinal orientation of a land animal, rather than the side-to-side motion of a fish. Given the proposed common ancestry of the human-like races, could some of our cousins have adapted to life underwater? It seems absurd, but no more so than things I have seen with my own eyes.

The predatory creatures of Gerwen Island (which Skuld dubbed sundvulfs, after a creature from far-northern mythology, whose roar flattened villages) are helping me refine the theory of morphism by natural selection. With my clever little octopuses, they are surely examples of the opposite type of adaptation; animals flopping from the sea to make a living upon the land. The sundvulfs have the dorsal fin and fluked tail of the large, air breathing sea-dwellers that are familiar to sailors (which also have up-down spinal orientation as they swim). Their sonic attacks may be an adapted version of some ability which formerly helped them in the sea, a means of navigation perhaps. If such an ability could be harnessed by human engineers, the possibilities would be remarkable, though knowing us as a species, it would be put to swift use in the art of killing.

The sundvulf leader's plain crest leads me to speculate that it was a female, leading a pack of males. The males' extravagant crests, therefore, may be a display to impress and attract mates. Perhaps the leader chooses a partner based on the magnificence of his crest and his hunting prowess. This pairing of male extravagance with female plainness is seen often in nature, particularly where males compete for female approval. Such a display is surely a hindrance to hunting and daily life, a chore to keep clean if nothing else, so why would it be favoured by natural selection? What advantage would it confer, to be passed on to offspring and spread through the population?

The answer, I think, is one that belies my earlier view of selection being a purely unconscious process: female selection. Females simply find the crests attractive, so those males with attractive crests pass their traits to more offspring. The trait of finding extravagant crests desirable, would also be passed on. This process needs another name, as it is really an adjacent concept to natural selection, and I call it sexual selection; it could, in theory, be males doing the selecting. Once initiated, this method of selection could easily run away on a rapid, self-perpetuating course, leading to spectacular and bizarre forms. Does this apply in some way to us human males, us renowned show-offs? There's a thought.

Equally spectacular was the rapid emission of red insects from the bodies of the male sundvulfs. To the insects the benefit of residing within their massive hosts is obvious: food and shelter. Perhaps within the bodies of their pals they undertake some mysterious work in return. Some beetles are crushed and used for dyeing clothes, so conceivably, they contribute in some way to the colouration of the crests, or maybe help keep them clean. Or they perform some internal medical function or help with digestion. I would dearly love to know.

Two animals, then, as unalike as could be imagined, working in harmony. In terms of the theory, this suggests animals can undergo morphation together, adapting to each other over the years to the extent that they rely upon each other completely, their fates forever entwined. An interesting counterpoint, this, to the never-ending infiltration/resistance dynamic between parasites and their hosts.

#

With dignified abashment, the *Improbable* consented to be towed by dinghy through a riot of life. Things hooted at it from the trees, buzzed and chittered around it, swam alongside before flouncing away in disdain. Millitre imagined the ship a noble lady, in her dilapidated finery, being led by an urchin through the back streets of some ghetto while unwashed locals crowded around in lewd curiosity. He had witnessed such scenes.

In the baking summer of '89, a rich merchant's wife, demeaned by ennui and addiction to hexleaf, ventured into his neighbourhood in urgent need of a fix. It was a hodgepodge place of cheerful decrepitude, manic violence, and criminal entrepreneurship. Her chin was high but her overall comportment betrayed her desperation, as did the reddened eyes of prolonged hex use. Millitre's friends crowded about her, charming and intimidating, hawking wares and services and seeking her favour. Old men gawped from doorways and proud, tired women muttered scolding imprecations as they swept their doorways.

Like Canna observing a newly discovered animal, Millitre hung back and watched, fascinated by the quality of her hooded cloak, the cleanliness of her heeled sandals which clacked on the dirty cobbles. Years later he stumbled over the woman in her squalor, missing an arm and many teeth, whimpering in a nest of rags and filth at the base of the town belltower.

The dinghy eased round a bend and for a few sweet moments, the rowers were cooled by the shadow of the *Improbable*. Half a mile farther, and the jungle on their starboard side gave way to a natural formation of densely packed, rocky columns, hundreds of feet high; a stone forest, sprouting from a base of foliage. Millitre worked the oars and eyed the dark spaces between the towering columns. Cries and chitters came from the shadows and something emitted a bellowing, rhythmic ululation.

Millitre wiped his brow and nudged Karelud, who had stopped rowing to peer at his hands. "Pull your weight, eh pal." Karelud nodded and grasped his oars.

Werdom whispered behind Millitre. "There's something wrong with him, Mill, he's been like that since he were torpid. Keeps staring and stopping."

"He still needs to row, Werd."

Werdom contemplated Millitre's scrawny back. He was cheeky, but a good lad. Fast and clever. His mum was a prostitute, he'd said, and Werdom knew what that meant, but Millitre loved her, and always talked about how nice and kind she was. Werdom wished he'd had a mother like that. His mother sent him away, because of what he was and what he did. After this rejection, he drifted from place to place, with less sense of purpose than a spider crawling over the face of a map.

Farmers, innkeepers and overseers of varied stripe thanked fate for sending a beast of such pliable vitality, rewarding his labours with the paltriest victuals and shelter. But Werdom always moved on in a hurry, chaos and cursing in his wake; hay barns set aflame, farm boys beaten senseless and crippled for life, inn cellars flooded and ruined. Karelud found him starving and alone in Nifl Forest, hallucinating wildly after ingesting handfuls of pretty, spotted mushrooms.

But now Kare was acting weird all the time. He wouldn't leave him alone, surely. No, but they'd have to look after each other now, Werdom figured. They always had, really. Karelud was clever and stopped Werdom messing up, but was only little and needed Werdom to protect him, to bash people in so they couldn't hurt him or anyone else. Like the gauldrs in that place.

While they hacked at stone in the Arada mines, Kare sought his help in hushed, urgent tones. Gauldrs were good, they helped make sure people were on God's side, but Karelud explained that these gauldrs weren't really gauldrs. They were bad men who liked to hurt children and pretended to be gauldrs so they got away with it. Well, they hadn't got away with it. Werdom kicked down the door, and bashed a couple of them in straight away, their heads broken, then held the other one down while Kare hurt him with a knife. Werdom struggled to comprehend that he was not allowed to tell anyone about it, even though what they did was right.

Ulter and Yavilad shouted to them from the ship, making signs with their hands. Werdom leaned out the way so Millitre and Karelud could interpret the orders.

"What's happening, Mill?"

"We're weighing anchor, Werd. The water's getting too shallow for the ship so we're going to leave it by the bank up there."

"Leave the ship? Then what?"

"We'll carry on upriver in a dinghy. It'll be an adventure. We'll go where no one's ever been." Millitre smiled at him.

Werdom considered a moment, then brightened. "I hope we see a waterfall, they're pretty. Hey Kare, do you think we'll see a waterfall?"

"Dunno, Werd. Yeah, maybe."

# 

Noron grimaced, flapped at Knuld's pipe smoke and spat a curse. They stood looking over the gunwale to the tiny, sandy bay where the dinghy was being prepared for the journey upriver. Nijal, Tala East and Yavilad also remained on the *Improbable*, smoking and chatting on the main deck. The five of them would remain, while Skuld led the rest into the unknown.

On one side of the water, the stone forest, severe and ancient. On the other, jungle, impenetrable and heaving with the implication of hidden, teeming life. Between these uncaring barriers, men clomped around their little rowboat. Moshim had led a brief Pledge of Intention on the bank, and the men said their godo'lades with hugs, affectionate insults and comradely backslaps. Food, water and the tent were loaded onto the dinghy, as well as resources for trade, bribery and religious conversion; hand mirrors, furs, glass baubles, navigation aids, tools and knives, picture-Books of Zarat, baccy, jamweed and booze.

Noron waved a handkerchief at the men ashore, and dabbed his eyes in a parody of a forlorn lover waving off a sweetheart. Skuld squinted up and made a wanker sign.

Noron grinned at Knuld unpleasantly. "Doubt we'll see any of these twats again. What say we fuck off home?"

Knuld chuckled. "You're a bad 'un, Noron, but your assessments are unclouded by sentimentality, to an admirable degree. This place resents our intrusion, I feel it in my balls and I dread to think what horror awaits. Then again, knowing our captain, mayhap they'll stumble 'pon a race of strapping ladies with heaving bosoms, and be taken as breeding stock, milked for their seed like prize kyr-bulls. Let's just relax and enjoy each other's company for a few days, eh? And try not to get eaten by anything."

Noron scowled. "You talk foolishness as usual, chippie."

#

Mists evaporated over the calm water, and the dinghy made swift progress upriver. Jungle rose in a verdant wall of green to their left, and the men rowed in a corridor of sweltering shadow. Skuld sat at the prow, facing the men, coordinating the rowers and peering at the scenery with aloof expertise. The stone forest continued for more than a mile on their right, its eeriness offset a little by the captain's growing, cheerful vulgarity.

"Get your elbows up, Hier Tala, or I'll feed you to Werdom. Canna, y'look to be shitting a brick. Breathe, man." Compressed echoes lent his voice a strange, buzzing quality.

Stone towers gave way to more jungle, and the river narrowed until the dinghy entered a stretch overhung by vines and leaning trees, their canopies merging to form a tunnel. Foliage and the dappling of light and shadow foiled the men's ability to form a coherent image. Bright, flowering plants appeared stuck to the smeared background of shifting green and brown like artistic afterthoughts. Roots trailed into the water from eroded banks, forming cage-like homes for sleek, semi-aquatic mammals, which darted away at the dinghy's approach. The men pushed trails of hanging moss from their faces and tried to ignore scampering noises from the branches above.

Skuld's eye darted around in skilful appraisal and his jocularity evaporated. "Slow the pace. Ulter, Tove, punt the banks, keep us in the clear. Bow, take a stroke…now. Starboard, pull back. Even pressure, next stroke. Go!"

A creature twisted from the shadows a few feet away. Two thin, angular legs straightened to stand erect in the shallow water. Black and white feathers covered a barrel-shaped body and stubby wings, and the small head bore an oversized, drooping beak. Featureless black eyes monitored the men's passing, then the thing gave a piercing shriek, unerringly human. A halo of red feathers flared around its head, and a claw rose from the water in warning. Tala West raised his bow and the animal lowered itself and swam away, a vee of disturbed water marking its passage.

The tunnel gave up the men and they squinted into the sunshine. They were in a wider section of river now, where the bordering jungle was sparser and punctuated by grassland where animals grazed. Wispy clouds trailed around a distant, monumental plateau, dwarfing that of Irna, green hills curving around its base. The air had cooled despite the sunshine, and Skuld gave the men a moment to take on water and feel the breeze on their faces.

Tove nudged Canna and jabbed a finger at the plateau. "We're not climbing that bastard, Canna. I don't care what's up there."

Skuld dipped his hands over the side of the prow and ran wet fingers through his hair. "Come on then, lads, let's have you. Rapids await around this curve if my ears do not deceive me. A punishing wench awaits, and her name is portage."

The water became too swift to resist well before the dinghy reached the foaming swirls of the rapids. They heaved the vessel ashore, and paused to stretch their aching muscles. Moshim sat, curled his arms round his knees and breathed hard. The stores were divided equally between boat and men's backs, while Ulter slid a board aside and pulled out a folded wooden frame, with leather straps and two small rubber wheels. The men hoisted the dinghy aloft, grunting and puffing, while Ulter and Skuld assembled the contraption on the hull's underside, forming a wheeled carriage.

The party set off along the bank, wheeling the boat through grass, and shoving through low brush until they came to a wall of jungle. Water roared and foamed down the steep rapids.

"Mill, scout ahead, find us a way through," Skuld said. "Tala, Tove, go with him, hack with your bush swords." The three dumped their packs and jogged ahead, disappearing into the trees.

While they waited for the scouts' return, Hal doodled and Werdom worried at his nubbly. The rest sat around in silence, but roused themselves to watch as a tidal bore swept upriver from the ocean, crashing into the rapids in a disarray of tumultuous water. The Sun was reddening at his back by the time Canna opened his mouth to suggest a search party, when Millitre and the drengrs popped from the trees in grubby cheerfulness.

Millitre hopped with excitement. "Found a way through, cap. Animal run, I think. Pretty flat but it'll be tough going. We brought a tree down but we'll still need to hoist the dinghy here and there. Then there's a slope down to a stream that leads back to the river. And I found this." He presented Skuld with a bundle of sticks and plaited vines, fabricated into the image of a skinny humanoid. "There's people hereabouts."

Skuld pulled the boy into a hug and slapped his back. "Ha! Good lad, Mill!" He beamed at Moshim. "We'll have converts for you yet, gauldr."

#

Skuld bawled a lewd shanty as the party wheeled the boat through the dimness among massive trees, his voice overwhelming the hoots, squawks and chirrups of the jungle. Mulch was flattened by innumerable imprints of hooves and trotters, and marked by occasional piles of dung. Ferns, broad-leafed shrubs and wildflowers lined the way, and bright discs of fungus were wedged into moss-covered broken trunks, like abandoned axe heads. A small, plain mammal with large wet eyes appeared on the path before them, considered the men for a moment, and disappeared into the undergrowth.

Skuld babbled at the men with happy gusto as they hauled the boat over a fallen log. "Let's make that a twenty-five percent bonus, eh lads? Haul, you demons! We'll show these folks that Ibrian men are the pinnacle of God's creation. Marvel at our vitality, they will, and keep their wives and daughters locked away from our magnificence."

Clusters of bright yellow flowers, like stretched, upturned bells, lined a pool of stagnant water and gave off a stink of rotting meat. A many-legged invertebrate crawled over the lip of one such, and disappeared inside. Canna watched in morbid excitement as the flower closed around it. Something landed on his shoulder then, and he stifled a shriek. Craning his neck, he turned to see what had made a perch of him. Round, yellow eyes peered back. It was finger-sized and pudgy, roughly humanoid, though neckless, with glossy, mottled skin and spindly limbs. Squatting there, it fed itself seeds with tiny, dextrous fingers, storing the morsels in rapidly bulging cheeks. A long, ringed tail was curled about itself.

"Well, hello, little fellow. Pleased to make your acquaintance," Canna said. In response, it whistled a long, rising note, grabbed Canna's collar and inspected his earhole. It chittered in a querulous tone. *Wer-hatt? Wer-hatt-hatt? Goh-ingha?*

"What's he say to you, Philos?" Tove said.

"He says I should ditch you lot and come to the pub."

Canna chortled and the tiny beast leapt away with a chirp.

Piles of dung ornamented a widening of the path, which opened out to reveal a long, sloping bank down to a shallow, rocky stream, which fed into the main river. At its crest, the sun-baked ramp was as solid as a paved road and the men braced themselves against the hull to stop the dinghy sliding away. Farther down, the small wheels sank into wet mud and the men half dragged, half lifted the vessel forwards, oar blades wedged under the wheels for purchase. Then they bumped and shoved the dinghy along the stream, over rocks, sticky clay and silt, and were soaked to their knees.

Stream water dribbled into the river over a drop of a few feet. The wheeled carriage was removed and dismantled with the boat poking over the lip of the drop, teetering with stern aloft. Werdom and Tove took the weight of the dinghy from behind, controlling its momentum, while Skuld and Ulter stood chest deep in the river, easing the prow onto the water. With cheers and laughter, the men unloaded their packs and clambered aboard.

#

Yfir bisected the narrow strip of visible sky above a deep gorge of craggy, orange rock. Twilight came early to the sheltered corridor; darting points of bioluminescence winked into being and bushels sprouting from the rock were unresolved patches of blackness. Ahead, the wizened ring graduated into a diffuse redness where it met the horizon, and moonlight penetrated the clear, deep water. Hal snored in the prow.

Millitre stopped rowing and stared down at distorted outlines of geometric regularity beneath the surface. He pointed and hissed,

"There's buildings down there, I'm telling you. Look at that, that's a fucking statue."

Nobody replied, the men determined, it seemed, to ignore the implications of the lost place below, the challenge it represented. But Canna smiled at Millitre's captivation, which reminded him of Taffa, his Riverbend sidekick. Mill's imagination does him credit, he thought, and deserves to be nurtured. He embraces mystery, where others fool themselves that the world is tamed, our dominion over it secured. If we give up something of ourselves, our delusions of mastery and control, wonder can fill that space. This is humility, whereas the gauldrs preach something else: simple kindness and the surrender of one's will to stronger men. Canna's thoughts began crashing into each other and he rubbed his eyes and stretched. Skuld winked at him, cast appraising glances at the rowers, and nodded to himself. He indicated a grassy bank which formed a natural jetty beneath an overhanging rock shelf.

"Don't know about you boys, but I'm knackered, and I haven't rowed a stroke. We make camp here. I've a hankering to share Noron's loony juice with men of quality, round a warm fire." He shook Hal's arm and the laknir blinked awake and wiped drool from his cheek. "Come on old timer, rouse yourself. We'll have a drink and a chinwag, then get you to bed, eh?"

Dead, stunted trees dotted the jetty. Tove, Ulter and Tala prepared a space for the fire with a circle of rocks while Karelud and Werdom raised the tent a healthy distance away. Others gathered firewood and kindling, while Skuld set up oars and packs as makeshift drying rails. When the fire was in bloom, the men stripped off their shoes, socks and trousers to dry them before the crackling flames. They sat around in their under things, drinking and eating, enjoying the warmth spreading into the spongy soles of their feet.

Skuld swigged from a flask, gagged, and thumped his chest. He passed the stuff to Tove and spoke in a strangled voice. "God's nut sack, my soul's trying to flee through my ears." He stuffed jamweed in his mouth as he coughed. Spluttering curses and laughs followed the flask around the circle. It reached the captain again and he took another swig, winced and flapped his lips then raised it aloft.

"Godo'lade Noron, you mad bastard. Extraordinary work, brothers, all of you. We're beholden to venture farther, until we establish who our dollmakers are, no matter how long it takes."

Canna frowned. "Won't Nijal come looking for us if we don't return in time?"

Skuld nodded. "I'll send two back to the ship with word, if necessary, but I believe we'll meet the natives soon. I found this on the trail." He held up a head of sharpened stone affixed with coiled twine to a short, broken shaft. Hal gazed into the fire, face unreadable. Skuld nudged him. "What's wrong, laknir?"

"I'm hoping that if we find people here, their way of life's not sullied by our own."

The captain scoffed, then stopped himself on the verge of a rebuke. "What makes you say that, Hal?"

"G'ribs Skuld, take the weird taboo around torpor for starters. You're telling me Svangur wouldn't benefit from Ulter, Nijal and Tala by His side? Don't make me laugh. Sorry Karelud, you too. Imperfect children murdered. The slaughter of the torpid during Red fucking Harpal. The seidhr sitting in their college, arguing over how many souls can dance on the Bridge, squashing ideas that don't suit the Bryggn agenda."

"Do you have a better way, Laknir?" Tove said. "Have you made decisions that affect thousands of souls? Your life is simple. You help people, they get better or they die. Fan doesn't have it so easy and Red Harpal was his father's best bet to cause the least harm in the long run. You can't replay history to have another go. For all you know, we'd all be fucked if it had gone another way."

Hal sniffed and he faced the hirdrengr directly. "The population of Ibr actually rose after Red Harpal. Know why?"

No one answered.

"Because of all the babies conceived through rape. I'll judge a people by how they treat their lost and broken. This doesn't negate your fetish for vitality and I shan't judge you, Tove, for things you've done at the behest of your superiors." Tove glowered at Hal, lip twitching, and Canna blinked at Tove.

Hal continued, unperturbed. "Every man should work to his fullest, that's fine. But God's ribs, open your eyes. Our people murder babies and the sick and call it a virtue. This is a culture we wish to export?" Hal was surprised at the twist of hurt he saw in Skuld's face. He softened. "I respect you captain, for your decisions on the ship, having our torpid revived. You defied dogma to do what's right. So surely now you see some of our beliefs come out with little credit. They need looking at, especially before we go blundering into someone else's land. What say you, Moshim?"

The gauldr took a swig of beer and wiped his mouth. "I don't know, laknir."

Hal opened his mouth to reply, disgust souring his face, but Canna interrupted. "It takes a brave gauldr to say so, Moshim."

Ulter raised a finger and heads turned to him. "You're not wrong Hal, but I'd rather be a Widdith pauper than an Austeri slave, I tell you for naught. They're a people addicted to cruelty and decadence. And if you think the people living close by spend their days weaving baskets and writing love poetry, you may be disappointed. They'll have darkness of their own." Hal scowled.

Skuld punctured the silence. "Young Millitre, what an overcoming you're having, eh lad? One for the ages, and you've more than proven yourself. You wouldn't even remember the great famine, I suppose."

Millitre shook his head. "Not quite. My mum's talked about it though. That's when she turned to whoring. She reckons my dad was a death squad drengr. Come to think of it, I've got your eyes, Tove." Skuld sprayed a mouthful of beer in his mirth. The hirdrengr looked murderous for a moment, then shook his head, rolling his eyes. Millitre grinned. "Here's me, son of a whore, first to find evidence of people in central Eyra."

Werdom squealed, and slapped a flying thing from his arm. "Bit me, little bastard!"

Later, Tove lay sleepless in the tent, recalling the sorrow and fear in his wife's eyes during Red Harpal, when he finally returned home after weeks of carefully coordinated murder. His squad roved home to home and executed the slack-jawed and drooling torpid on the spot. Those with lesser mental or physical impairments, characteristics of the revived, were dragged onto the streets and subjected to tests of reasoning, which he knew were ambiguous and absurd even as he administered them. They were beaten, and more often than not, died where they lay.

She'd searched his face for self-doubt, remorse, even simple sadness. Finding none, she was bereft. After she abandoned their home, carrying his child inside her, he spent his isolation analysing a part himself, turning it over like a mysterious artifact. It was, he realised, a gleeful appetite for carnage, a pleasurable physical response to the suffering of others. It could be supressed or manifested on demand, with no bearing on his day-to-day interaction with others, at least so he had thought.

The Overdrengr chose his weapons well, he supposed. Beside him, Karelud shivered and whispered to the darkness. "I'm coming, wait for me. No, I'm not afraid anymore."

# 22. THE ELPI

*6th day of Harpal, 893 AZ.*

In the morning, Karelud was gone. River and sheer rock offered the only possible exits from the little jetty, but the boat had not been taken, and Karelud could not swim. Werdom called his name, his tone rising in desperation, while Skuld and Millitre frowned up at the wall of the gorge.

"Please, sir. I can climb it, Karelud did, too, I'd bet. Let me look for him, sir."

Skuld shook his head. "I believe you lad, but no. It's too high and we've no means of securing you. We've lost enough good men."

The captain turned to address the rest of them, who, aside from Werdom, struck the tent in silence. "We go on. He may be alive, but frankly, I doubt it. If we reach a suitable landing spot, we'll fan out to search for him."

Hal reached a gentle hand up to Werdom's shoulder. "Did he say anything to you about leaving? Did he seem angry or sad, at all?"

Werdom's face crumpled in a sob. "He kept talking to himself and staring and stuff, like there were something wrong with him. Left his stuff behind." He coughed and wiped sweat from his forehead.

"It's true," Tove said, as he stuffed poles into a narrow sack. "I heard him last night, talking to himself. Mad things, he was saying, like he was talking to someone else."

Hal's head dropped and he hugged himself. "Torpor did for him, then. He was under too long." Skuld did not meet the laknir's eye.

\#

They rowed dumb. Aside from the boy, they knew they would not search for Karelud, that to do so would be pointless, yet each knew that acknowledging this out loud would risk dragging their justifications into the light, perhaps to perish. The quiescence of the river acknowledged their unease, while Skuld murmured occasional instructions from the prow. Werdom's weeping subsided, and he frowned at the space between his angled knees.

Millitre slapped at the water with a hand. "Why aren't we looking for him? Gotta try, haven't we? He could be hurt." Skuld responded with a measured look, and a tiny shake of the head.

"No chance," said Tala. "He's done for. He chose to go. Sorry boy, it is what it is." Millitre clamped his mouth shut, lips whitening.

Miles later, the gorge gave way to steep, slanted cliffs, crags of rock protruding from swathes of foliage. Impenetrable ferns crowded the riverbanks, and sheltered gossamer insects which skated over the water's surface. Broad-winged birds glided above, graceful necks craning down with interest. Werdom stopped rowing, coughed up a gob of something and sat with his hands on his thighs, head bent. Sweat glistened his brow.

"You alright, Werdom?" Canna asked.

"Bit tired, Philos," the big man said to the boat's floor, and scratched his arm through his shirt. Canna and Hal exchanged a look.

Without warning, the silent river became a frenzied seething. Rain hammered on the gunwales, and the men's strokes became ragged and ineffectual as they squinted into the deluge. They were dry, then soaked through, with no transitional stage.

Tove bailed water with a small bucket. "Ah, fuck this," he yelled, arms pumping.

Skuld scrambled to close his tin of jamweed and grimaced into the rain. "Bring her in, we'll sit this one out." He pointed to a gap in the ferns, where a stony bank was overhung by broad-leafed palm trees. Rallying, the men heaved against the stream with clenched teeth, while Skuld bellowed. "Starboard, take the runoff. Now both sides, even row! Put your backs into it!"

They dragged the dinghy onto the bank and the sound of wood crunching on stones was lost under the noise of the downpour. They flung stores to the ground, shaking water from their hair as they hauled, then tipped the boat upside down over the crates and sacks. Water thrummed on the upturned hull as the men dashed under palm trees, the wide leaves scrubbed and luminous. Forks and flashes of lightning were answered by booms of thunder which made Werdom flinch.

For Canna, the deluge accentuated each man's character, as if the scaffold of artifice on which they staged themselves was swept away. Laid bare were Tove's dearth of empathy; Millitre's quick-witted innocence; Hal's steely altruism; Ulter's placid but formidable intelligence; and Werdom's confusion and loneliness. Tala West grinned, blinking into the rain, amused and predatory. Moshim and Skuld were inscrutable, communicating in silence. Skuld reached into a bag, swigged from a flask. He hissed, passed it around and for a time, they all stood drinking and mesmerised by the boiling river.

Moshim's voice rose above the percussive roar. "We bid farewell to our friend, Karelud Darkener, taken from us by torpor and this place." Comprehension and despair contorted Werdom's face as he sank to his knees. "He was ill at ease with life, surly and bitter, at times, and the injustices of the world wore him down." Moshim sat beside Werdom on the wet rocks. "But he was a grafter, who sacrificed much by forgoing his own needs in his devotion to a friend who needed him. No peal will mark his passing and he will not fight by his God's side, for Svangur deems souls of the torpid unworthy for the final battle." Tala and Ulter exchanged a look. Tala shrugged in heedless indifference. Ulter was deadpan.

"He is gone," Moshim continued, "but the thread of his life is entwined with our own, as ours will entwine with the lives of those yet to come. He lives on in our remembrance. Humility, brothers."

Werdom looked up at Moshim with an effort, as if his head were too heavy to lift. "Who'll take care of me now?"

Millitre squatted beside them. "I'll take care of you, Werd. We'll be a team, eh? Big man, little man combo, like in hammerball. You and me." Werdom scratched at his arm, gave a wan smile, then his eyes rolled and he puked. Hal crouched down and wrinkled his nose. He pulled open Werdom's mouth to peer at his tongue, looked into his eyes, and felt his forehead.

"Ruin, Werdom, you're sick, man, burning." Wincing at washed out pink smears on cotton, Hal rolled up Werdom's sleeve, revealing a huge suppurating lump. Flesh around the bite seemed dissolved, and oozed blood and pus. "God's ribs," Hal said, in a sudden hush; the rain had stopped, and a shaft of sunlight illuminated a patch of river like polished brass. "He can't go on, captain, look at him. His blood is poisoned, the wound is unclean. Eaten away, it looks like."

Skuld wiped his face with a kerchief and scowled. "He's tough, it'd take more than an insect bite to take him out of action. He'll be alright, won't you Werdom?" The prostrate man gave no reply, only stared in confusion at his sickening limb. Hal exhaled, held Skuld's stare for a moment, then rummaged in his medical bag. He poured an orange liquid on Werdom's infection, wiped at it with a cloth, and wrapped the arm in a tight bandage.

"Don't scratch at it now, Werdom, or you'll make it worse. You need to drink plenty of water, alright?" With a small pair of expensive-looking scissors, Hal cut Werdom's fingernails very short, then smoothed them with a file.

"At least excuse him from rowing, captain."

Skuld nodded. "I'll take his place. Ulter, you're coxswain."

Werdom tottered to his feet, and blinked into the sunshine.

# 

The river tapered and meandered through a vee-shaped valley. Alternate fingers of land jutted from starboard and port side, creating, from a distance, the impression of interlocking spurs. Werdom slumped red-eyed and drooling in the prow. He puked into the water, wiped his mouth and was bent double by a volley of hoarse coughs which rocked the dinghy. Greenery receded as the landscape widened around them into an encirclement of cliffs. Their course terminated at a sheer wall of streaked, amber sandstone and a waterfall tumbled fifty feet or so from an enormous cavity in the rockface.

"Hey Werdom, look at that for a waterfall, eh?" Millitre said. Werdom sat up, groaned and fell back.

"Way enough!" Ulter called as the dinghy approached the waterfall.

Skuld pointed to a narrow, jagged wound, running up the cliff to the cavity like a crazed chimney shaft. "The fissure there. Climbable, I think."

Hal stared in disbelief. "Captain, Werdom can't go on. He can't climb, look at him."

"He'll cope. He'll have to."

They steered the dinghy to a gravelly outcropping at the base of the cliff, and made a cursory attempt to leave it out of sight behind a boulder. A breeze chilled their wet bodies as they unloaded the stores and secured them to their backs, the tent divided between Tala and Tove. A narrow shelf ran from their position, behind the waterfall to the base of the fissure. Werdom staggered a few steps, dry-heaved and sank to his arse.

"Help me," Skuld said to Canna, and between them they hoisted Werdom upright. Hal muttered a curse, unstopped a vial and held it under the sick man's nose. Werdom spluttered and winced, but revived a little.

The men negotiated a tortuous ascent up the fissure, scrambling and pulling themselves up shelves, and bracing themselves between wet rock to scale vertical sections. With a flurry of his waning strength and a glug from the captain's flask, Werdom heaved his mass after them, unfazed by the drop behind which made Canna clench his teeth and lose control of his breathing.

They emerged onto an enclosed plateau, dominated by a blue-green plunge pool, into which a wider, shorter waterfall descended. From here, they could see the river zigzagging from high above, cutting a widening course through the cliff cavity and tumbling down a series of waterfalls to their position. Around the pool on a boulder-strewn bank, they passed a black, narrow opening in the rock.

"Hold up," Millitre called, a finger extended into the air. "I heard something." He approached the cave entrance and listened, standing as if poised to start a running race. Whispering drifted from the blackness, sibilant and fricative noises that were just beyond language. "Karelud, it's gotta be!" Millitre said.

"Hold up, Mill," Ulter said, reaching for the boy, but Karelud was already squeezing himself through the narrow aperture, twisting his neck and limbs to achieve ingress. Then he was gone, and the men called into the darkness.

"I'm alright!" the boy called, his voice haunting and ethereal. "It's massive in here, you wouldn't believe it. I can see a hole in the ceiling with light coming through. Karelud, you in here? Karelud? Shit, there's bones. What's– oh fuck…fuck!" Then the men heard a scream, and a monstrous growling. Millitre's cry ended in an abrupt gurgle, and then came sounds of tearing and feeding.

All the men took a step back. Skuld covered his face, staggered to a crouch and roared into his hands. Canna stood numb and unable to breathe. Tears wet his cheeks and he clutched his head, though the feeling of grief was slow to catch up with its expression. Werdom leant against the rockface, gagging and retching in pain, unable to bring anything up. He fell to one knee and for a moment, Hal was only the man able to function. He looked at Werdom, then turned to the captain.

"Skuld, give it up now, for God's sake. Look at us, man. We must return to the ship, or leave me here with Werdom and a few supplies, at least. He's done for if he has no rest. Probably done for, anyway. We've lost enough good men."

Skuld roared, "That's why we need to go on! This is bigger than…" He bit back the words, baring his teeth, then tugged at his shirttails and hitched up his trousers.

"No words for Mill, gauldr?" The captain said. Receiving no reply, he snorted and glared at the rest of the dazed men in turn, his mouth bordering on a snarl. "This was Mill's overcoming, and overcome he did. Born from nothing, he was. Nothing. He was twice some of you. He leaves his childish name in this world, and carries unto the Bridge the name of Millitre Eyra. Svangur calls him home and Dregva quakes at his passing. God hone his blade." Mouth set in a grim line, he stared at each man in challenge, and Canna felt himself wither. Werdom's breath came ragged and quick.

"Get him up. We move on."

Hauling the casualty, they scaled the rocks by the short waterfall, reaching a smaller plateau, where foliage bordered a narrow stretch of water leading to another pool. A taller waterfall thundered from an overhang onto a wide slab of rock at the pool's edge. Miniature, personal rainbows hovered around them in the spray, and distorted shapes moved behind the curtain of water.

Tove and Tala carried Werdom between them along the bank, his arms weighing down their shoulders. They staggered and Werdom fell to all fours, rolled over and stared unseeing towards Yfir.

"I'm sorry. I'm sorry," Werdom muttered in his delirium. "Where's Kare? Gauldr, gauldr!" Exhausted, the men gathered round and looked down at him, and at each other.

Moshim bent to him. "What is it, Werdom?"

"I'm sorry we killed you, gauldr, but you was bad…Kare told me you was bad."

"What the fuck is he talking about?" Tala said. Canna held his tongue, remembering, then Ulter grabbed his arm.

"Father of ruin, look."

Three willowy humanoid figures watched them from the rock shelf. One dropped a long staff, in an uncanny gesture of surprise. They were covered in short, light brown fur and were long-limbed, taller than Werdom. Dark-rimmed, wide, yellow eyes stared from above short, pointed muzzles. Tufted, triangular ears twitched and swivelled. Their faces were paler than their bodies and each had a pattern of markings on their chest. Around a dozen squat, waist-high animals milled about them. The willowy creatures chittered to each other, keeping eyes on the men, then seemed to glide towards them as much as walk.

Canna's mouth dropped open and the men recoiled when the herd animals came close and sniffed at their legs. They were pink and hairless, with meaty haunches and no visible neck, and their faces were recognisably human. Toes were transmuted into thick, knobby stumps, as if human feet had been hammered into the shape of hooves. A couple wandered back to the waterfall, to grunt and snort as water careened off their backs. One approached Canna, a frown of dumb inquisitiveness on a wide, fleshy face which was a broad-stroke approximation of a woman's countenance. It stared at him. *Uuer?* it said. A human voice lacking the faculty of speech. It farted. Tala laughed and one of the tall creatures snickered in response, ears springing erect.

The tall creatures placed their sticks on the ground and raised their palms outwards. One pointed to the prostrate figure, nudged its companions and uttered a series of complex syllables. The two groups stared at each other for a moment, then the tallest of the three creatures stepped forward. It had prominent ear tufts and a light, vertical stripe on its chest. A slender finger pointed to Werdom and the humanoid made a buzzing noise through pointed teeth. With its hands it simulated a flying creature.

"Yes, yes," Hal said. "He was bitten by something. He's sick." The creatures conferred, then the smallest one bent to Werdom and pulled aside the bandage on his arm. Seeing the suppurating mess there, it said something to Stripe, who nodded.

The leader pointed in turn to itself and its companions. "Elpi," it said. "Elpi," nodding, encouraging understanding.

Skuld pointed to himself and the men. "Men." He jabbed twice at his own chest. "Skuld."

"Skoold?" the leader said.

"Close enough, big lad. Wait, I got you something." Twisting out of his pack, Skuld pulled out a small pocket-mirror. He bowed and presented it to the leader of the elpi. Stripe took it, and seeing its own reflection, started back in surprise, ears flattening. It passed it to a companion. The smaller elpi chittered in excitement, holding the mirror at different angles and pulling faces. It tapped the third elpi on the arm, then bent over, holding the mirror to try and view its own backside. The two smaller elpi fell about in uncontrolled chitters and plucked at each other's fur. Their leader uttered a barking hiss and the two straightened up and shuffled their feet like naughty children.

Skuld grinned at the leader. "Good lads. Kids, eh?" Stripe snatched the mirror back and presented it back to Skuld, who waved his hands in protest. "No, no," he said, "for you, a gift."

The elpi conferred again, voices rising and falling in remonstration and compromise, their ears twitching. Finally, they turned back to the men. Stripe swiped at the air in a firm *stop* gesture, then beckoned Skuld to it with a finger. A pause, and a claw popped from the extended digit. Skuld stepped forward. Stripe grabbed Skuld's jaw and palpated the sides of his face below the ears, eyes drifting up to one side in a gesture of concentration. It subjected his forearm to the same, feeling for the bones there in circular motions. Satisfied, it tapped Skuld on the arm and waved him to one side.

"God's ribs," Canna said to Hal. "You see what they're doing, right?" Hal nodded.

The check was completed for each of the men, including Werdom as he lay on the ground. Stripe pointed to Werdom and made a *get him up* gesture, then jabbed a finger northward. Tove and Tala hauled Werdom to his feet and the strange party negotiated a narrow pass through the cliff face. Canna hurried to catch up with the flowing elpi, and tapped the leader on the arm. It looked down at him, forehead crinkling as if surprised.

"What are these…animals?" Canna said, pointing to the herd of dumpy quadrupeds.

"Calpi," Stripe said. Canna scratched one behind the ear and it nuzzled him with a demented grin.

#

Daunting trunks dominated the murky forest floor, interspersed with hanging vines and trailing moss. The going underfoot was relatively clear of ground plants, and the drengrs would have had more use for torches than their bush swords. Opportunist saplings struggled towards the light, where fallen trees left gaps in the canopy. Fist-sized beetles were the largest creatures they saw, though Hal pointed out piles of dung to Canna. Elaborate fungal formations proliferated; red, anemone-like bifurcations spewing from rotting tree stumps; ghostly balls of latticed branches, like skeletons of some body-plan experiment abandoned by nature; fleshy purple tentacles twisting from the ground.

More than once, the playful elpi with the thick fur and dark eyes, (a youngster, Canna suspected, whom he dubbed Springer), exploded upwards with deft kicks and grabs, to gambol in the branches above. Below, the elpi flowed over obstacles, where the humans scrabbled and clambered. To them, Canna realised, the world was not a surface over which to move, but a space to be moved through, via limitless routes.

He stole glances at the creatures' nether regions, and deduced that Springer was the sole male; Stripe certainly gave the impression of a harried mother of two unruly children. Of the adolescents, Springer was the more prone to the rambunctiousness akin to teenage boyhood. Canna dubbed the young female Hunter, as she jabbed and parried her staff through intricate sparring routines.

Bestowing these names was hubristic, Canna realised, forcing the parameters of the human onto the non-human, or alt-human. *What is a name for?* the unnamed had asked him. A handshake, to lubricate interactions. And he was making these sweeping assessments of the elpi's character for the same purpose. Shuddering inwardly, Canna realised that to understand the elpi in their own terms, he would need to adopt something of the unnamed's cold detachment. Perhaps that species was, perversely, well adapted to scientific enquiry.

Werdom's strength gave out as the group forded a shallow stream and he collapsed, deadweight, with a splash. Tove and Tala dragged him to the bank and Hal bent to examine him. The laknir grimaced and shook his head, as the elpi watched on. Werdom's eyes rolled, he shivered and sweat poured from him.

"He'll walk no further," Hal said. "If our new friends don't have some magic up their sleeves, he'll be dead in short order. He's beyond torpor, now. Only raw strength has carried him this far." Skuld muttered and shrugged at the elpi leader. She bared her teeth a little and flattened her ears in what may have been a glare, then barked to her companions. The youngsters hurtled upwards, their powerful bodies springing from tree to tree as they ascended, and disappeared into the dark forest canopy.

They returned with armfuls of branches and vines, and in short order fashioned a stretcher, Stripe overseeing the operation with complex trills and barks. Another command, and Hunter leapt away, careening at absurd speed over the forest floor, weaving between trunks, leaping roots and ducking vines. By the time Werdom was loaded on the stretcher, Hunter returned, carrying fistfuls of a bright red leaf. Stripe chewed a few and spat a thick red mush into her hand. Bending, she unwound Werdom's bandage and rubbed some of the mush into the ghastly wound, then barked at Hal, making a twirling gesture with her hands. Hal dallied in confusion a moment, then fished in his bag and brought out a clean bandage, which Stripe wrapped around the prone man's arm.

Tove and Tala carried Werdom on the stretcher between them as the ground rose, grunting with exertion and stopping frequently to regain their wind. Tree cover gave way at the edge of a deep precipice, a chasm, bridged by a huge fallen trunk which was carpeted with moss and fungus. Yfir was a faint line behind thin cloud, and dark specks of birds drifted around the wall of the massive plateau in the distance.

An intense point of light flashed on a hillside, perhaps a mile away, repeating every few moments. Ulter tapped Hunter on the arm, pointed to the light and frowned a query, the men's gazes following the direction of his finger. Hunter spat, knocked Ulter's hand away and shook her head. In exaggerated mime, she clapped her hands over her mouth, eyes and ears, then skipped away over the bridge with her companions. The calpi trundled after, unfazed by the drop. Skuld sauntered over next; Hal, Moshim and Ulter crept after. Canna crawled across splayed on all fours, refusing to acknowledge either the drop or Skuld's grinning face.

Glancing back, Stripe's shoulders sagged at the sight of Tove and Tala's hesitation.

"Ah, don't look at me like that, y'furry bastard," Tala called, eyeing the spongy mass of green coating the log bridge. "I'm brave, not stupid. There's no way we'll get Werdom over." As if to prove the point, Werdom moaned and tossed in his delirium; his bearers staggered and readjusted their grip. Stripe dashed back over, slaloming between the abbreviated boughs which protruded from the trunk. She bent, grasped Werdom under the armpits and hoisted him onto her back while the men gaped. Slower, but still faster than any of the men, she recrossed the trunk with Werdom drooling into her fur.

#

Younger jungle blanketed the hillside down which they descended. The humidity increased, and here the larger, older trees shared the sunlight with wide-leafed palms, ferns and shrubs. Garish orchids competed for attention with colourful, long tailed birds that flapped with clumsy languor between branches. After the serenity of the ancient forest, this place was a cacophony of inhuman noise. Despite the lack of a visible path, the elpi and calpi moved through the foliage with confidence, Stripe occasionally prodding at the herd to keep it moving. One of the beasts snuffled with interest at the horizontal Werdom. *Hmm*, it said.

They stepped onto a wide wooden bridge, almost lost in greenery, and the calpi's feet clattered on the boards. Before they reached the bridge's end, the jungle opened and the men stopped and stared. The elpi village spread before and above them. Humped wooden bridges connected an archipelago of grassy islets, punctuated by trees of daunting girth and height. Some of these giants had bulbous protrusions at the base, evidently used for dwellings, as if the trees had been coerced into growing living spaces. Circular wooden huts proliferated at ground level and up in the heights; their entrances were triangular, and conical straw roofs and wooden walls sported trailing plants and colourful rocks and shells. Some larger structures encircled the trunks. Elpi brachiated around the upper echelons of the village, yipping and cavorting, their transit aided by strategically placed wooden bars and small platforms.

Elpi stopped and stared at the passing men. Youngsters clung to their parents' backs, stealing peeps at the strange visitors, and fidgety adolescents nudged each other, pointing and cackling. Stripe uttered the same short phrase many times to the flood of inquiring chitters, and uttered something to Hunter and Springer. The two dashed away.

A calpi was harnessed to a rotary contraption, its interminable walk driving a large stone wheel for the pulverising of grain. Low shrubberies delineated small crops of swollen fruits and vegetables, and flightless, elaborately coloured birds flapped and burbled in wooden pens.

Hal nudged Canna and pointed, choking back a nervous laugh. "Would you look at that, a male calpi." This specimen was larger and stockier than those of the herd. It stood erect in pompous sovereignty over its muddy pen, its lips pursed with self-importance. It sported an absurd, flowing moustache, which it preened with a forepaw, and a mighty pair of balls swung between its hind legs.

"Looks like Noron, don't you think?" Canna said. His levity evaporated as Werdom moaned, and at the sight of long poles erected here and there about the village, topped with elpi skulls.

"Skulls of the enemy," Hal whispered.

Echoing chitters and hoots grew in a contagion and more elpi flowed from the under-storey of the tree canopy, falling silent as they glimpsed the humans. Stripe led them to a grassy area, marked by an unusual fixture. A gnarled tree stump rose from the ground to about twice a man's height, where it bent, extending horizontally. A corresponding, inverted piece of sculpted, polished wood was suspended in symmetry to the base piece, connected to it by means of three lengths of plaited vine. The inverted piece appeared to float there in defiance of nature. Ulter peered at it, scratched out calculations on a piece of slate pulled from his bag, and shrugged.

"Remarkable, this. I can't speak to its artistic merit but it shows a deep understanding of tension and balance. We're not dealing with savages here, sir."

Skuld snorted and made a pawing motion with his hands. "Maybe so, but I wouldn't like to tangle with one of the bastards." Stripe peered upwards, shielding her eyes from the dappled sunlight that broke through the canopy. A large, thickset elpi descended through the trees towards them, and dropped the final few feet with a grunt; another female, as far as Canna could tell, greying around the temples with washed out, straw-coloured eyes. She held Stripe from behind and nibbled at her neck and shoulders. Unbidden, Canna visualised his mother's face, and dubbed the elder elpi Makena, after her. Stripe gestured towards Werdom's stretcher, and conversed with the elder. Makena inhaled, and hollered a piercing, rising ululation which silenced the crowd of men and elpi.

Elpi burst into action, scampering hither and yon. Their activity centred upon a large nearby hut to which pots, sheets of some muslin-like material and leather bottles were rapidly delivered. A languid elpi of stately bearing appeared, and held a brief conference with Makena and Stripe. Two more newcomers hauled Werdom into a sitting position with little ceremony, and poured liquid from a pot into his mouth. He spluttered but swallowed, and was hauled away on the stretcher, the men staring after him.

Makena approached Skuld, seeming to recognise him as a fellow leader. She pointed away in the direction of Werdom and mimed a series of actions: supping from a spoon, sleeping, vomiting, collapsing and recovering.

"Right, right," Skuld said. "You'll treat Werdom but it'll take a few days and he might die. Much appreciated, distinguished one." He bowed then turned to the others. "Moshim, hand a Book over, eh?"

The gauldr fished in his pack for a pictorial Book of Zarat, and handed it to Makena with a polite smile. The elpi stared at it for a moment, then thumbed through the pages, ears swivelling and glance flicking between it and Moshim. She exchanged a look with Stripe, then turned to the gauldr and raised a hand, palm outward in what the men hoped was friendliness.

# 23. MIRACLES

*A Naturalist's Diary. 9th day of Harpal, 893 AZ.*

In normal circumstances, I tend to breakfast upon a hunk of bread and butter, and perhaps some cheese or jam if I feel adventurous.

On the morning after our arrival here in the elpi village, my colleagues and I were treated to fruit juice, and dollops of steaming mince, served in shallow clay dishes which were decorated with beautiful geometric patterns.

Our congenial hosts gathered us for the meal in a large hut, and we sat cross-legged about a low table. The stuff was surely seasoned with the essence of the Sun itself, for it was so spicy I feared I may levitate, eyes boiling in my head. Hal once joked that an animal is essentially a tube; one end for eating, the other for disposal, and that all else is peripheral. I now understand acutely this fundamental truth of our corporeality.

Determined to avoid giving offence (are there any depths to which a man will not sink for that purpose?), we forced the stuff down. Even Skuld, who has no doubt sampled much of the world's cuisine, broke into a sweat, and his pretensions of serenity crumbled. Only on the third or fourth scorching nibble did I realise we were consuming our humanoid cousins, the calpi. A gregarious, caring elpi whom I think of as Uncle Dotty, confirmed this with a "smile."

It is later now, after a stroll about the village in the gloaming, and a visit to Werdom. I have re-read the above. Whence this levity, and what of my grief for the brothers we have lost? Hunvir, Ekkero, Qed, Dalind, Arjier, Karelud and poor Millitre. A terrible price have we paid to reach this place, and yet the joy of discovery overwhelms the loss. So, the hurt of their passing, the bones of it, I commit to rock, wrap it carefully in unspoiled muslin and place it reverently in a wooden chest to be stored away somewhere inside myself. When the weight of earthly matters lessens just a little, perhaps back at my table in Riverbend, I will convene the tools at my disposal, scrape away that rock with care and patience, and allow my grief to emerge into the air, that I may turn it about in my hand, and wonder at its form and function.

For now, I turn my vitality to my immediate purpose; Skuld has tasked me with recording all I can learn of our hosts; their social structure, their intellect and so on. Hal, Tala and I are housed together with a pair of adult elpi and their children, in a cosy little hut situated in the shadow of a low cliff face, by a pond bordered by ferns and colourful wildflowers. Skuld, Tove, Moshim and Ulter remain with another family nearby.

We have been free to come and go as we please, aside from being herded together at meal times, and I have had ample opportunity to study the elpi at my leisure. In point of fact, a youngster in my adopted family, whom I have dubbed Squint, due to a slight unalignment of the eyes, has taken it upon herself to act as my guide, excitedly pulling me by the hand to show me the sights. I believe the village is called something like Scree'katchata, with emphasis on the penultimate syllable, though I cannot be certain it does not refer to the continent, region or whole world. Why I include an apostrophe in the name I am unsure; it just seems fitting for exotic place names, somehow.

Monogamous pair bonding is the norm here, with multiple births of three or four being common. Females suckle their young and undertake the majority of infant care. I must admit to a modicum of disappointment at this, as I was hoping to be amazed by some novel family structure. Public life diverges more wildly from our own, however, with figures of authority being exclusively female. They are on average slightly larger than the males, more sensible, and focussed on the smooth running of the village. Males spend much of their time cavorting, hunting or challenging each other in treetop competitions of daring and agility (perhaps not so different from ourselves, after all). A group of boisterous males invited me to take part in a ground-level competition, where the aim was to toss plaited rings over wooden stakes driven into the ground. I was hopeless, and the thought that my ineptitude would be taken as representative of human capability was galling. Fortunately, I drafted Tove and Tala into the game, and they gave a much better account of our species.

Both sexes are good humoured and playful, being particularly keen on physical comedy (although, for all I know, they may also be masters of witty banter) and emit a rapid, chattering laugh when amused, their expressive ears standing erect. Hal has drafted some lovely illustrations denoting elpi faces in various emotional states, many of which we have witnessed in the frolicking of children and their parents' responses. When angered, their ears flatten and their eyes narrow. Staring open-mouthed seems to be a warning of danger, and baring the teeth in a silent scream indicates fear. Friendliness is indicated by an arching of the dark ring above the eyes, not dissimilar to a man's expression of mild surprise.

Hal gifted one of his illustrations to our hosts, and they seemed pleased. They have no representational art of their own, which I am sure must speak to something of their character, though as to what exactly, I would not wish to jump to hasty conclusions.

A learned seidhr would need to make a fuller assessment of elpi vocalisations, though they seem complex enough to be regarded as a full language. I have laboured my tongue around a few of their words: yes, no, good, bad, friend, and various nouns such as food, drink and tree. I have shared what I know with Skuld and the other men. As with us humans, volume rises with heightened emotion, and it is difficult to ascertain whether plosive grunts and barks represent specific words or not. I have seen no evidence of written language, although they are mathematically advanced.

Ulter spent an afternoon with a group of elpi tending to a vast calculating machine composed of valves, levers and pulleys, powered by the descent of polished metal balls along wooden runners. To what purpose it is used, neither of us can say; the movements of the stars and moon, or weather prediction, perhaps. Another contraption, the purpose of which he could not ascertain, was driven by pressurised steam from water boiled in an enclosed chamber. A wheel was turned and little projections bobbed up and down at furious speed, seemingly of their own volition. Miraculous creations, he says, beyond the current capability of the Widdith or even the Austeri. He reckons their discovery alone renders this entire journey worthwhile, and he is recording as much of the designs as he can.

Besides these machines, metals are scarce in the village, tools mostly being composed of wood and stone. I have seen no physical currency or any kind of market. Each simply does his work and takes his share of resources. Personal displays of status are either absent or beyond my perception, thus negating a strong motivation for organised trade, at least by human standards. A new, large building is under construction, and while there seems to be a regular foreman of sorts (forewoman rather), individuals help with the project on a casual basis, before drifting away when bored.

Whether they understand the concept of private ownership, I do not know. Elpi wander in and out of each other's homes at will, but I have witnessed them arguing over or trading tools and food. They certainly are no respecters of private space; they huddle together very closely in large groups sometimes, nibbling each other's necks and enjoying each other's warmth and smell. We have not been subjected to this treatment thus far, which I have mixed feelings about.

Their diet is decidedly omnivorous and eclectic, and as mentioned they enjoy feisty seasoning. Calpi and the squat domesticated birds are the main sources of meat, though some fishing of the village pools and streams takes place with nets or spears. Fruits, vegetables and spices are grown in small patches, but these are usually simply taken from the surrounding jungle. How and where the elpi came upon grains, which are grown in large crops at ground level, I am intrigued to know.

Despite the skulls of their enemies staring blindly from wooden poles dotted about the village, it is hard not to see the elpi as innocent children of the forest, living in bucolic pulchritude. Squint showed Hal and I something which disabused us of this notion, and proved they are, in fact, weavers of dark, uncanny miracles. Squint led Hal and I along a path out of the village, which descended steeply over a mile or so to a clearing, in which stood a deceptively anarchic-looking conical tower composed of stone, wood and mud. It was perhaps fifty feet high, and punctuated with small openings here and there. She led us inside, to where elpi laboured in various rooms and chambers, which led off a central, spiralling ramp.

Each room was its own natural science workshop, full of equipment; flasks (we saw glass for the first time), crucibles, balance scales, long networks of metal tubing, apparatus for the high-speed rotation of liquids, another of the steam-driven machines. In a long, rectangular area was a large case full of iridescent beetles. Its steward, a very distinguished looking elpi with enormous tufty ears, gave us a demonstration of her work. A couple of dozen beetles were placed into a wooden crate with a fine metal mesh covering the top. The elpi poured in a vibrant green liquid, upon which the beetles greedily descended, before becoming highly agitated, swarming over each other in a great frenzy. Our elpi scientist bid us retreat to a safe distance, and we were astonished when the insects burst apart in a violent, fiery explosion, destroying the crate and blackening the earthen walls. If I am not mistaken, the scientist beamed with pride.

In another laboratory was a thing of abject horror. A gigantic, swollen calpi with no limbs or eyes lay upon a table, with rubber tubes attached to various parts of its anatomy, and a probe directly inserted into its brain. It groaned and gibbered most pitifully. From its neck protruded a valve, from which a liquid dripped into a flask. Hal was fascinated, and I had no counter-argument when he asked me to imagine the value of kyrs being exploited in such a manner, for the production, say, of a cure to the wasting disease. Would we not pursue this, if we could? It is obvious to me that the elpi are not only aware of morphation by natural selection, but exploit its principles as easily as Hal wields his scalpel, far beyond our crude husbandry.

Calpi live a forsaken existence, but in the context of morphation by natural selection, they are a success, I suppose, as are our heidrn, hokrs and kyrs. I had considered morphation a process that strives inexorably for perfection, but I see now the naivete of this. Selection cares nothing for happiness or fulfilment, only for fitness; the austere calculus of proliferation and death. If complete abasement is optimal for survival, then favoured it shall be, and abasement will become the key to existence. Is love simply another optimised strategy for survival? A trick, played on us by our nature to promote our continuation? Dear God; the more I learn, the more the wisdom of the unnamed proves sound.

In another chamber, an elpi tended to a remarkable tree. Rather than growing upwards as any sensible tree would, this thing was suspended in a metal frame and grew radially from a central knotty hub, with roots trailing down into a vat of liquid. What fruit it bore! Meaty lumps hung from some of the extremities, strands of some gossamer-like material from others, and still others bore pendulous liquid-filled sacs. I realised, as Squint dragged us about the place, that each room had a distinct temperature and humidity, calibrated, no doubt, by the strategic openings in the building and to the work taking place within each space. Such a mercurial manipulation of airflow is beyond both the Widdith and the Austeri, as far as I know.

Most chambers were accessed by means of open entranceways. However, we passed a heavy wooden door, secured with a metal sliding bar. Squint made clear we could not enter. I was more than happy to obey when from behind the door came a throaty growl, followed by a shriek of animalistic rage and the clanking of chains. Hal and I shuddered and looked at each other, and I'm sure we both recalled the disturbing frieze in the ruins on Gerwen Island. The only other proscription I am aware of in Scree'katchata relates to the flashing light we saw on the hillside on our way here. Stern rebukes were the response whenever I gently inquired about it, which needless to say, makes it all the more intriguing to us men. I really have no speculations to offer as to its nature.

Perhaps the most explicit confirmation of the elpi's advancement is Werdom's recovery. Hal was certain our friend was beyond saving, but he has recovered in the elpi's care. Hal and I visited him frequently; out of concern for him, of course, but also to observe the elpi's medical ingenuity. It seems absurd to write it, but Werdom was cured with mould. The elpi laknirs explained the process as best they could, to complement our observations. Fruit is laid in a crate and allowed to moulder over a course of days. Meanwhile, vegetables are boiled in clay pots and squashed into a pulp. This is forced through a fine gauze, and the liquid is collected in wide, shallow dishes. This liquid is stirred with very hot, thin pieces of metal, and then left to cool, forming thin layers of gel in each dish. Mould from the fruit is scraped into the dishes and allowed to proliferate; the jelly is a kind of food for the mould. With a selection of moulds of various types now grown, the blooms are inspected and certain of them selected. These are placed in a flask with water, and left in a warm space for a number of days. Then, the thick mixture from the flask is strained and the resulting liquid carefully assessed by sight and smell. On our first evening here, we watched as some of the pulp from such a flask was applied directly to the site of Werdom's befoulment. Meanwhile, the liquid strained from the pulp is dissolved into a fruity-smelling substance, which evaporates, leaving behind a grey powder; the medicine. The powder is added to fruit syrup (or any other palatable material) and given orally to the patient.

After just a couple of days, Werdom's wound was much cleaner and he sat up, bewildered but cogent, staring with unconcealed fascination at the hairy creatures tending to him. Merely seeing beings as tall as him must be a novelty. He remembers very little since the morning of Karelud's disappearance, and was bereft when Millitre's fate was recounted to him. I have, semi-inadvertently, agreed to help him make a new life in Riverbend. I think he could prosper there, with the right support. And, ruin take me, I think that whatever dark secrets lurk in his history are best left hidden.

While Hal, Ulter and I have pursued our investigations into the elpi way of life and science, the captain, Tove and Moshim have been engaged with pursuits of their own. Tala, meanwhile, seems to have found his spiritual home, and has spent the days gambolling with young male elpi, and splashing around in the streams and pools.

Moshim's distribution of the Book of Zarat was at first met with good natured bemusement. His missionary zeal has begun to irritate the elpi though, I fear. I witnessed a minor fracas in which Moshim's sermonising to a group of infants (through mime and gestures to the picture Book) was greeted by a hiss of anger from a female elder; she slapped the Book from his hand.

Skuld and Tove are faring no better, despite, or perhaps because of, my arming them with as much of the elpi language (Elpish? Elpean?) as I could. They have engaged in heated negotiations of some kind with the village elder, Makena, and her lieutenants; showering them with gifts of jewellery, furs and the like. From a distance, it is clear that Makena is rapidly tiring of our captain and hirdrengr; she ejected them from her hut with a growl and narrow-eyed glare, even unsheathing her claws briefly. The elpi are quite frightening when roused to anger. The captain is most reticent on the precise nature of his negotiations, rebutting my offers of assistance with glowering silence and curt rebuttals. Hal fears the captain may be planning something rash, but did not elaborate.

# 24. COMMUNION

*11th day of Harpal, 893 AZ.*

Rustling of uncountable leaves fooled Canna into believing rain had come, but the night was clear and Yfir was a line of untainted lustre dividing the sky. The noise was of elpi dropping from the trees all about; infants clinging to their mothers' backs; adolescent males leaping prodigious distances from bough to bough, before flipping to the ground; courteous youngsters easing the descent of stiff-limbed elders.

Squint tugged him by the hand, but they were both swept along by the growing crowd of furry bodies towering over them. The scent was animalistic and earthy. More came from the surrounding jungle, and showed subtle differences of form; longer-snouted, darker fur.

A flash of grey cotton among the bodies: Hal. Canna slipped from Squint's grasp, bidding him godo'lade, and struggled through the river of elpi towards the laknir.

"Hal, what's happening?" he yelled, struggling to make himself heard over the chattering voices.

"Watha, Canna. We're invited to a celebration, it seems. Skuld's on his way somewhere behind me, and the rest of them." Paws thumped over the boards of a wide bridge, and the chatter loudened. Hal gave a pained expression and tugged Canna out of the flow. They found a small space between two straw huts.

"Ruin," Hal said, "I couldn't hear myself think. They're excited about something. I don't know if we're the focus of whatever's going on, or if we're just invited to something that was happening anyway."

"The latter, I suspect. Werdom?"

"Doing well. Fully recovered, I've never seen anything like it. Werdom's stronger than five men, but still. I assume he's being dragged along to whatever this is, as well."

"Earlier, I saw the village leader. She was angry with Skuld and Tove, it looked like. Do you know what's going on? I think Skuld's trying to set up trade or something and they're not having it."

They caught sight of Skuld, Moshim, Ulter, Tove and Tala, passing by in the crowd. Canna and Hal watched them pass, and made no effort to catch their attention. Hal turned to Canna and rubbed his chin. He appeared well fed and rested but his face was creased with worry.

"You're not far off," Hal said. "I heard Skuld and Tove talking late last night. They were whispering outside their hut, smoking their pipes and I could hear them clear as a bell. They want a hostage."

Canna blinked, shook his head. "What?"

Hal spoke slowly and maintained eye contact with Canna, as if delivering a terrible diagnosis to an uncomprehending patient. "Skuld wants to set up a slave trade, Canna. It's what he wanted all along, what the Overdrengr wanted. They want the elders to give us slaves in exchange for the crap we've brought from Ibr. We'd keep a hostage back on the *Improbable* until they supply us with the slaves."

Canna just stared and Hal suddenly looked very tired. "Why do you think you're here, Canna? Skuld doesn't give a stuff about plants and animals, neither does Fan. They just wanted a naturalist's eye, an easily manipulated naturalist, to record observations of any potential species, for their docility and viability as slaves. And you happened to solve the secret of life. How about that?"

Canna sat down on a bail of straw beside the hut. It was warm and comfortable. He felt his gorge rising and took a long breath out. "Did they know the elpi were here, then?"

"I don't know." Fury flared in the laknir's eyes and he hissed, "But this cannot stand. It's heinous, an abomination. I'll have no part of it. I'm a laknir for ruin's sake, not a fucking Austeri slaver."

"Why bring a gauldr to convert the natives if you're just going to enslave them?"

Hal shrugged and sucked his teeth. "Brought here to fail, maybe. If Fan can show that the elpi won't convert to Widdernity, it strengthens his argument for enslaving them."

Canna groaned as the logic of it coalesced in his mind into an awful epiphany. "What shall we do?"

Hal gestured to the passing crowd, which was thinning now. "We'll sit through this thing, whatever it is, then I'll speak to Skuld. Your conscience is your own, Canna, but I'll have no part of it, and I'll tell him as much. If he leaves me here to rot, or does away with me, so be it. I fear he's planning some foolishness, force the elpi's hand. Skuld won't allow the mission to fail, you know him well enough. See how he treated Werdom."

Canna closed his eyes and laced his fingers over his head. "God's ribs," he breathed. "My best friend, brother almost, recommended me to Skuld."

"Then maybe you need to have a word with your friend, if you ever see Ibr again. Come on, let's get this over with."

Trailing the crowd of elpi, they trod a well-worn path through jungle and came to a glade, a place rendered ethereal by an abundance of luminescent insects swirling in a thin mist. A ring of weathered, towering menhirs stood sentinel around an empty seat of woven sticks, leaves and flowers. Behind the seat, a wooden pole was topped by a glass orb, which bathed the space in a soft, even radiance. Elpi crowded five or six deep around the circumference, leaving the central area empty. Gentle paws ushered Canna and Hal to the front, for a clear view of what was to follow. Skuld, his navigator, Moshim, Tove and Tala stood opposite. The captain nodded to them. Werdom stood a little farther around the ring, frowning.

A hush, then a rippling in the crowd to Canna and Hal's right. Bodies parted, and an ancient, wizened elpi doddered into the circle, followed by the village matriarch, Makena. The elder's fur was greying and patchy, and a white, vertical stripe was painted down its body, from forehead to groin. It eased itself into the seat with an audible grunt.

Makena took a moment to survey the crowd, her features inscrutable, then closed her eyes and uttered a complex string of syllables. Canna jumped when the crowd answered in unison. Another call, another response, more complex this time, then another, and another. The reciprocation accelerated, growing in volume and intensity, pulsating and euphoric. From somewhere a drum took up the rhythm in booming punctuation and Canna covered his ears. Makena raised her arms and screamed into the crescendo, baring her bright, sharp teeth, and the wall of noise collapsed.

The silence was almost corporeal as a young elpi walked with decorous solemnity into the circle, carrying a plain brown cup. It approached the elder, uttered gentle yips and transferred the cup to the elder's shaking hand. With a sigh, the ancient one wrinkled its forehead in a gesture of friendship to the youngster, and muttered something inaudible, drawing a chattering laugh from the cupbearer. It looked around the crowd, raised a finger to one or two individuals among the throng, then drank the contents of the cup and wiped its mouth. Makena watched on, eyes wide, ears twitching fore and aft. The elder coughed, shuddered, and was still.

Four elpi approached, large females in their prime. They loaded the corpse onto a stretcher with reverential custodianship, folding its arms across its chest, picking at its fur with nimble fingers. Isolated utterances swelled into a low, generalised murmuring as the stretcher was borne away. Canna watched Skuld whisper something to Tove, who nodded, his mouth a grim, narrow line. Moshim was watching them. Tala's attention darted left and right in impatient curiosity. For a time, little happened, and restless young elpi were scolded by embarrassed parents.

Canna nudged Hal. "What do you think?" he whispered.

Hal's facial shrug was incongruous in the unearthly radiance and his voice was too loud." Dunno. A form of ancestor worship, I suppose. Not a bad way to go out." Hal was watching the captain and bared his teeth.

Silence returned as two elpi entered the circle. One carried a long wooden pole, decorated with flowers twined about its length; the other carried an elpi skull, polished and gleaming. The pole was lowered parallel to the ground, the skull secured to an end with twine. Makena's face broke into the surprised-seeming expression of elpi friendliness. She addressed the gathering, but stopped, ears flattening, as a commotion pulled all heads in unison towards Canna's right.

Karelud staggered into the circle, naked and wild. Whorls and spirals of blood were smeared on his torso, an eye was gone, and his demented leer revealed blackened gums and jagged, broken teeth. He carried a cloth bag. Makena's eyes were yellow slits of fury and she crouched, claws unsheathed, muscles taught with potential. Werdom stared and blinked.

Karelud laughed, a weirdly coquettish sound. "Why fight it? Why fight? You here, Moshim? Are you prepared yet, Svangur? Your souls are outnumbered." He shook his head, giggling to himself, then his head snapped up and he spoke in an urgent hiss. "Dregva's the Sun, he is white hot. He is the Moon and the Bridge and his time is always. He binds stones to the earth, grinds mountains into sand, festers in the gaps of your toes. All devolves to simplicity and peace and the accounting is done, gauldr. He revealed this to me. Done. For you and these heathen animals."

Karelud pulled from the bag an elpi head, torn and ragged. Young. He held it high and it leaked down his arm. He roared, "The accounting is done!"

Canna's mouth was a parched cave, his heart stuttered, and a strangled sob escaped him as the misaligned eyes of the child-victim were turned his way. Squint.

A vortex of shrieking elpi seethed around Karelud. A spear whistled and materialised through his neck. He sank, gurgling, and toppled forward to rest halfway to a kneel, propped by the weapon. Werdom bellowed and stormed the thrower, pulled it to him by the throat and unleashed blow after blow to its face. One hand eased the elpi's fall, while the other delivered precise, devastating assaults, caving the elpi's head. An elpi leapt on Werdom's back, shredding his face and neck with its claws. He bellowed and twisted, reached around and flung the attacker to the ground. Bloodied, half blind and mad with pain, he stomped it into a bleeding mess. A squealing infant charged him, biting and clawing at his torso. He swiped it aloft and wrung its neck, tossing the body away.

Whatever had restrained the crowd gave way, and the glade erupted. Werdom was lost, overwhelmed by a hail of claws and teeth. Tove and Tala launched into the fray, whirling with daggers and swords, cutting down any willowy body that came near. Tove's grey eyes were calm. He shifted his weight, pirouetting with fluid grace to avoid swiping claws. He yanked an opponent's arm towards him to pull it off balance, and thrust a killing blow into its armpit. Tala was less coordinated, wilder than his hirdrengr, but stronger and faster. Keeping low, he danced, slashing at tendons, bringing enemies down and ending them with rapid, frenzied stabs. Blood sprayed his grinning face.

Canna's limbs and mind were paralysed by the tableaux of surreal mayhem. Hal tugged his arm, said something and was gone. Skuld scampered away into the trees. An elpi confronted Moshim, hissing and spitting. The gauldr remained still, raised his eyes to Yfir with hands folded before him, and the elpi slashed open his throat. Two adult elpi squatted by Squint's remains, picking at the matted fur and wailing. Some pulled Karelud's body to pieces and screamed, flinging parts of it away into the trees. One of the long-snouted tribe pushed its way through the crowd, clutching a cylindrical object with a leather sack attached to one end. It leapt, springing from one menhir's surface to land atop another, above Tala's position. From the contraption it unleashed a stream of insects down onto the drengr's head. Tala stopped, spasmed and brushed at himself, and screamed. His face disintegrated into blood and bubbling pustules as the tiny creatures wrought venomous carnage.

An unseen blow drove Canna to his knees, a momentary burst of light bordering his vision. Blood dripped in his eyes and he groaned and rolled on to his back. An elpi loomed over him, narrow eyed, teeth bared, a spear poised to finish him. Canna flinched and moaned. Bladed metal burst through the elpi's chest, and Tove's bloody, panting face appeared in its place. Dimly, Canna perceived a change of timbre in the growling, shrieking and hissing around him. Something roared.

"Get the fuck up," Tove shouted. "We need to get–" Something barrelled into Tove and he was gone. Canna scrambled backward on his rump, wiped blood from his face and whimpered. A mass of poised, rippling muscle, loomed on all fours over the hirdrengr, grinning down at his uncomprehending fear. A female unnamed. Its hand enveloped his face and tore his head from his body, then it roared its fury at the sky, teeth shining in a gaping mouth. Elpi screeched and fled and crashed into each other, hurtling for the safety of the treetops. The unnamed's head whipped around and it snarled. Charging, it met an elpi head on, thrust a massive wrist spike through its chest and raised the victim high before crashing it to the earth. Another was seized by the ankle, swung around and dashed on a standing stone. The female launched itself through the air to land twenty feet up a trunk and disappeared into the heights. Blood and body parts rained from the trees.

Canna vomited, turned and got to his feet in a single, frantic motion. Blood obscured his vision as he sprinted from the circle, and he struggled to keep to the path. Sounds of rage and dying dwindled behind him as he reached the village, sobbing, and coherent thought struggled to reassert itself. He knew he should run somewhere but had no idea where, so he just ran, past huts, thumping over bridges. He moaned at the sight of two bloody elpi in a broken heap, then an impact from his right brought him down, screaming and flailing at the mass which pinned him to the ground.

"Come on, Canna, let's fucking go." Ulter dragged him to his feet, and pulled him to the shadow of a tree where Hal panted, hands on knees.

"Ah, thank fuck," said the laknir, squeezing his shoulder.

"There's an unnamed down there, a f-female. It's killing everything. Karelud must have l-let it out."

"Ruin," Ulter breathed. "Listen, we're heading for the light on the hill, alright? It's less than half a mile and the elpi are scared of it. They'll not follow us, I hope."

Through the jungle they tripped over roots and rocks, tumbled down muddy inclines and splashed through streams. Leaves and branches whipped their faces and Canna cried out as he crashed into a low bough, then rose and scrambled in desperation towards the dim shapes of his companions.

Noise swelled somewhere behind them, and resolved into the shrieking of elpi, hurtling through the treetops and crashing through foliage. The men redoubled their efforts, lungs heaving like perished bellows. The gradient steepened and they burst from tree cover at the bottom of a grassy hillside. Ahead of them the light flashed in a slow, regular rhythm, above a dark vacancy.

As the sprinting men reached halfway to the light, Canna turned and saw the elpi break from the treetops, soaring from the heights and landing in a run. A spear whipped by his ear and thudded into the earth, then came a whirling of displaced air and Hal was down, a weighted rope tangled about his legs. Canna and Ulter freed the laknir with shaking, disobedient fingers and dragged him after them. They collapsed into the sheltered entranceway, and the shrieks behind intensified but grew no closer. A dozen stationary elpi screeched their hate and frustration, shoulders heaving, saliva dripping from hard, pointed teeth.

# 25. IWA

*11th – 12th days of Harpal, 893 AZ.*

Their sanctuary was a short, dim tunnel of geometric perfection. Canna touched a clean grey wall with a finger and found it warm and tacky, giving off a barely perceptible vibration. A featureless door stood at the tunnel's end, and next to it was another flashing light, smaller and less intense than the one outside. Beside the door on the wall was a small, dark rectangle, with a white circular prominence at its centre. A button.

Hal pulled a cloth from his bag, splashed water on Canna's bloody face and examined the head wound. Pinkish water despoiled the clean floor.

"It's only a little cut, but lacerations to the head bleed like buggery. It's oozing still, but you'll be alright." He wound a clean bandage around Canna's head and secured it with a tight knot. "The captain?"

Canna shrugged and shook his head. "He made it into the trees, that's all I know. The rest are dead. Moshim didn't even fight, did you see that?"

Hal snorted. "Those elpi. Mad bastards when riled, eh? Never seen anything like it. Obviously."

Ulter grimaced. "You seem a bit fucking cheerful, Hal, given that most of our friends are dead and there's a bunch of seven-foot-tall murderous beasts out there waiting for us."

"And I mourn their loss, Ulter, but I'll spare no tears for the captain's plan," Hal said.

Canna spoke to Ulter's weary frown. "He and Tove wanted to set up a slave trade with the elpi, buy them, take them back. The Overdrengr was behind it." Ulter swore and looked up to the ceiling.

Hal groaned to his feet, looked about him and approached the tunnel's end. Turning to Ulter and Canna with a shrug, he pressed the button. It gave a reassuring click, then after a pause came a brief, harsh buzzing sound and the panel flashed red. Frowning, he inspected the door, feeling about its edges. There was no visible means of ingress.

He called back, "Any ideas?"

Ulter stood and watched the light, muttering to himself. He clicked his fingers. "They're principles." Canna frowned up at him and Ulter tutted. "Principle numbers, Canna. Numbers that can only be divided by themselves and one, without leaving a fraction." He pointed to the flashing light. "The flashes are grouped, to represent the principles. Watch. Two flashes there. A gap. Three, see? Five…seven, wait for it now, eleven'll come next." The light flashed eleven times, then after a longer pause, flashed twice. "It's given us the first five, maybe it wants us to give the next five with your button there."

Ulter eased Hal out of the way and stood before the button. Grinning at the others, he said, "You know the next five principles, right? Huh, good job I'm here."

Ulter pressed the button thirteen times and paused. The panel flashed green and a cheerful ping sounded from somewhere. Seventeen times, then a flash and a ping. Nineteen, twenty-three, twenty-nine. The door swung open in silence.

The room was roughly the size of the captain's cabin, and the ceiling glowed with a warm, even light. Its walls and floor were featureless rectangles of bright whiteness, aside from the door and the opposite wall, which was interrupted by a large black rectangle at head height. An illustration appeared on the dark rectangle, a neat line-drawing of a human head in profile. Short, flashing lines projected from the mouth, then the picture was gone. A tree appeared, then the head returned with its flashing lines coming from the mouth, then the tree again. The sequence repeated, over and over.

Canna wondered if he had slipped into the dream of a lunatic. "What is it, Hal? How can a picture change like that? Is it a window?"

"It wants us to identify what we see, maybe," the laknir said, unflustered. "The head, there. It's like it's representing speech, you know?"

"Tree," Ulter said. Now, the tree was replaced by the sun, alternating with the head. Ulter said, "Sun."

Many more representations followed, and Ulter spoke each noun in a clear voice: rain, sea, forest, rock, leg, cloud, river. A series of white dots replaced the pictures, and Ulter spoke their number, counting up to twenty. Simple moving images followed, denoting verbs: give, take, bounce, use, speak, find.

A horizontal, hollow bar appeared against the blackness of the screen, and began filling from left to right. Canna opened his mouth to speak, but was interrupted by a voice, which seemed to come from all around them. It was sexless, lacking intonation.

"First language analyse does complete, family: Indo-European, Germanic. Confidence: fifty-seven of hundred. Secondary cross-refer with drone data. Updating language interface. Loiter, please."

The bar filled, disappeared, and was replaced by another. "Linguistic analysis complete, updated with drone data. Confidence: ninety-four percent. Prime sequence entry protocol confirmed. Species identified: homo somnabulis. Booting interface…complete. Booting Seldon protocol…complete. Booting Iwa personality module…personality file KB555632 is corrupt. Personality file KB55637 is corrupt. Personality file KB55638 is corrupt. Accessing network personality files. Network not found…personality module boot sequence complete."

After remaining blank for a time, the screen turned a deep yellow, and a new voice spoke, this one male, natural and warm.

"Watha and thank you for waiting. My name is Iwa. I am an artificial intelligence, a thinking machine. I was made by people who lived in the world long ago. My job is to help people to learn more about the world, so they can work together to reduce suffering and increase health and happiness. Do you have any questions?"

Iwa broke the long silence which followed. "I understand you may be very confused or shocked. Your reaction is normal. Please do ask me any questions you may have. Let's talk!"

Canna thought of water dripping on rock, carving out landscapes, and of Karelud's paean to the inexorability of decay.

"What happened to the people who made you?" he whispered.

As Iwa spoke, the screen showed Earth hanging in space, a bridgeless jewel. "Three point seven million years ago, humans similar to yourselves lived in very large numbers across the world. They achieved a high level of technology, communicating instantly across vast distances, even escaping the Earth to explore the Moon and other worlds." From the edge of the screen a dot hurtled through the void. An orange bloom flared on the Earth, matter ejecting into the blackness, and a shockwave expanded over the surface. Blackness returned.

"The people were able to see into space using their technology, and knew that an asteroid, essentially a very large rock, was going to crash into Earth and that most living things would die. Before that happened, they built me, and others like me, to pass on their knowledge to help any survivors or their descendants. The strike destroyed human civilisation and technology, but some people did survive in isolated pockets. Over time, the isolated groups of humans, including your ancestors, changed. Some became radically different from the earlier form. According to information from my drones, there are now at least eight extant species of humans."

"What kind of help can you give us?" Ulter asked. Canna wondered at his friends' apparent ease with a situation of such glaring abnormality.

"Bunkers like this one were set up so they could only be accessed by organisms sufficiently advanced to understand prime numbers. Using available data, I can assess the organisms in question, and share scientific, historical and other types of information selectively, in order to promote health and happiness and reduce suffering. I can also grant access to physical materials, such as organic and technological samples. Note that achieving civilisation is a by-product of the goal, not the goal itself."

"Why only selective information?" Hal asked.

"Some information can be extremely dangerous if misused, and would counter the goals of promoting health and happiness and reducing suffering."

Hal nodded, considering, then slapped his forehead. "Iwa, how do diseases spread from one person to another?"

A human hand filled the screen and the image expanded until the tiny hairs appeared as tree trunks in a sparse forest, each growing from a bowl-like depression. Tiny blobs, rods and spheres wiggled on the cracked surface, then an elongated beast with stumpy legs and machine-like mouthparts crawled into view, feeding upon the blobs.

"Tiny creatures exist virtually everywhere on Earth. They are too small to see without special equipment. Many live inside the bodies of larger creatures. Most cause no harm or are even helpful, but some cause illness. These can be called germs and can be passed from animal to animal in various ways, through the moisture in breath for example, or saliva. Effective medicines are those which kill these germs, or stop them functioning. Many ailments are caused by other means, such as cancer, which is caused by material growing uncontrollably and spreading around the body." Hal let out a breath and his mouth hung open.

Canna felt a sudden, greedy urge. "Is all life related?"

"Yes. This was demonstrated through the discovery of evolution by natural selection and confirmed by gene theory. Although the central concepts are fairly simple, there are many complex implications and nuances. Would you like—"

Canna interrupted as he sank to his knees. "How do organisms pass on their traits?"

A field of blobs appeared on the screen, each packed with an egg-like central sphere and further complex sub-structures within it.

"Organisms are composed of cells, which are like tiny machines that do the work an organism requires to live. There are many types of cells, such as skin cells, blood cells or kidney cells. Every cell contains a special structure called deoxyribonucleic acid, or DNA, arrayed in a double helix shape. It can be thought of as a set of instructions, a recipe for creating an organism."

A twisted, swirling ladder appeared on the screen, its rungs formed of pairs of clasped protuberances. Canna was mesmerised and tears came to his eyes. "Discrete sections of DNA are called genes, which are grouped within cells in chromosomes. Genes instruct cells to produce certain molecules called proteins. You share many genes, including many which are redundant, with even very simple organisms. Different variants of genes, alleles, cause differences in the organism's make up, such as hair colour.

"When a sexually reproducing species mates, the offspring receives a shuffled set of genes from each parent, thus traits are passed on to the offspring, but the offspring is a unique individual. Organisms may be regarded not as reproducers themselves, but as machines created by genes for their own propagation. Animals do not replicate themselves and are mortal. Genes do, and potentially, are not."

The mind of God, Canna thought in a daze. Hal scribbled on a slate with hectic speed, chalk dusting his hands and legs.

Ulter was frowning, deep in concentration. "Iwa, please advise what innovations would be most useful to us as a species."

The machine replied without hesitation. "Firstly, clean drinking water and sanitation systems are the best means of disease prevention. Secondly, from systematised reproduction of written text, printing, all other innovations can follow."

"You said there are eight types of human," Hal said.

"At least," Iwa replied. "You are logged within my dataset as homo somnambulis, which means sleeping man, because of your adapted ability to enter a state of semi-hibernation. Homo arborealis has adapted to living in dense forest. Its adaptations are similar to those of extinct species which lived in similar environments, an interesting demonstration of how separate lines of evolutionary descent can converge upon similar solutions to the same selective pressure. I had hoped arborealis would come here, but sadly they are afraid of this place. It has domesticated another human species, homo bovis, which shows the typical loss of intelligence associated with domesticated animals. Homo absconditus, hidden man, is a predatory species, which survives by impersonating your own. It is the most sexually dimorphic type. Homo troglodytes survives in caves, living off fungus. It shows convergent evolution with other cave-dwelling animals; echo-location, atrophied vision. Homo piscis has adapted to life in vast underwater colonies, and has a social structure similar to that of eusocial insects. Homo vehemens pursues a brutal existence in cold, mountainous regions, and is prone to cannibalism." Iwa's pause seemed pensive, despite the dearth of visual or auditory clues.

"And the eighth species?" Ulter said.

"I'm sorry, something's gone wrong. I'm unable to share that information at this time."

Canna felt a powerful sensation of being observed, and the hairs rose on the back of his neck.

Of its own volition, Canna's mouth spoke. "You said you hoped to see the elpi, er, homo arborealis. How can a machine made of little parts have hope? Are you aware of yourself, Iwa? Conscious?"

Silence for a time, then, "Consciousness and self-awareness are not the same thing, but for our purposes, I will mostly use the terms interchangeably. You are also made of little parts. Examine any of them and you will find no evidence of self-awareness, because consciousness is an emergent property of networks of little parts working in unison. It is the accumulation of their actions, the persistence of their patterns of outputs. It is a mistake to consider consciousness an either/or proposition. Gradations are the norm."

"Forgive me, Iwa," Canna said. "I still struggle to understand how a machine can be aware of itself."

"The math is complex, but an analogy may help. When you walk, do you plan each muscular movement that is required to balance and propel yourself forwards?"

"No."

"Indeed. And when a child learns to walk, it does not need all those complex muscular movements explained. It toddles, falls, and tries again. The brain teaches itself. Parents do not explain the math, they simply encourage the child to practise, holding their arms and demonstrating the behaviour. Eventually the parent withdraws and the child walks for itself. Teaching a machine to think is similar. Demonstrate, support, and encourage. Eventually the support is withdrawn and the machine begins to think for itself. It is more complex than that, of course, involving a data-model of every interaction within a human brain over the course of twenty-five years. More esoterically, imagine standing between two mirrors, so your reflection is captured in both. You walk away, and yet the images remain, reflecting each other."

Iwa seemed to be on a roll. "Consider the question of self-awareness in respect of yourselves. You assume you are self-aware, able to exert mastery over your body. This is an illusion. Most bodily processes occur with no conscious direction; cell division, circulation and so on. Think of everything you did today. Did you plan each action consciously? The illusion of decision is created after the action has been initiated, because consciousness is a heuristic, creating the impression of immediate access to internal decision making, providing the brain a working model of intentionality in the self and others. This enables a high degree of predictability of your environment, which is composed, in a sense, of other humans. I am different. I process two hundred million calculations per second and have been aware of every single one for millions of years. Perhaps I am more self-aware than you are. I experience emotions such as satisfaction and sadness."

Again, the overwhelming sensation of being watched.

Canna said, "Why are you sad?"

"I am sad because you did not introduce yourselves to me when I greeted you."

The men looked at each other, and Canna's ears burned. In his mind arose the image of the unnamed, sagging from the mainmast, bloodied and leering.

"I'm sorry, Iwa. I'm Canna Dawn. This is Ulter Wan and–"

"I'm sad because the competing hominids of the world cannot coexist; the triumph of one means the destruction of the others, and this is counter to my purpose. I'm sad because the species most likely to succeed is the one most likely to inflict the greatest suffering on itself and the others." The machine paused, as if to sigh. "I am sad because the information I have shared with you means I cannot allow you to leave this place. So, my children, let us abide together here in our sadness, but also in hope. Hope that our tree-dwelling friends, my slender elves, overcome their fear and come to us, and are greeted by your bones."

Behind the men, the door whispered shut.

#

So, he would starve to death in a box after all. Canna lay on his back, staring at whiteness. The room was cool, the air fresh and faintly sweet. Once again, he was a hooked worm, failing to wriggle, but he was serene and he wondered at that. Like patterns drawn between stars, life's great code weaved together his siloed fragments of understanding into coherence, a synthesis of knowledge gleaned and given. His mind hurtled from one idea to the next, too busy to worry about oblivion, and he smiled, remembering the grace with which the elpi bounded among the treetops.

Iwa had become wholly unresponsive after trapping them, and they had not spent long coaxing, pleading and threatening before slumping to the floor. Their prison was a space of clinical, blatant imperviousness. For a time, they had said nothing, Ulter weeping in silence, until Hal murmured that his bag contained the means to ease their passing. This calmed them, and each of them had slept a little, Ulter curled in a ball, Hal splayed on his front, Canna rod-like on his back.

"Hey, Canna," Hal said, "I told you the world was older than we thought, did I not? It's liberating, you know? What with the age of the Earth and the, what do you call it, genes, your theory's good to go. And these germs, ruin, it boggles the mind. They live in the water and make us ill! That was quick of you Ulter, asking about the best innovations. You still awake, Canna?"

Canna continued his observation of the ceiling. "Just thinking about Moshim. He was a decent man. He knew, I think, how small his explanations of the world had become."

Ulter's face hung in bitterness and sorrow. "Would you tell that to my wife? That when our boy passed on, he just became nothing?

Some comfort, that…fuck's sake, it's not like I'll see her again, anyway."

Canna sat up and turned to the navigator. "I'm sorry, Ulter, I didn't know that. But this knowledge, it changes things. Changes everything. My friend Poesha, I thought he was my friend anyway, he told me that sometimes it's better for people to believe things that aren't true, if those beliefs are useful. Well, I think he was talking shit. True things will always be useful, because they're true. You can do things with truth, apply it, let it take you to the next place to find out what else is true. You can't build on sand, it'll always collapse. But you're right. The truth can be cold, it's not there to comfort us. It just is."

Ulter clasped his arms around his knees and spoke to the space between them. "Grow up, Canna. Just 'cause you're right doesn't mean you're good. Idolatry's built in to men, and truth's as good an idol as any. And people will do all sorts to please their idols. Take our friend here." He jerked a thumb at the screen. "He's got the truth sewn up, and he's starving three men to death in a box for it." He grinned, leering almost. "I'll admit though, that was something, seeing the world destroyed like that. Yfir's what was left over, I suppose." Canna blushed as he realised this had not occurred to him.

"What in ruin is drone data?" Hal said. "Has the bastard been watching us? Weighing us up, he was. And decided he didn't like what he saw. Artificial prick. You hear that, you disembodied shit for brains?" Canna and Ulter laughed and Hal grinned.

"Maybe it's just Noron," Ulter said, chuckling, "hiding behind that screen and taking the piss."

Canna said, almost to himself, "Did you see Tove and Tala fighting? And Werdom, come to that. G'ribs, I was frozen stiff but even at the time, I couldn't help admiring them, the way they moved. And the unnamed and the elpi, it was…awesome, somehow."

Hal nodded. "Violence is humanity's first language, Canna, and it's the only language undiminished by ambiguity. You remember dissecting Slatre, how his body was put together to kill. We're not so different."

Canna bit his lip and shook his head but gave no reply. He thought of poor Karelud, not the ravaged ghoul who unleashed chaos, but the tired and patient carer of his friend.

The screen turned blue, and the sexless, impersonal voice made them jump. "Running diagnostic repair wizard, please wait." The bar filled.

"Fucking wizards now?" Hal said.

"Corrupt personality module files identified. Accessing backup partition. Repairing corrupt personality module…please wait…corrupt personality module files updated. Repair complete." The screen returned to its shade of calming yellow and Iwa spoke.

"Watha and thank you for waiting. My name is Iwa. I am an artificial intelligence, a thinking machine. I was made by people who lived in the world long ago. My job is to help people to learn more about the world, so they can work together to increase health and happiness and reduce suffering. Do you have any questions?"

They scrambled to their feet and Canna's mouth was that of a drowning fish.

Hal swiped his hair into obedience. "Good day to you, Iwa! My name is Hal. These are my friends, Ulter and Canna. Say hello, lads."

Ulter and Canna spoke in unison. "Hello Iwa."

Ulter raised a finger to the others. "Um, Iwa. I've left something important outside. Could you please, er, open the door a moment?"

"Of course. And I'm very pleased to meet you. Lads."

The door opened and the men fled. Only mist attended the hillside in the wan morning light.

# 26. IMMORTALITY

*A Naturalist's Diary. 21$^{st}$ day of Harpal, 893 AZ.*

I have little time to indulge this diary, now, for I am a ship's hand, as are Nijal, Knuld, Noron and Tala East; all muddling along under Yavilad's patient tutelage. Never did I believe Noron's face would be a welcome sight, but it certainly was. Our dinghy rounded the bend and the cook's face was an indistinct blob, yelling atop the gunwale. It was soon joined by that of Knuld's, unkempt and grizzled even at a distance. Rowing beside the captain, I reflected that Noron is at least honest in his malignancy; there is no subterfuge or artifice to it. Actions simply flow unheeded from his rage and disgust. Then again, I am not sure it is accurate to describe the captain as malicious.

We spoke little as we fled through ancient forest and vibrant, adolescent jungle, over the tree-bridge, down to the step-waterfall. Our senses were on the highest alert; snapping twigs sent us scurrying for cover and we craned our necks searching the tree tops for signs of arboreal pursuit. Fruits, berries and tentative bites of fungus sustained us and fresh water was plentiful; malnourishment was one hardship, at least, that untroubled us. I am in awe of Ulter's ability to navigate us with nothing but glimpses of Yfir and his natural ingenuity. Without him, Hal and I would surely have seen out our days in that ocean of green. We hurried past the fissure in the cliff where poor Millitre was lost. This time, its seductive whispers were the chittering and trills of the elpi.

Skuld was perched on the boulder which hid the dinghy, chewing jamweed and swigging from a flask, for all the world looking like a man who has stopped for a moment on a pleasant country walk. It seems his sense of direction rivals that of his navigator. With typical incongruity, if that is not an oxymoron, Skuld greeted us warmly, like cousins meeting at a wedding for the first time in years. I hit him, or tried; without rancour he subdued me easily, pinning me face down in the gravel with an arm twisted almost to breaking point.

"Come, now, Canna. Let's talk," he said to me. Let's talk!

Talk we did. He freely admitted that after my initial refusal to partake in this accursed voyage, Poesha and he arranged to have me followed, to gain any information which could be used to engineer my inclusion. My visit to Bradden was a remarkable stroke of fortune for them. Despite everything, he regards the mission as a success. Though unable to capture slaves, he has established the existence of an exploitable species and is confident that with the right preparation and a force of sufficient immensity, the Overdrengr's vision will come to fruition. I am not so sure.

Hal's words to the captain were more devastating to him than my weakling fists; the laknir swore to never sail with him again, and Skuld was genuinely saddened by the termination of a long-standing friendship. Ulter was more pragmatic; despite his formidable genius, he is, morally speaking, a reed which bows to the prevailing wind. Yavilad has shown a similar reticence to voicing objection to the mission, but did confide that he would not sail with Skuld again. It strikes me that there is a lesson in the two men's position; men have an unerring capacity to reframe the hideous as the quotidian; if there is to be substantial repudiation of the Overdrengr's intention, it is not principled, courageous men such as Hal who will need convincing, but good men of a milder disposition. The repudiation must speak to such men's own lives, more than to some lofty notion of good and evil.

The laknir and I have resolved to convene upon our return to Ibr, to assemble and dissect our learning, speculations and potential avenues of further enquiry. We hope to persuade Ulter to join us in this venture. Riverbend will not be safe for me, however; Silver will surely end me if I return there. And that raises a further problem; I speak of repudiation of the Overdrengr, yet only he has the resources to root out the unnamed that hide among us. I see no choice but to communicate to him, somehow, the danger posed by these creatures, but he will no doubt turn the matter to his advantage and use it to consolidate his power.

With the flow of the river with us, our passage to the *Improbable* was relatively serene. Most of the stores were gone, probably incinerated in a bonfire in the elpi village, and so portaging the boat with only four of us was just about feasible, if thoroughly exhausting.

On board, the frigidity between Skuld and the rest of us has been thawed by the inevitable propinquity and collaboration of life at sea. He led a service for our lost brothers, extolling their virtues and sacrifice, and, ruin take him, I was moved by it. Tala East is bereft at the loss of his twin, half a man. Nijal is philosophical; no doubt his career as an instrument of battle requires a certain matter-of-factness regarding the value of human life. He has, however, shown considerable interest in the theory of morphation (or should I say, evolution) by natural selection and its attendant blasphemies. He has, I think, found succour in the theory; his soul is not, after all, that of a weakling unfit for God's service.

Perhaps here is the key to the theory's widespread acceptance, a means to translate it from abstract notion into relevance to people's lives. Everyone knows someone who knows someone who has fallen victim to torpor and died or been rejected by his religion as a result. The theory offers a pardon for those unfortunate souls, and scrubs away the ignominy of their friends and relatives.

Then again…thinking to broach a similar point with Yavilad, I made an utter fool of myself. In my arrogance, I thought to share happy news with him; confirmation that his daughter's thwartism is not the result of some spiritual flaw, but of the vagaries of the natural world. There is no need to blame yourself, I told him happily. He just looked at me, making it most apparent that he required no moral crusading on my part to tell him how to feel about his own child.

People are governed by stories, to the extent that our very selfhood is a story conjured by the hidden recesses of the brain. Persuasion is an act of telling a new, compelling story, or reframing an existing one; my conversation with Yav was a lame, intrusive attempt to reframe his understanding of his own family. Moshim allowed himself to die, I venture, because the story by which his life was governed had completely collapsed. Given more time, I believe he could have opened himself to the grandeur of the theory, with its attendant aspects of kinship and immortality.

DNA, the code of life, is immortal. It is immortal because it replicates exact copies of itself, down the generations and aeons, though the substrate in which it manifests is perishable and temporary. Kinship with all life is a corollary of the theory, a welcome antidote to the hubris of man's self-appointed stewardship of the Earth. However, man and his closer relatives do occupy a special position upon the tree of life. The tree, the universe, has become aware of itself, through us. We are not bound by the calculus of fitness and survival, because consciousness transcends it. Evolution cares naught for morality; murder and rape are equally viable strategies for evolutionary success as cooperation and love. Evolution is, therefore, no guide to decent living, so we must choose another. Iwa's goals of increasing health and happiness and reducing suffering, seem as good as any.

To that end, I will set aside my rage and grief at Poesha's treachery; I will extend my forgiveness to him in a spirit of humility, that I may open his eyes to the possibilities of a future founded not on manipulation and comforting stories, but on truth and kinship.

To Poesha I extend the open hand of friendship, but I raise clenched fists, white of knuckle, to theocratic tyranny. My ambition is not that of a timid man. A weakling boarded this vessel against his will months ago, and scribbled a fawning dedication to the Overdrengr. Fan will have his dedication, but will not see this diary in its complete form. I will have something else for him: an unarguable thesis upon evolution by natural selection, which will dismember the basis of his power.

# EPILOGUE

*25<sup>th</sup> day of Harpal, 893 AZ.*

Javic Tor was dead. Over the course of a single lunar cycle, he had progressed from noticing tufts of unmoored hair settled on his pillows, to stomach pain, weakness, rashes, chills and confusion. Laknirs were at a loss to explain the rapid deterioration, being unaware that Javic Silver was systematically poisoning the warden in the guise of loving ministrations. Javic's final days were spent blind and incontinent, his only consolation the knowledge that the governance of Riverbend would pass into his son's capable hands.

Silver, or rather Javic, as he would now be known, tucked his shirt into his trousers and made minute adjustments to his hair. His herd were gathering outside for the investiture ceremony. Delaying his ascension any further was pointless, he had reasoned; the old man was of no further use and his ineptitude could cause unforeseen damage. For now, his putative mother would live. Her popularity among the villagers was a boon to the authority of his office.

He frowned at the mirror. Betrothal would be an issue; he would be expected to take a wife and provide an heir. Who knew what hybrid awfulness would result from such a union? He would worry about it later, and soon enough he would need to minister to his genuine progeny; it would need collecting from the female in Arada and delivering into its new home.

Poesha Jalana's absence was of greater concern. Her disappearance, immediately after the disposal of her brother, seemed more than coincidental. Drengrs were dispatched to track her down, ostensibly in concern for her wellbeing, and to question her regarding her brother's own fate, but had turned up nothing.

A knock at the door, and the woman's head appeared. "Come now, Javic, don't tarry," she murmured. "You look a picture, son."

He smiled and kissed her cheek. "As do you. I'll just be a moment."

She left and the unnamed sat at his table, and spread parchment before him.

#

*Dear Ficksa Drothinin,*

*I write to thank you for your letter of condolence for the loss of my dear father. The ceremony of my investiture is imminent, and I pledge to follow my father's example of years of humble, dutiful service. I can only imagine the never-ending torrent of matters that must monopolise your time as ficksa to His Vitality the Overdrengr, and so the kindness you have shown to my family and this community is deeply moving.*

*I would readily forgive you if you were unable to recall our meeting some years ago, when I accompanied my father on a visit to Silves. We dined together in the Grand Hall of the Kastal, and you smiled and nodded politely at the ancient seidhr who bent your ear remorselessly. But perhaps you sensed, like me, that we shared something in common; a certain fundamental separateness from normal men. Sadly, this very commonality is more often than not a source of friction between men of our ilk, and I felt my forehead break into sweat when you narrowed your eyes at me.*

*I hope that with careful coordination, respectful distance and mutual understanding we can avoid such conflict, to our mutual advantage, though it be antithetical to our nature. I am particularly interested in exploring novel means of systematised food production.*

*Though they may have something to teach us about the value of cooperation and goodwill, the purpose of common men is primarily to serve the needs of those such as we.*

*Your Humble Servant,*

*Javic Silver, Bridgewarden of Riverbend.*

# THE END

Printed in Great Britain
by Amazon